PRELUDE TO A WITCH

WICKED WITCHES OF THE MIDWEST BOOK EIGHTEEN

AMANDA M. LEE

WINCHESTERSHAW PUBLICATIONS

PROLOGUE
SEVENTY-FIVE YEARS AGO

Tillie Winchester was in a tizzy.

It wasn't all that much of a surprise to her mother. Caroline Winchester had learned long ago that Tillie was always in a tizzy. In fact, the day she gave birth to Tillie they were in the midst of a tornado ... and infant Tillie had more energy than the storm. Still, Caroline couldn't help but be concerned as she rolled dough for a pie and watched her daughter stomp through the house.

"What's wrong with her?" Caroline asked her other daughter as she watched the spectacle. "Is she in one of her moods?"

Ginger, always the calm one of the two, shrugged as she washed blueberries. There was little more she loved than helping her mother in the kitchen. She had grand plans to learn every family recipe and claim the title of best Winchester chef. Upon sliding a look toward Tillie, she realized that wasn't going to be difficult. Tillie had never shown any interest in cooking.

"I don't know what's wrong with her," Ginger admitted as she studied her sister. They were close, something their mother was happy to know. That didn't mean they always got along. "I haven't seen her in a few hours."

Caroline's gaze was speculative as she studied her calmer child. "Are you two fighting?"

"No." Ginger answered. "Well ... maybe," she hedged.

"What are you fighting about?"

"Willa."

Ginger's gaze darkened as she flicked her eyes to the window at the rear of the house.

Caroline wanted to match her daughter's expression but forced herself to remain calm. "What about Willa?" It was difficult for Caroline to feign caring when it came to the third Winchester child. Oh, she'd tried over the years. She'd spent time with Willa in an attempt to make her part of the family. But the girl belonged to her husband and another woman — he'd always had a wandering eye. Caroline had agreed to bring her into the family home despite her dislike for her husband. He didn't know she was plotting a way out. She wasn't quite there yet, but soon would be. Then she would divorce him and keep the family land. Her husband would be on his own after that. As for Willa, well, Caroline still didn't know what to do about her.

"Willa is sneaky," Ginger explained to her mother. She wasn't a tattler by nature — Tillie melted down when she was tattled on — but she couldn't help herself. The one thing she did better than anybody was worry, and she was legitimately worried about Tillie's relationship with Willa. "She kind of lurks in the corners and waits for Tillie to do something so she can blackmail her."

"Lurks?" Caroline arched an amused eyebrow. "Have you been reading in bed again when you're supposed to be sleeping?"

Ginger hesitated. Her mother never gave her grief about reading — in fact, she encouraged it — but her father was another story. "I know Papa said he didn't want us to read too much," she started.

Caroline shook her head. "Don't worry about that. His opinion doesn't matter. What I say goes."

Ginger's lips quirked. "I don't know that he would agree with that."

"I don't really care what he agrees with." Caroline pinned Ginger with a pointed look. "Who are you more afraid of?"

Ginger's answer was automatic. "You."

"Good."

"Well, maybe Tillie."

Caroline snorted. "She is going to be a force to be reckoned with. She's a tyrant at the age of nine. Who saw that coming?"

Ginger lifted her hand.

"Yes, well, you always were gifted when it came to seeing the future." Caroline winked at her fair-haired daughter and then turned serious. "What seems to be Willa's problem today?"

"She was hiding in the barn when Tillie went in there with the Harper boys," Ginger started.

Caroline's eyes narrowed. "What was Tillie doing with the Harper boys in the barn? She's nine."

"Oh, it wasn't anything gross," Ginger reassured her quickly. "She's been making stuff and selling it."

This was news to Caroline. "What sort of stuff?"

"Oh, just stuff," Ginger replied evasively.

Caroline folded her arms over her chest and pinned Ginger with her harshest look. "What has your sister been doing in the barn?"

"She's just been inventing stuff," Ginger replied. "It's not bad. You don't have to worry."

"Why would I worry about your sister inventing stuff?" Caroline deadpanned. "I mean ... that's silly talk. There's nothing frightening about your sister selling ... whatever it is she's selling, right?" The question was pointed.

"Wine."

Caroline was taken aback. "Excuse me?"

Ginger shrank back in the face of her mother's fury. "Um ... or not."

"Your sister is making wine?" Caroline was dumbfounded. "Where did she even learn to do that?"

"She found a book," Ginger explained. "It was in the basement, with Papa's stuff."

Caroline's expression shifted. "Of course. I forgot about that book. I told him to get rid of it. Did he listen? Of course not."

"Tillie says it's not hard," Ginger offered. "She said we can make extra money selling the wine, enough so that we can afford a new house and get away from Papa." It was only after she finished that she realized what she'd said. "Or ... we could do something else with it."

Rather than chastise Ginger, Caroline took pity on her. "Don't worry about your father," she said. "He can't touch you. He has no say regarding what you are, or who you'll grow to be. Don't be afraid of him."

Ginger was familiar with her father's drinking. Because of that, she had no choice but to be afraid of him. "Tillie thinks we'll be able to buy a new house if she keeps making the wine."

"Tillie is a menace." Despite the words, Caroline grinned. "Don't worry about getting a new house. This house is mine. It was left to me. We just need enough money to kick your father out." Caroline was thoughtful. "How long has Tillie been making wine?"

"About two months. Lots of people buy it."

"And she's managed to hide the fact that she's selling it for two months." Caroline couldn't help being impressed. "Don't tell Tillie I know about the wine," she said.

Ginger was taken aback. "But ... shouldn't she know you want her to keep selling it? She won't have to sneak around as much."

"I want her to sneak around. Your sister is a master at hiding what she's doing. I need your father not to find out. Do you understand?"

Ginger's eyes went wide but she nodded.

"Good." Caroline squeezed her shoulder and then went back to the pie crust. "Tell me about Tillie and Willa. What seems to be the issue?"

"They hate each other."

"I hope they'll outgrow that," Caroline mused. "Their bond is not as strong as your bond with Tillie." Caroline studied Ginger a moment and then smiled. "You're not as close with Willa either."

"I don't like her." Ginger opted to tell the truth. "She feels ... different."

Caroline's forehead creased. "What do you mean?"

"I don't know." Ginger held out her hands. "When I'm with Tillie I feel stronger. It's like we're always supposed to be together. I don't feel that way with Willa. When I'm with her, I just feel angry because she's so sneaky."

"I could point out that Tillie breaks the rules," Caroline argued. "Maybe Willa feels she's putting this family in danger with her actions."

"No, that's not it." Ginger's headshake was instant. "Willa wants to be better than Tillie. She wants to win all the time."

"And do you think that will happen?"

Ginger snorted. "No. Tillie always wins."

"Even more than you?"

Ginger hesitated and then nodded. "I don't need to win like Tillie does."

"Willa does," Caroline noted. "Why do you think that is?"

"Because she doesn't feel like she belongs here. She's different from us and she knows it." Ginger studied her mother with fresh eyes. "You know it too."

"Willa is part of this family," Caroline countered quickly. Even though Willa wasn't her biological daughter, she'd accepted the girl into their home and promised to care for her. She might not like Willa, but she would never mistreat her. "She's not an outsider. I don't like that you guys cut her out of the action."

Ginger made a face. "She's a baby."

"She's younger, but you and Tillie aren't the same age and you play together."

"No, I mean she's a baby," Ginger insisted. "If we don't let her win games she cries and carries on. She tattles on us in school. Tillie hates her."

"Tillie only thinks she hates her. She'll figure out that Willa is still her sister. She'll grow to appreciate her."

Ginger had her doubts. "I don't think that's going to happen."

"No?" Caroline pursed her lips.

"I think they'll be enemies forever."

"Well, that might be fun, too." Caroline smirked as Tillie stomped between the kitchen and living room. "Hey, little monster, do you want to help with the pie?" she called out to her dark-haired daughter. Tillie's long hair swished behind her like a tail.

Tillie stopped pacing long enough to eye her mother. "Why would I want to make a pie?"

"You need to learn a skill," Caroline replied. "So far, the only thing we know you're good at is irritating people."

"Oh, I'm good at more than that." Tillie's smile was smug.

For a moment, Caroline considered calling out Tillie about making the wine. Seeing her daughter's face when she realized her business endeavor had been discovered would've almost been worth losing the money. *Almost*. She didn't want Tillie to quit, though. The girl was sneaky in her own right, and if she could continue bringing in money under her father's nose it would benefit them all.

"You're a wonder," Caroline agreed dryly. "Still, you should probably learn to cook."

"Why?" Tillie never did anything without being convinced it would somehow benefit her.

"Because someday you'll marry and your husband will want you to cook dinner."

"Yeah." Ginger stuck out her tongue. "I'm going to have a very happy husband."

"Because you cook?" Tillie sneered. "Mama is the best cook in the county and Papa isn't happy. Why would I waste time cooking? If I marry someone — and it's doubtful I will — he'll be the cook."

Caroline chuckled. "I don't know any men who cook. That seems a tall order."

"Oh, I guarantee there's one out there. I'm going to find him, hit him over the head with a stick, and lock him in the house so he can wait on me."

"I like the stick part." Caroline's smile was impish. "Where is your sister?"

Tillie's expression remained blank. "She's right there." She jabbed a finger at Ginger. "Is your eyesight going?"

"My sight is fine. I was talking about your other sister."

Tillie made a face. "I have no idea where she is."

"Maybe you should find her."

"Um ... no." Tillie shook her head and did a little dance. "She can find her own way home. She's not a lost kitten."

"She's still your little sister." Caroline insisted. "It's your job to take care of her."

Tillie didn't bother to hide her disdain. "At some point Willa is going to be an adult and responsible for herself. All that tattling she does will be for nothing because we won't have to take care of her."

"Don't you think you should always take care of your sister?"

"This one." Tillie pointed toward Ginger. "She's my *real* sister and I'll take care of her."

Caroline froze. Could they know? She'd been careful never to slip in front of them when it came to Willa's true parentage. Had she somehow overlooked something? "What do you mean?" she asked, carefully avoiding eye contact.

"A real sister doesn't tattle," Tillie insisted, missing the relieved breath her mother let out. "Willa isn't a real sister. She's a tattler, and there's nothing that I hate more than tattlers."

"Willa is the youngest sister," Caroline noted. "You guys often play without her. She tattles because that's the only way she can be included sometimes."

"Don't kid yourself," Tillie said drolly. "She tattles because she thinks it'll help her win. I have news for her. I'm going to win. I'm smarter than she is."

Caroline felt weary. The thought of having to watch Tillie and Willa battle it out for decades weighed heavy on her. "Don't you think you could at least try for your mother?"

"It's like you don't know me at all," Tillie groused. "She's evil. She won't get better, no matter what you say about her growing out of it. You have to see that too."

Caroline studied her wild child. "She's still your sister. You're stuck with her for life."

"That doesn't mean I have to like her," Tillie insisted. "Blood only goes so far. Ginger and I will be together until the end. Once Willa is an adult, she can go wherever she wants and do whatever she wants ... as long as it's nowhere near me."

Caroline studied Tillie's face and then shook her head. "I think you'll change your mind."

"I won't." Tillie looked to the window. "I'm going to rule the world one day. Willa won't be part of that world."

Despite herself, Caroline couldn't stop the laughter from bubbling up. "You're going to rule the world?"

"I am." Tillie bobbed her head. "I'll be good at it, too."

"Well, at least I don't have to worry about you sacrificing your ego on the altar of a man," Caroline muttered.

"Definitely not," Tillie agreed, her lips curving. "I'm going to be awesome when it's my turn to rule."

"I hope you're right. There's nothing worse than a non-benevolent ruler."

"I don't know what that means."

"It means you're going to be a fair and just ruler," Caroline explained.

Tillie made a face. "That's not going to happen. I'm going to make people cry, and I'm going to start with Willa."

Caroline sighed at the circular nature of the conversation. "How about you at least try to get along with Willa for me? Can you do that?"

"No."

"Either try or you won't get any pie."

Tillie worked her jaw. "That's blackmail," she said finally. "I don't like blackmail."

"You like it when you're the blackmailer," Caroline pointed out.

"Then it's fun."

Caroline allowed Tillie to see her frustration. "You might very well rule the world one day, but you won't always get your way. You need to learn to deal with disappointment."

"That sounds like no fun at all."

"You still need to learn." Caroline lowered her voice. "There will come a time when you have a decision to make regarding Willa. I'm still hopeful you'll make the right one."

"And if I don't?"

"Then you'll have to live with it."

Tillie waited but her mother added nothing. "That's it? You're saying my punishment for getting my own way is having to live with getting my own way?"

"Oh, good grief," Caroline muttered. "You only see what you want to see."

"I do," Tillie agreed. "I see that I'm going to win and Willa is going to lose. I'm going to laugh and she's going to cry." Tillie's smile went feral. "I'm going to dance and she's going to pout in a corner."

"I believe we're already living in that world," Ginger offered.

"True." Tillie extended her hand. "One day, Willa will realize this is my world and I'm only allowing her to visit. One day, I'll make her cry buckets."

Caroline considered sending Tillie up to her room without supper to shut her up but ultimately opted against it. Tillie's spirit was the one thing that would always keep her afloat. "You might change your mind one day."

"Oh, I definitely won't." Tillie was firm. "Willa will be my enemy until the end. Eventually, I will take her down ... and I'm going to throw a party when it happens."

"Good to know."

"There will be wine."

"I'm sure there will."

"And dancing on the bluff."

"Keep looking forward to that."

"Oh, I will." Tillie bowed low in front of her mother, offering a bit of theatrical flair to the conversation. "I'm the queen and Willa is the jester. It's always going to be that way. Just you wait."

ONE
PRESENT DAY

"There's only one way to do this if we want to survive." Aunt Tillie was grave as her gaze bounced between my face and those of my cousins Thistle and Clove. "We must be quick. We must be precise. We must be bold."

Thistle, her hair a bright shade of red that reminded me of autumn leaves, rolled her eyes and folded her arms over her chest. "We must be lazy," she said. "That's what you're getting at."

"There's nothing wrong with being lazy," Aunt Tillie snapped as she straightened. "In fact, I wholeheartedly support laziness. Do you want to know why? I'll tell you why. We're witches. We need to save our strength for the big battles, the ones that save lives. We don't need to be wasting our energy on crap like this." She gestured toward the old campground we'd frequented as children. "Goddess help us, this place is a hole."

I shot her a dirty look and moved closer to one of the old cabins. It was empty now, the most recent overnight guest taking off after we stripped her of power. The building was dilapidated, collapsing and surrounded by trash. I, Bay Winchester, was trying to be responsible ... at least mostly.

"It's not a hole," I argued, pinning her with a dark look. "It's a great piece of property. It just needs a little work."

"It is a great property," Clove said as she moved to the shade and sank into one of the canvas camping chairs we'd brought along, her needs pressing on all of us. She was largely pregnant. Like ... close. She could go into labor now and the baby would survive. She still had a few weeks left before she was ready to pop, but we'd started watching her with the careful eyes of expectant aunts who were both excited by the imminent arrival and terrified about what it would mean for us going forward.

"It's a hole," Aunt Tillie insisted. "There's garbage everywhere."

"That's why we're here," I reminded her, grabbing the rake. "In exactly one week, construction workers are coming to demolish the old buildings. I promised Landon I would get as much of the trash out of here as possible before they come."

"I thought you guys couldn't afford to build a house for at least a year," Thistle argued as she begrudgingly used a stick to spear garbage and bag it. "Why are you tearing the buildings down now if you can't even start building?"

"They're dangerous," I replied. "They could go at any moment, and if there are teenagers hanging out — and the beer cans we keep finding seem to signify that there are — we could be sued if the buildings fall on top of them when they're doing the dirty."

Thistle snorted as she shook her head. "Doing the dirty? That's something Landon would say."

She wasn't wrong. My fiancé had a way with words, which made me laugh every day. That was only one of the reasons I'd fallen in love with him. The others included the fact that he was ridiculously handsome and had a heart of gold. Just thinking about him made me smile. When caught by Thistle, that made her frown.

"Stop being schmaltzy," Thistle snapped. "You're bugging the crap out of me."

"Maybe you're bugging the crap out of me," I shot back. She was my cousin and I loved her, but she knew what buttons to push to drive me crazy. "I can be schmaltzy if I want to. I'm getting married in a few weeks."

"Yeah, I still don't understand why you're pushing that so fast," Thistle complained. "You guys just got engaged. Why not drag it out a year or so? Then you can plan the wedding of your dreams and not have all this pressure."

"We want to get married now." Landon and I had talked long and hard about what we wanted. "I want an outdoor wedding, which means we have to do it before the weather turns. He's fine with whatever I want as long as there are scallops wrapped in bacon as hors d'oeuvres and we go somewhere tropical for our honeymoon."

"Yeah, but ... everything is so rushed," Thistle said. "Our mothers are absolutely melting down over this. You must've noticed."

"I know they wanted more time, but Landon and I don't want to wait." I avoided making eye contact as I turned back to picking up garbage. "Just in case."

"Just in case what?" Thistle demanded as she skirted around Aunt Tillie. Our elderly great-aunt appeared to be using her magic to clean ... or bring the trees to life. It was always hard to tell with her. "Be careful with whatever spell you're using," she barked. "If this goes *Fantasia*, we're going to have a heckuva time explaining it ... especially given who lives on the other side of the lake now." She pointed at the expansive house across the water.

"I don't care what they think," Aunt Tillie said darkly as she glared at the house. Nobody was outside — something I considered a genuine relief — but I couldn't help but wonder if the occupants were inside watching us.

"Has anybody seen them?" Thistle asked. She looked just as unhappy as Aunt Tillie.

"I haven't, but I know they're still hanging around," I replied. "I was talking to Mrs. Gunderson the other day. They had those bacon maple doughnuts Landon likes, so I picked him up a box. She said that they've been having coffee and doughnuts in her shop almost every day."

"I guess that means they're still here." Thistle's expression was sour. "I don't trust them."

That was the understatement of the year. Ever since Aunt Tillie's half-sister Willa had returned to Hemlock Cove, our touristy witch town in northern Lower Michigan, we'd done nothing but watch and wait. We were all suspicious of Willa's motives. The fact that her granddaughter Rosemary was with her and was engaged to my former boss only added to the heightened sense of worry washing over our family.

"Nobody trusts them," Aunt Tillie barked, waving her hands so the wind served as an invisible garbage collector and started moving all the trash into a pile near the fire pit. I had to admit — even though I would never say it out loud in her presence — it was an impressive spell. "They're bad people."

I sighed. "I don't know if it's fair to call them bad people," I hedged.

"Oh, no?" Aunt Tillie was having none of it. "What have they ever done that's good for humanity?"

"Nothing." I couldn't argue that point. "They also haven't gone out of their way to mess with us for the most part. Brian, however, is another story." I looked at the house. It was big, bold and impressive ... and I believed beyond a shadow of a doubt that Brian had purchased the house because he knew it would bother me. Thanks to Landon and Hemlock Cove Police Chief Terry Davenport, a man who had helped raised me, I was now the proud owner of The Whistler, the town newspaper. Brian inherited the newspaper from his grandfather William Kelly almost two years ago, but he ran it into the ground while threatening me in the process. Landon had stepped in, helping me buy the newspaper and essentially stealing it out from under Brian. The man was still bitter about it, which had to be why he was back in town ... and haunting the property Landon and I planned to build a house on eventually.

"This is obviously on purpose," Clove said from her spot in the shade. When inviting her to help, I knew she wouldn't. She was too big. But she whined when left out of things, so I figured it was best to let her act in a supervisory position. So far that had included snacking, drinking caffeine-free soda, and barking orders at the rest of us.

"That's the stupidest thing I've ever heard," Thistle said. Clove's laziness — a word she used and I never would — had turned Thistle into a beast of late. We all were looking forward to the birth so that Clove would return to normal. Sure, she was a whining kvetch a lot of the time and I expected her to be a neurotic mother, but that was still better than … this. What she was right now — an uncomfortable woman about to spew forth life — was even worse.

"What's stupid?" Clove demanded, annoyance obvious. "Brian only bought that house because he wants to torture Bay. Why else would he come back? He knows everybody here hates him. This is all payback."

"I stole his newspaper," I said. "He wants to make me pay."

"I think he's more interested in making Landon pay," Thistle countered. "Landon threatened him. That's the only reason Brian agreed to sell to you."

I'd spent a great deal of time thinking about that. "I'm afraid he's going to do something to cause Landon to lose his job," I admitted. "An FBI agent isn't supposed to threaten someone so his girlfriend can buy a newspaper."

"If you ask me, that's the best thing your boy wonder has ever done," Aunt Tillie offered. "He made me proud to say he was a Winchester that day." She puffed out her chest. "He was a badass."

"You should tell him that," I said with a laugh.

"No way." Her expression darkened again. "That will only puff his ego and we all know what he's like when his ego is out of control."

"I happen to like his ego."

"That's because you're blind to his faults."

"He doesn't have any faults." That was mostly true. "Well, other than the fact that he's a little bossy."

"A *little* bossy?" Aunt Tillie screeched. "He's a lot bossy. He needs to learn that he's becoming a member of our family. I'm the only one who can be bossy from here on out."

That was such an Aunt Tillie thing to say. "I'm pretty sure my mother has reason to argue with that," I pointed out. The only person I knew bossier than Aunt Tillie was my mother. In fact, she was the only person who could rein in Aunt Tillie. It was fairly impressive ... and altogether terrifying when she got in a mood.

"I'm the boss of your mother, no matter what she says," Aunt Tillie groused, her attention back on the house. "We need a storm."

"Excuse me? Why would we want a storm? The weather is beautiful."

"Yes, it's a lovely day in the neighborhood," Aunt Tillie drawled. "It's absolutely delightful. We still need a storm."

"I think you need to expand on that," Thistle said. "What would we do with a storm?"

"We could turn it into a tornado that just happens to hit that house." Aunt Tillie pointed across the lake. "A storm could level it, and then we would go on our merry way."

"I'm guessing if a storm leveled exactly one house in Hemlock Cove before disappearing, it would be considered suspicious," I offered.

"I think you're doing what you always do – overthinking," Aunt Tillie shot back. "If you think two decimated houses would help, I know another one we could take out."

I shot her a dirty look. "Yes, because Mrs. Little's house being flattened along with Brian's — which are miles apart — wouldn't be at all suspicious."

"Who cares if it's suspicious? They'd have to prove we did it, and we all know that won't happen."

"Just leave the house alone." Even as I said the words, a pang rocketed through me. I'd done my best the last two weeks to pretend Brian's return hadn't bothered me. I didn't want to be seen as paranoid — that was Aunt Tillie's job, after all — but I couldn't shake the notion that something terrible was about to happen.

"Who raised you?" Aunt Tillie demanded with a scowl. "Only an idiot would think we shouldn't do something about that house. If Brian Kelly has his way, he'll be spying on you and Landon the rest of your lives. You'll be neighbors with Rosemary. Is that what you want?"

It was the last thing I wanted, but that didn't change my reality. "So far he's done nothing to warrant payback."

"Oh, puh-leez." Aunt Tillie's eye roll was so pronounced I was surprised she didn't fall over. "Who says there has to be a reason to pay somebody back?"

"I believe that's part of the standard rules," Thistle said dryly.

"Well, it's a stupid rule." Aunt Tillie was determined when she turned to me. "We need to get rid of him. Like ... right now. We can't sit around and wait for him to move on us. We need to move on him and get him out of our town."

"And how do you suggest we do that? We can't attack him out of the blue. We could get in trouble."

"You're not worried about us getting in trouble." Aunt Tillie made a face. "You're worried about your love muffin getting in trouble. That won't happen either. Do you think Brian is going to drive to the FBI field office in Traverse City and report your boyfriend for dating a witch?"

That' exactly what worried me. "I don't want Brian creating trouble for Landon. Things are good for us right now."

"That won't change," Aunt Tillie insisted. "I've met the fed's boss. He's easily manipulated. We can bend his will and turn him into a slave if we need to."

"Don't even think about it," I warned. "Just ... stay out of it." It would turn to war if Aunt Tillie pushed too hard. "We can't do anything until Brian does something. All he's done since returning that might be considered dastardly is hang out with some teenagers."

"I still want to know what that was about," Thistle muttered, her eyebrows drawing together as she stared at the house. "Hanging around with teenagers — some of whom turned out to be evil witches — is not the mark of a standup man."

"He knows we saw him with the girls," I pointed out. "He knows we're suspicious. He'll be doubly careful now."

"What about those girls?" Clove asked, her hand busy rubbing her huge stomach. "Have you talked to them since you wiped their memories?"

I shook my head. Talking about the girls who had decided to use magic as a means to escape Hemlock Cove — not caring in the least who they hurt in the process — gave me a sour stomach. "Believe it or not, I would rather talk about Brian than them."

"They're still blank canvases?" Thistle asked. "They don't remember what they did?"

"No, and more importantly, they don't remember what we did to stop them. They seem to be normal teenagers again."

"That doesn't mean they're not evil," Aunt Tillie pointed out. "Teenagers are freaking sociopaths."

"And now you know why we loved you as much as we did as teenagers," Thistle drawled.

"Shut it!" Aunt Tillie jabbed a finger in Thistle's direction. "Nobody needs your mouth."

Quite frankly, I didn't need any of their mouths. "What's the deal with the garbage?" I asked, changing the subject. "Why are you moving it into the fire pit? We still have to bag it."

"Oh, ye of little faith." Aunt Tillie snapped her fingers, causing the pile of garbage to go up in flames.

I opened my mouth to tell her that conjuring fire was a bad idea and then realized that the campground was completely clean and the garbage would be gone within five minutes. "Nice work." I clapped her shoulder. "You're more than just a pretty face."

Aunt Tillie scowled. "Keep it up and I'll arrange to have all that garbage replaced."

"That won't be necessary." I reached into my pocket when I felt my phone vibrate, smiling when Landon's name appeared on the screen. "Maybe he misses me," I said, beaming at Aunt Tillie in a way that I knew would drive her crazy. "Who is your favorite witch in the world?" I asked by way of greeting.

"That's not even a competition," Landon replied. "You're my favorite everything."

Right away I knew something was wrong. He wasn't his normal playful self. "What is it?"

"It's ... um ... I need you to come out to the Dragonfly."

My heart practically beat out of my chest. "Did something happen to my dad?" I flicked my eyes to Thistle and Clove in turn. "Any of our dads?"

"No, sweetie, I'm sorry." Landon was instantly contrite. "I didn't mean to make you think that. We did find a body, though. Behind the Dragonfly. I need you to come out here and ... well, I just need you."

I knew what he was saying. The party spot behind the Dragonfly had been cause for concern for weeks. There was something he didn't want to say over the phone.

"I'm on my way," I said.

"Thank you. And Bay, don't drive like a maniac. Take your time. I'll be here when you get here."

"I'll be careful. You don't have to worry about me."

That earned a short laugh. "Oh, if only that were true."

2

TWO

I didn't have time to drop off my cousins and aunt so the whole crew was with me when I parked in the lot at the Dragonfly. Landon stood with my father, their heads bent together in conversation.

"This looks bad," I said as I got out of my car.

Landon slid me an unreadable look. "It's not good," he said. "I'm sorry I had to call you out here."

"We're a team, right?" I attempted a smile. "If you need me, I'm always here."

"I always need you." He pulled me in for a hug. "I really am sorry. I know you were spending quality time with your family."

That at least nudged a grin out of me. "We were picking up garbage at the campground."

"We're done," Aunt Tillie added as she joined us. "You're welcome, by the way."

Landon flicked his eyes to her. "You're done already? I thought that would take days. I had plans to take Bay out there this weekend to finish up."

"You had plans to take Bay out there and act dirty in those cabins and you know it," Aunt Tillie challenged. "You don't care about the garbage."

That elicited a weak smile from Landon. "Those cabins are death traps. I wouldn't risk taking Bay in them."

"Oh, you're so full of it." Aunt Tillie shifted her attention to my father. They had a tempestuous relationship, which was putting it mildly. "Jack."

"Tillie." Dad held her gaze a moment before turning to me. "And my favorite daughter." He beamed. "How are the wedding plans coming?"

"They're going well," I replied. "It's hard to believe it's only a few weeks away."

"Yes, well, I've been wondering about that." He shifted from one foot to the other, uncomfortable. "Is there a reason you have to get married so quickly?"

The question caught me off guard. "What do you mean?"

"I thought maybe ... ." He didn't finish the sentence, instead tipping his head to where Clove was being helped out of the car by her father, Warren.

"I think he's asking if you're pregnant, sweetie," Landon said. "My guess is that he's looking for a reason to hate me again."

"I don't need a reason," Dad shot back. "The way you look at my daughter is reason enough."

"Your daughter is going to be my wife in about a month, so get over it."

"And I'm not pregnant," I added, horrified at the thought. "You have to wait a bit for that."

"Totally," Landon agreed. "We want to be in our new house before we add kids to the mix. That's still a few years off."

"Hey, a father can dream." Dad's smile was charming. "A little one to spoil would be fun."

"Then spoil Aunt Tillie," Thistle suggested, gesturing toward our wily great-aunt who had been steadfastly edging her way toward the inn. I saw she had mayhem on the brain, because she glared at Thistle for drawing attention to her. "She's little and acts like a child."

"Keep it up, mouth," Aunt Tillie warned. "I'll put you on my list if you're not careful."

"That's no longer a threat." Thistle was blasé. "I've been on your list for more than twenty-five years now. Guess what that means to me. Absolutely nothing. As in there's nothing you can dish out that I can't take."

I shot her an incredulous look. "Why must you say things like that?" I demanded. "You know that's just like waving a red flag in front of her face."

"She says it because she needs constant attention," Aunt Tillie replied. "Now that Clove is about to give birth to the first baby of the next generation and you're engaged to the boy wonder over here, she feels left out."

"I do not," Thistle shot back. "I love my life."

"If you say so." Aunt Tillie's gaze never left Thistle's face. "You know what? Screw it. You're on my list. Does that make you feel better?"

"It doesn't make me feel anything," Thistle shot back. "Being on your list means nothing."

"We'll just see about that."

Sensing that the conversation could derail and venture into the "I know you are but what am I" realm, I asked, "You have a body?"

Landon's smile slipped. "We do, and I need your help."

Yup. That definitely wasn't good. "Dad and Uncle Warren are here, so I assume Uncle Teddy isn't the victim."

"Teddy is inside baking," Dad said. "He'll want to see you before you go, Thistle."

Thistle nodded. "If he's baking, you don't have to twist my arm."

"Me either." Clove's cheeks turned rosy. "Is it cookies? Or wait ... cake? Even better, is it cheesecake?" She was fixated on food these days, but I really couldn't blame her. If I had an excuse to eat nonstop without judgement, I would run with it.

"I believe it's bread." Warren shot Clove an apologetic look. "Sorry."

"There are fresh doughnuts inside," Dad offered brightly. "Can I entice anybody inside for those?"

Clove's hand shot in the air. "Me!"

"I figured." Dad turned to me. "What about you?"

I risked a glance at Landon, who kept his face neutral. There was enough worry lurking in his eyes that I shook my head. "I don't think I'll have much of an appetite after Landon shows me what he needs to show me."

"Probably not," Landon agreed. "I know I don't have much of an appetite."

"Even for Teddy's new maple bacon doughnuts?" Dad challenged. "He had you in mind when he started experimenting. He pretty much has the recipe perfected."

Landon pressed his lips together and shook his head. "I'll try them another time."

That's how I knew this was serious. Finding a body was always serious, of course, but whatever was in the woods behind the Dragonfly had killed my future husband's gluttonous appetite. That meant it was bad. Likely *really*, really bad.

"Let's get this over with," I said.

Landon held out his hand. "Why don't the rest of you head inside? Terry is on the scene now. The medical examiner will be here shortly, but we need Bay to see something before they get here."

Dad stopped him. "Why are you forcing Bay to look at dead bodies?" There was an edge to his voice that I recognized.

"Dad, we've talked about this," I replied. "I'm a witch. Sometimes I have to do witchy things."

The statement only served to darken his expression. "This is a murder, not a witch thing."

"How do you know?" I asked.

"I found the body." Ghosts whipped through the depths of Dad's eyes, showing me exactly how haunted he really was. "It's terrible, but there's nothing magical about that scene."

Instinctively I reached over and patted his shoulder. "I'm sorry you had to see it."

"I don't want you to have to see it." Dad was firm. "She's not a police officer, Landon. This is your job."

Landon chewed his lower lip. "I need her to see it. I'm sorry you're upset."

"Why does she need to see it?"

Landon just stared back at him.

Dad growled and then took a step back. "Do what you want. This is between the two of you."

"It is," Landon readily agreed. "Take the others inside. I shouldn't have Bay out there too long. You can spoil her rotten when we get back."

Dad and Landon had worked themselves to a relationship in which they didn't overtly attack one another regularly. I didn't know if they would ever be friendly, but they had made terms. "Fine, but you owe us for babysitting Tillie."

"Hey!" Aunt Tillie was almost to the front door when she pulled up short and glared at my father. "I don't need a babysitter. In fact, I was the babysitter when your kid was little and you were never around."

Dad let loose a sigh. "I stepped into that one."

Landon tugged me toward the woods. "We shouldn't be gone long. Keep an eye on Aunt Tillie until we get back."

"Yeah, yeah, yeah."

Landon was quiet until we moved past the foliage line. He released my hand and started rubbing the back of my neck. "I really am sorry about this."

"Don't be sorry. We're a team." That distinction had been harder for him to accept. He was taught that law enforcement personnel were supposed to go it alone, not include civilians in their investigations, but in our time together he'd slowly changed his outlook.

"We're definitely a team." He slowed his pace to study my face. "I love you."

The naked emotion I found overtaking his features tugged on my heartstrings. "I love you too. What's wrong? I know this is bad. Just ... tell me."

Rather than tell me, he reached out to push the branches in front of us aside. I registered several things straight away. The first was that I'd been to this clearing before. The local teenagers had been drinking in this spot for weeks, taking advantage of the location to party hard. The second was that the body of a woman lay spread eagle on the ground.

"Oh, geez." My heart clogged in my throat as I registered the regret on Landon's face. "Is that ... ?" I recognized the girl. Not long ago she'd tried to take us on with magic she couldn't correctly wield. We stopped her, modified her memory, and then let her return to her life.

That obviously hadn't lasted very long.

"I'm sorry." Landon sounded tortured as he moved in front of me to shield my view. "I thought you would want to know."

"Paisley." It was the only thing I could manage as I pictured the girl's predatory smile from our previous altercation. "Paisley Gilmore."

Landon nodded as he brushed my hair from my eyes. "Are you going to be sick?"

"I've seen dead bodies before," I reminded him.

"This is different."

"How?"

"You went out of your way to save her a week and a half ago," he replied. "You thought you were doing the right thing, giving her a life despite what she tried to take from us. Now she's gone."

I sucked in a bracing breath. "I don't blame myself for this, Landon. I didn't do it. It's likely she did it to herself."

"I don't think she did this to herself," Chief Terry said from behind Landon. I could hear him but I couldn't see him.

I wrapped my hand around Landon's wrist and squeezed. "You did the right thing calling me out here."

"It doesn't feel like the right thing," he grumbled.

I forced a thin-lipped smile that felt hollow. "I have to look at her now."

Landon nodded and stepped aside. "Don't get too close, okay? We've got a forensic team from the state on the way."

My mouth was dry as I moved closer to Paisley. She'd been a

vibrant girl, full of life. I hadn't particularly liked her — actually, I'd outright loathed her — but I'd admired her energy. Now there was nothing but an empty husk that had once been a human being. "She was stabbed," I said.

"She was," Chief Terry agreed as he moved to my side. He was a father figure for me. He'd helped raise Clove, Thistle and me when our fathers disappeared from our lives years ago. He was obviously unhappy with my presence. "You don't have to be here, Bay. I told Landon this was unnecessary."

As much as I loved Chief Terry, his determination to protect me was occasionally a sore point. Unlike Landon, who was learning, Chief Terry wanted to keep me out of his investigations. Landon had figured out that I was good at the witch thing, even though it hadn't been all that long since I'd been ignoring my powers. My future husband and I still butted heads about appropriate safety measures when investigating but he'd grown into an accepting individual. That's why he'd called me out here today. He understood something Chief Terry didn't.

"It is necessary," I argued, shooting him a rueful half-smile. "Not only did we fight with this girl less than two weeks ago, she was killed in ritual fashion."

Chief Terry's expression never changed. "How do you know about that?"

"I watch a lot of television."

Landon snorted. "She does like old reruns of that *Criminal Minds* show. I think she's hot for Shemar Moore, but she also pays attention to the profiling angle."

"It's not just ritual in that way," I argued. "It's ritual in a witchy way."

Landon was taken aback. "What do you mean?"

I pointed to the trees surrounding the clearing. "Someone used her blood to draw runes on the tree trunks."

Landon moved closer to the nearest tree and frowned. "I don't see anything." He removed a flashlight from his pocket and switched it on, viciously swearing under his breath when he finally got a good look.

"You're right. His gaze was steady when it locked with mine. "How did you see that?"

"What answer will freak you out the least?"

"The truth."

I bit back a sigh. "Things are different for me now," I explained. "Since the necromancer stuff kicked in, I'm more powerful."

Landon tugged on his bottom lip. "So ... you can see blood that other people can't?" he asked.

"I can see the remnants of death," I corrected.

Landon's expression shifted into one of horrified sympathy. "I'm sorry."

I laughed even though it felt out of place. "Why? I was born this way. Besides, I'm pretty sure you're the reason I can handle it now. Before you, this would've freaked me out. Because I have you, I know more than I did before and I can accept it."

"Oh, that's ridiculously cute and makes me want to retch," Chief Terry drawled. "There's nothing I love better than watching you two fawn all over each other."

I slid him a dubious look. "But?" I prodded.

"But I need to know what these runes mean." He gestured toward the tree. "I can't see what you guys are talking about."

"We may have to use luminol to light it up for photos," Landon said. "I can get copies of the photos for you, baby, if that helps."

I nodded. I edged closer to Paisley, but not so close I risked treading on their evidence. "Her eyes are open. She saw what was coming."

"I don't know how long she lived after the initial blow," Landon said. "She was stabbed multiple times. The medical examiner will be able to tell us about that."

I nodded. "She would've seen it all."

"Bay ... ." Landon reached out, but then dropped his hand. "Is her ghost hanging around?"

I cocked my head, considering. "I don't see her."

"You could call to her, make her come if she's around."

"I could," I agreed, "but I prefer not to."

He studied my face before nodding. He knew better than anyone that forcing ghosts to do my bidding was uncomfortable. I'd had more than a few nightmares about it. "Okay. There's one other issue we need to consider."

I waited for him to continue.

"Even with the blood on the trees, there's very little on the ground. Given the number of stab wounds, there should be more blood."

I'd been around him long enough to know what he wasn't saying. "You think someone took her blood."

"It's a distinct possibility."

"That means a blood ritual."

"Which leads us back to witches," Chief Terry mused. "I don't suppose you can give us a heads up on what all this means."

I shook my head. "No, but I'm going to find out. No matter how troubled Paisley was, nobody deserves to die like this."

Chief Terry let loose a heavy sigh. "This is a mess."

3

THREE

Chief Terry stayed with the body to wait for the medical examiner while Landon and I made our way back to the Dragonfly.

"I really am sorry I had to bring you out here," Landon offered in a quiet voice. "Terry didn't want me to. I debated, but ... I felt it was important you see how she was staged before the medical examiner moved her."

"You did the right thing," I reassured him.

He linked his fingers with mine. "I don't want you having nightmares because of this."

It wasn't the first time he'd brought up my bad dreams of late. It was clear he didn't want to hurt me. I appreciated the sentiment but found it completely unnecessary. "I'm stronger than I look. Bad dreams won't bring me down."

"Bay, you're the strongest person I know." He pulled me to him for a hug right outside the door that led into the Dragonfly kitchen. "I just don't like it when your dreams chase you."

We had that in common. "It's fine. Maybe what happened to Paisley explains why I've been having bad dreams."

He pulled back to study my face. "What do you mean?"

"I've felt antsy the last week and a half. I thought it was because of Brian and Rosemary. What if they weren't the reason?"

A scowl took over his face. "They're reason enough to be upset. Don't kid yourself on that front. I'm curious if you're upset because you think you could've stopped this?"

"I really wasn't thinking that. I guess maybe I should."

He vigorously shook his head. "This isn't on you. That's not what I meant. In fact, I was saying the opposite. I hate when you blame yourself for things you can't control."

"I don't do that."

"Oh, please." He slung his arm around my shoulders and pressed a kiss to my forehead as he led me toward the inn. "I love you more than anything, but you always blame yourself for things you can't control."

"You're exaggerating."

"I'm not."

Everybody was in the kitchen, grouped around the small table opposite the counters. Somebody had put out quite a spread — doughnuts, cookies, cake and brownies — and Clove was elbow deep in sweets.

"It was horrifying," Dad said. He hadn't realized we were standing behind him. "I don't understand why Landon feels the need to show her something like that."

"Probably because Landon correctly ascertained that it was a ritual killing and we need to do some research," I answered, feeling a small jolt of amusement at the way my father's shoulders jumped.

"I didn't realize you were back." Dad hopped to his feet and glanced between us. "I thought you would be out there longer."

"I don't enjoy torturing your daughter by making her look at dead bodies for hours on end," Landon muttered as he sank into one of the open chairs. "I wasn't saying that," Dad protested.

I growled, the sound cutting them off before they engaged in a full-on snipefest, and walked to the drawer at the end of the counter.

"What are you looking for?" Teddy asked, his brow creasing. "If you're hungry, I can cook something for you – if you're not interested in sweets."

"If you are interested in sweets, you should get them now," Thistle added. "Clove will devour them all soon."

"I'm not hungry." I flashed Teddy a smile I didn't feel. "You guys had a notebook in here a couple weeks ago. I saw it when I was looking for something to jot down some information."

"You need a notebook?" Teddy looked perplexed as he rummaged through a drawer until he came up with a yellow legal pad. "Will this do?"

"It will. Thank you." I carried the pad to the table and sat next to Landon. "Can I have your pen?"

He removed it from his pocket. "What are you doing?"

"I'm going to draw the runes I saw."

"I thought you were going to wait until I can get some luminol on those trees and take photos."

"I'll use that information when it comes through. Until then, I want to see if I can match the runes I saw on the trees with anything in the books we have."

He rubbed my back before shifting his attention to my father. "I need you to tell me what happened this morning."

Dad's eyes were still on me. "It was just my normal routine. We go to that clearing once or twice a week to pick up after the kids who party there."

"We should point out that nobody has been out there in almost two weeks," Warren added, his eyes wide as he watched Clove scarf down a doughnut in record time. "Are you supposed to eat that much sugar?"

He obviously hadn't meant to ask the question out loud because his cheeks colored when Clove fixed him with a death glare. "Eat whatever you want," he said hurriedly.

Thistle's smirk had Clove battling back tears.

"The baby is hungry," Clove complained. "It's not my fault that I'm eating for two."

"You're eating for ten," Aunt Tillie countered, appearing in the doorway that led to the staircase. It was only then that I realized she hadn't been sitting at the table. "You should be eating for one and a half. Per usual, though, you don't think about what the future holds. You're impulsive, like your mother, and you're going to regret it when you have to drop fifty pounds in baby weight."

Clove's mouth dropped open. "Excuse me? I've only gained twenty pounds with this pregnancy."

Even though I was intent on my sketching task, I jerked up my chin. "Twenty pounds?"

"In each thigh," Thistle shot back.

"That's not true!" Clove's voice took on a shrillness I recognized as portending an imminent meltdown. If Thistle didn't pull back immediately, Clove would make us pay.

Because she was Thistle, though, she refused to pull back. "Oh, get a grip. You can't even fit in your elastic band sleep pants."

"I prefer sleeping in Sam's shirts," Clove growled, referring to her husband, a man for whom I had infinite sympathy because Clove's moods were impossible to gauge from one moment to the next.

"Uh-huh." Thistle was having none of it. "Listen, I don't want to pick on you — and the Goddess knows I don't want to agree with Aunt Tillie — but you eat three times as much as Landon now. You're eating way too much."

"Hey!" Landon's face clouded with annoyance. "I eat just enough to survive."

That earned a raised eyebrow from me, but I chose to focus on my work.

"It's true," Landon insisted when he registered the uncomfortable silence that had descended over the table. "I eat just enough to stay alive. Tell them, Bay."

"Hmm." I feigned as though I hadn't been listening. "Sorry. I need to focus on what I'm doing."

Thistle snorted as Landon growled. "At least you work out a lot," she said. "You and Bay hike and you go to the gym for your job. Clove hasn't been doing anything but sitting on the couch like a great lump for weeks."

"That's not true." Despite Thistle's accusations, Clove kept shoveling bits of doughnut into her mouth. "The baby is hungry. It's not my fault."

"If you keep feeding that baby it'll be twelve pounds when you give birth," Aunt Tillie warned as she sidled closer to me. "Do you have any idea how much that's going to hurt?"

I looked to her, enraged. "What have we told you about frightening her with birth stories?" I demanded.

Aunt Tillie became the picture of innocence. "I have no idea what you mean. I wasn't doing anything."

"Yeah, right," Thistle muttered. "You know I have to deal with her when she has panic attacks in the middle of the afternoon. Do you know how many times she's held up a watermelon and compared it to an orange to explain the birthing process? I don't know either, but it's a heckuva lot."

The men at the table cringed in unison as Thistle painted the terrifying picture. Warren ultimately stepped forward to soothe his daughter.

"You're beautiful," he reassured her. "Don't listen to them. They're just messing with you."

"That is the Winchester way," Dad agreed. "We should stop picking on Clove and start picking on Bay. Have you decided on a honeymoon location? I'd really like that to be my gift."

"We have been talking about that," Landon said, his hand still moving over my back. "There's an island Bay wants to visit – Moonstone Bay. You shouldn't have to pay for the trip, I have money put away."

Dad insisted. "I want to pay for it. I've been gone for much of Bay's life. It's the least I can do."

Landon darted his eyes to me. "Bay won't come out and say it, but she wants me to allow you to pay for the honeymoon. How about we split the difference and you pay for the plane tickets and I'll handle everything else?"

I thought for certain my father would argue, but he nodded. "Fine, but when you guys build that house, I'm going all out for a house-warming gift."

Landon leaned back in his chair, relief radiating from him. He hated arguing with my father, if only because he knew it agitated me. "I'll give you the dates and you can purchase the tickets."

"Great." Dad beamed at him. "I'm also going to buy cooking equipment for your new house. I was at the guesthouse the other day; you two have three pots."

"That's because we don't cook," I replied, finishing up my first sketch and ripping it from the pad.

Landon took it from me and stared. "Do you recognize this?"

"No." I stared at the drawn rune for a moment and went back to drawing. "I only got a good look at two of them. I think there were four, a different one on each tree."

Before Landon could speak again, Aunt Tillie took the drawing from him.

"This looks familiar," she said. "Where did you find this?"

"They were drawn in blood on the trees," Landon answered. "Bay saw them even though they shouldn't have been visible. The Michigan State Police are sending out an evidence team. I'm going to have them spray luminol on the trees and photograph the runes."

"That's smart." Aunt Tillie cocked her head. "I swear I've seen this before, but I can't place where."

"You can help with the research later," I suggested.

"Yeah, that doesn't sound fun." Aunt Tillie said. "Who has the bedroom right at the top of the stairs?"

Dad straightened as the conversation shifted yet again. "I wondered where you disappeared to. I believe we told you to stay on the main floor."

"If I only did what I was told I would have no fun at all," Aunt Tillie groused. "Your laundry is gross, by the way. It smells like mildew. You need to make sure your clothes are dry before you toss them in the hamper."

Dad's glare was dark. "You went through my hamper? What is wrong with you?"

"Oh, there are so many ways to answer that question," Thistle drawled. "I've started a list. Would you like me to recite it?"

"Not really." Dad said. "Tillie, as thrilled as we are when you visit — and we are truly thrilled — it would be great if you didn't go through our things when you're here."

"Yeah, I'm going to keep doing what I want." Aunt Tillie moved to the other side of Landon and sat. "What were we talking about again?"

"Nothing important," Landon replied. "I need to get actual statements before you guys return to picking on Clove's eating habits." He reached out to snag one of the doughnuts at the same time Clove decided to claim it.

"That's the last maple and bacon one," Clove announced, refusing to move her hand.

"I know. I can smell it." Landon kept his hand in place. "Haven't you eaten, like, five of them?"

"One," Clove protested.

This time Warren couldn't contain his snort. "What?" His expression matched that of his daughter when she was trying to cover up for saying something stupid. "I had something caught in my throat."

"Yes, laughter," Aunt Tillie said. "Clove, I've seen you eat at least three doughnuts and I was upstairs for twenty minutes. I'm sure you inhaled another two while I was gone. Give the doughnut to the glutton."

"Thank you," Landon said as he took the doughnut. "It's nice to be loved."

"Oh, I don't want you to have it because I love you. I just don't want Clove eating until she explodes."

"Hey!" Clove's eyes went wide. "How many times do I have to tell you that the baby is hungry?"

"Just until I believe it." Aunt Tillie folded her hands in her lap, suddenly demure. "I believe Landon has official questions."

"I do," Landon agreed, groaning as he bit into the doughnut. "Oh, this is like heaven in a tiny little cake. Bay, you need to talk your mother into making these. I'm sure they'll be even better from her kitchen."

Teddy glowered at my future husband. "That's my recipe."

"And they're awesome, but Winnie is the best cook in the world. You'll never hear me say otherwise."

"Mostly because Aunt Winnie won't feed him if he says anything other than that," Thistle offered.

"I can neither confirm nor deny that." Landon brushed off his hands. "So, why were you in the clearing this morning?"

"To clean up," Dad replied. "Like I said, the kids haven't been out there partying in recent days. They've either toned it down or moved someplace else. I go out there to check for returnables and trash twice a week. We don't want to draw in bears."

"Or Bigfoot," I offered absently.

"Oh, you just had to go there," Clove seethed. "You'll give me indigestion."

"Sorry," I said. Clove's Bigfoot fear was the stuff of legends.

"Have you heard anything at all out there the last few days?" Landon asked. "I'm pretty sure she was killed out there last night. Did you hear any vehicles in the area? Any voices?"

Dad shook his head. "No. Sorry. I was shocked when I saw her."

"Did you touch her?"

Dad hesitated and then shook his head. "No. I'm sure that sounds awful. Most people would jump at the opportunity to help, but I could tell she was dead."

"It's good you didn't touch her," Landon said. "Keep your eyes open the next few days. It's unlikely, but some killers like revisiting the scene of the crime."

"Who was it?" Thistle asked. "All we know is that it was a young girl."

I ripped off the second drawing and placed it on the table as I regarded her. "Paisley Gilmore."

Thistle's mouth dropped open. "Are you kidding me?"

"She'd been stabbed several times."

. . .

"I GUESS we know why you wanted Bay." Thistle's lips twisted. "She wasn't a very pleasant girl, but I wouldn't wish that on anybody."

"You and me both," Landon agreed. "I just wanted Bay to see what we were dealing with given ... well ... given everything that happened with Paisley."

"I assume she was one of the girls involved in that kidnapping plot," Dad said. "I didn't recognize her."

ACROSS THE TABLE, Clove stopped eating long enough to grab my second drawing. She made a face as she studied it. "This thing is evil."

Amused, I held out my hands. "I never pretended to be an artist."

"I'm not talking about your drawing. I'm talking about the rune. It's definitely evil."

I was confused by her response. "Why would you say that?"

"I didn't say that. The baby did."

I shifted my gaze to Thistle and found her staring at Clove with the same dumbfounded confusion I felt. "The baby?"

"That's what I said."

Before I could question her further, Chief Terry barreled into the room.

"What is it?" Landon asked, instantly alert.

"I sent a couple of uniforms to inform Paisley's parents," Chief Terry replied grimly. "They weren't home – and it looks as if there's been a struggle."

FOUR

Even though it was clearly the last thing he wanted, Dad agreed to take Clove, Thistle and Aunt Tillie home. I told him to consider it a wedding gift, which made him smile, but he was clearly troubled as he watched me head off with Landon and Chief Terry.

"We'll drop your car at The Whistler," Landon said as he hopped in the passenger seat. "Terry can pick us up there."

I turned to Chief Terry. "Are you okay with me tagging along for the ride?"

"Of course." He shot me a warm smile. "I'm always happy to have you with us."

That was a bit of an exaggeration, but I let it go.

During the drive to The Whistler, Landon was mostly quiet. When he finally did speak, it wasn't about the case.

"Are you okay with the deal I struck with your father?"

"About the honeymoon?" I had to laugh despite the circumstances. "Of course. I was okay with you turning him down."

"See, I don't think you actually were okay with that."

"Well, I was."

"You weren't."

"I was."

"No, you wanted me to accept because it made things easier for you and your dad. It hasn't exactly been smooth sailing."

That was true. "Things are getting better between us."

"They are, but you're still dealing with some residual resentment from your childhood. It's okay to feel what you feel."

"I know. I just ... don't want to argue. It was a good compromise."

"I'm glad."

After we shifted to Chief Terry's vehicle, the conversation swiftly turned to Paisley and her parents.

"It's possible someone broke into the house, killed Richard and Anna, and took Paisley to the clearing," Chief Terry said.

"You didn't find any bodies at the house," I said. "None of it makes sense to me. I can't shake the feeling that what happened two weeks ago ties into this."

"How could it tie in?" Landon asked. "You wiped all their memories."

"I did, but I've never really done that before. Maybe I failed."

"Are you suggesting the other girls somehow went after Paisley for payback? How would that benefit them?"

I had no idea. "I don't know. Paisley wasn't technically the ringleader. She had a powerful personality, but that doesn't mean she was in charge."

"So, who did this?" Chief Terry swung into the Gilmore driveway. The family vehicles — both of them — were parked single-file on the pavement. "Someone decided to snuff out that girl's life. I need to know why."

He wasn't the only one. "Let's check inside."

Landon and Chief Terry took the lead, the former glancing over his shoulder twice to make sure I was okay. Once inside, weapons drawn, they swept the main floor. I figured the uniforms had already done the same, so I went straight to the living room.

It did indeed appear as if a struggle had taken place. The coffee table rested on its side, the items that had been placed on top strewn about the room.

"Was the television on when your officers came in?" I asked as Chief Terry joined me.

"I didn't ask. Why is that important?"

"I don't know that it is. I'm just trying to get a picture of what happened here. The remote control is on the couch." I pointed for emphasis. "There looks to have been a glass of some kind on the table thanks to the ring. It looks like it's from a wine glass."

Chief Terry followed my finger. "You think someone was home, relaxing, and then something happened."

I held out my hands. "That makes the most sense." I moved to the television and pressed the power button. An HGTV show flared to life before I killed the power. "I'm guessing it was the mother."

"Because that's a chick show?" Landon asked as he swept through the open archway. "I checked all the upstairs bedrooms and closets. There's nothing. No one is here."

"HGTV is not a chick channel," I shot back. "You've watched it with me."

"Only when we were really bored and you weren't in the mood for Netflix nudity."

I rolled my eyes. "Yes, because I often police your viewing habits," I drawled. "That sounds just like me."

"Fine. It could've been a man."

I bent over to study a broken wine glass. "There's lipstick on the glass. I think it was the mother."

"I kind of want to pull a Winchester and say something mean," Landon lamented. "Maybe add a little 'I told you so' dance to the mix."

It made me smile. "Don't ever let my mother hear you say something like 'pull a Winchester.' She will melt down."

"Good to know." Landon dragged a hand through his shoulder-length hair. "I don't know what to make of this. Both the vehicles are in the driveway. There's no blood."

"What about cell phones?" I asked. "Did you find them?"

"No, but that's a good idea." Landon shot me a wink. "It's a good thing I have you."

My gaze fell on a framed photograph on an end table on the other side of the room. It featured four smiling teenagers striking a pose in their designer outfits. I recognized all of them. "Do you want another bit of investigative advice?"

"Sure." Landon's reply was easy as he glanced at the photo. "I think I know what you're going to suggest."

"We need to talk to Paisley's friends."

"I take it you want to go with us."

"Do you have a problem with that?"

"Not in the least." Landon took another look around the room. "We need to get ahead of whatever this is. They might be our best shot."

CHIEF TERRY PLACED A CALL TO FIND out where the girls were. Thankfully they were all at Amelia Hart's house. It only took us five minutes to drive there, and once in the driveway Landon shot me a warning look.

"I want you to do what you need to do to ascertain if they're still under the memory spell, but you can't take control of the interview," he warned.

I had to laugh. "This isn't my first time interrogating people with you."

He made a face. "Let's not call it an interrogation. We are talking about teenagers here."

"Got it."

Tina Hart, Amelia's mother, opened the door. Chief Terry had spoken with her on the phone. She seemed baffled by our appearance.

"What's wrong?" she asked.

"Something has happened, Chief Terry replied calmly. "We need to talk to the girls."

Tina hesitated a moment and then pushed open the door wider. "Come in." She led us to the living room, where the three girls sat watching the Kardashians. They seemed lost in their own little world, not looking up when we appeared in the doorway.

"Amelia, you have visitors," Tina offered. She almost sounded frightened to announce our arrival.

From her spot between Sophia Johnson and Emma Graham, Amelia slowly tracked her eyes to us. Surprise registered across her face, but she masked it quickly.

"I surrender." She held up her hands and smiled. "Whatever it is, I didn't do it."

"Neither did I," Sophia said, her eyes wide as saucers. "We're completely innocent."

"That's good to know." Chief Terry moved to the center of the room and inclined his head toward the remote. "Turn off the television, please."

Amelia remained motionless for a second. Then, rather than follow his instruction, she muted the television. "What's going on, Mom?" She focused her full attention on her worried-looking mother. "Is something bad about to happen?"

"I don't know what's wrong," Tina replied, wringing her hands. "Chief Davenport has something he needs to discuss with you."

"Well, we didn't do anything." Amelia's tone was firm enough that I narrowed my eyes. She had "disappeared" three weeks before. She had turned Hemlock Cove upside down with stories of kidnappers and predators. It turned out she'd masterminded her own disappearance because she wanted money and planned to run off with her friends for a grand adventure — borrowed magic from Hollow Creek fueling her — but with a little witchy intervention I'd managed to make her forget those plans. Had the spell held up? Amelia was a master manipulator.

"We're not accusing you of anything," Chief Terry assured her as he sat on the coffee table and stared at the three girls. "Something has happened to your friend Paisley."

"Oh, no!" Tina's hand flew to her mouth.

"What happened?" Amelia asked, her expression bland.

"She's dead."

"What?" Sophia sat up straighter. "Are you serious?"

"Of course not," Amelia sneered. "This is some weird joke."

"I don't joke about death," Chief Terry replied calmly. "Paisley was found behind the Dragonfly this morning. She was in a clearing in the woods. She'd been stabbed." He laid it out concisely, no embellishment.

"I can't believe it." Tina whined. "We saw her just the other day. She was fine."

"Well, that's how this works," Landon offered. "One minute someone is fine and the next they're not."

"Oh, we'll always need hot police officers like you," Sophia said, offering up a wink that made Landon shift uncomfortably.

Landon managed to keep from scowling, but if I had to guess, it took a lot of work. "Thank you for that inappropriate comment in the wake of your friend's death."

Sophia had the grace to look abashed. "I didn't mean ... um ... ."

"What happened?" Amelia asked. She'd yet to react like the others, who appeared to be shocked. She was calm, something I couldn't identify in her eyes.

"She was stabbed," Chief Terry replied. "That's all we know right now. But there's more."

"More?" Tina was so pale I thought she might pass out.

"You should sit down," I prodded, grabbing her arm and leading her to the oversized chair at the edge of the room.

Tina was the malleable sort, which probably explained why Amelia was queen of this particular castle. She allowed me to situate her in the chair.

"What could possibly be worse than Paisley being stabbed?" Amelia demanded.

"I didn't say it was worse," Chief Terry cautioned. "I said there was more. We went to Paisley's house to inform them of their daughter's death, but they weren't there.

"Both vehicles were in the driveway, but it appeared there had been a struggle in the living room," he continued. "The coffee table was tipped over. There was a broken glass on the floor. We believe that Paisley's mother was in the house watching television."

"Are they dead too?" Emma asked in a timid voice. "Were they all killed?"

"There were no bodies in the house. We're not certain what happened to Paisley's parents. That brings us to why we're here. Do you know of anything that was going on in Paisley's house that might explain what has happened?"

"No," Sophia and Emma said in unison.

Amelia didn't respond.

"I need specifics," Chief Terry stressed. "When was the last time you saw Paisley?"

"Yesterday afternoon," Sophia replied. "We were all downtown together for coffee."

"What time was that?"

"Um ... around three o'clock I think." She looked to Amelia for confirmation.

Amelia nodded. "That sounds right." She'd yet to show a shred of emotion and I was becoming increasingly suspicious.

"What did you talk about?" Chief Terry asked.

"Normal stuff." Amelia lifted one shoulder in a haphazard way, as if they were having a conversation about the weather. "I mean ... it wasn't a big deal."

"Sophia has a crush on Taylor Watkins," Emma volunteered. "We mostly talked about that."

Sophia's cheeks colored. "I don't have a crush on him. Don't be ridiculous."

Even though it was a byproduct of their age, the trivial back and forth frustrated me. The trio had just been informed that one of their closest friends had been brutally murdered, but they remained wrapped up in themselves.

"It's important that you girls think hard," Chief Terry stressed. "Paisley is dead and we can't help her. But we can find out who did this. Her parents are still out there somewhere. We need to find them."

"Why do you think we would know where her parents are?" Amelia demanded. "It's not as if we hung out with them."

"Amelia! Show some respect," Tina scolded.

"It's okay." Chief Terry waved off the admonishment. "They're in shock."

"It doesn't feel real," Emma admitted. "I mean ... I keep thinking that I should be having one of those montages in my head, like on television, where I hear music and remember all the good times we used to have."

The statement struck me funny. Not ha-ha funny but funny weird. Perhaps the girls weren't reacting normally because of the spell I'd put them under.

"That's normal," Landon offered. "It won't feel real for a little bit. We need you to think hard. Was there anything weird going on in the Gilmore household? Were Paisley's parents fighting? Was she fighting with them?"

Horrified disbelief washed over Sophia's face. "You don't think her parents killed her?"

"It's unlikely," Landon replied, "but we have to consider all the angles. We need your help. Was there anybody new in Paisley's life? Perhaps a boyfriend."

That single word — boyfriend — sent Sophia and Emma into squirming fits. Amelia managed to remain impassive, but it appeared to be by force of will.

"There was a boy," I surmised, speaking before I thought better of it. "Did Paisley have a boyfriend?" Thanks to my previous journey into Paisley's head, I knew she didn't have a boyfriend as recently as two weeks ago. But these were teenagers. I remembered well how quickly things could change on that front for girls of that age.

"She didn't have a boyfriend," Sophia said. "She just hung around with us."

I ignored her and focused on Amelia, the group leader. If we wanted answers, she would have to supply them. "Who was she dating?" I demanded.

"I ... ." Amelia glanced at her mother, unsure.

"If you know something, you have to tell them," her mother stressed.

Amelia sighed. "I don't know who it was. She was hiding that information. I know she'd met someone and seemed to think he was 'the one,' but she wouldn't tell us who it was."

"Was that odd for her?" Landon asked. "Did she tell you about other boyfriends?"

Amelia shrugged. "Yes and no. She liked to build up to it before telling us. It was like a game to her."

"Was it a boy from the high school?" I asked. Could a teenager have delivered the destruction I saw in that clearing? It didn't seem possible and yet I couldn't shake the notion.

"We don't know him," Amelia replied. "We just know she met someone last week and she really liked him. We didn't pressure her because we knew she would tell us eventually. She liked to drag things out because she liked the attention."

Emma nodded solemnly. "Do you think he killed her?"

Landon slid his eyes to me, his expression unreadable. "We don't know. But we're going to find out."

"How?" Amelia demanded.

"We're going to investigate."

"That's not really an answer."

"It's the only answer I have. We need answers, so we'll dig until we find them."

"What should I do?" Tina asked. "There's a killer out there. Could he be coming for the rest of the girls?"

That was a very good question.

"We don't know what we're dealing with," Chief Terry answered. "I'll have marked cars patrol the areas around your houses tonight and for the foreseeable future."

Tina didn't look comforted by the answer, but she nodded. "I guess that's something."

"It's all we have for now," Landon said. "We will have more ... and soon. You have my word on it."

5

FIVE

Landon opened the back door of Chief Terry's official vehicle for me, pausing long enough to brush the hair from my face and stare into my eyes, and then leaving me to my thoughts.

I waited until we reached the diner in town for lunch to speak.

"I don't know if they remember." My voice was low. "I just ... don't know."

Landon shot me a sympathetic smile. "I figured. If you'd keyed into the fact that she was lying you would've pushed the situation."

"Most definitely," I agreed. "I don't know, though. She's ... detached."

"For all we know, she might've always been detached," Chief Terry noted. He smiled at the waitress as she delivered our drinks. "What's on special today?"

"I think you're special." The waitress, a woman who had lived in Hemlock Cove for as long as I could remember, winked at him. "But on the menu, we have chicken pot pie."

"Comfort food," Landon said. "I'll have that. Thank you."

Chief Terry nodded in agreement. "Sounds good to me."

The waitress turned her attention to me. "And you, honey? You look a little pale today."

"It's been a long day. I'll have the pot pie."

"No problem." She winked and moved on to another table.

"Bay, you can't blame yourself for this," Landon said. "This isn't your fault."

"Did I say it was my fault?" The challenge came out harsher than I intended. "I'm sorry. That was uncalled for. I just feel ... something." And that something didn't have a name.

"I know how your mind works," Landon said. "You think those girls had something to do with what happened to Paisley. You believe if you'd done something different, she'd still be alive."

"I don't believe that."

"You don't?"

I shook my head. "I can't see those girls stabbing Paisley multiple times. She was one of them. I do think it's possible that they know more than they're saying. I also think it's possible somebody else was helping them and we missed that person during our initial sweep."

Realization dawned on Landon's face. "There's a sixth partner taking out the others so they can't squeal?"

"It's a possibility. That still doesn't explain what happened to Paisley's parents."

"Maybe they were involved," Chief Terry suggested. "Maybe they staged their house to make it look as if there had been an attack and took off."

"I ... don't know. Why would they kill their daughter and flee?"

"Maybe they didn't feel they had any other choice."

"If they were involved, they could've set the scene and then fled as a family. That doesn't explain why Paisley had to die."

"Maybe they didn't believe her when she came home with a modified memory," Landon suggested. "Maybe they thought she was lying and figured they couldn't trust her."

That didn't feel right either. "Say there was a sixth person — though it seems they would've admitted what was happening when we had them at Hollow Creek, if only to point fingers away from themselves. Why kill Paisley and not the others? Why not draw them all out to that clearing and kill them at the same time?"

"That would draw outside attention," Landon replied. "If you kill four teenagers in ritual fashion and leave them in a clearing in the middle of the Michigan woods, that will be the lead story on every cable news channel ... and for more than just one night."

"He's right," Chief Terry said. "That's the stuff nightmares are made of and news programs thrive on. Besides, why add the ritual? That just makes it all the more hinky."

That was another good point, but I had an answer for that. "This is a witch town. Making the murder ritualistic points the finger at all the fake witches in town."

Chief Terry shook his head. "I don't know what to say, Bay."

I rested my elbow on the table and rubbed my forehead, watching as Landon pulled out his phone and checked his email. His lips curved down almost immediately. "What is it?"

He attempted a smile. "It's not good news."

"Is it the autopsy on Paisley?" I hoped he wasn't going to somehow make things worse and say there was a sexual component to her death.

"We won't get that until this afternoon at the earliest," Chief Terry replied.

"So, what is it?"

"It's Steve."

Steve Newton was his boss. I'd come to know him through his several visits to Hemlock Cove. I liked him but remained fearful of how he would react if he ever found out the truth regarding my family. "Does he want you to go into the office?"

"No. He's sending someone from the office here."

Oh, well, that was actually worse. "What did we do to deserve that?"

"There, there." Landon patted my hand with a chuckle. "It's not some grand conspiracy aimed at you. He saw the photos from the crime scene. He believes they suggest we may have a serial killer in the making. He's sending a profiler."

My brain went blank. "Like on *Criminal Minds*?"

"If you're picturing Shemar Moore right now, we're going to have issues," Landon warned.

That elicited a smile. "I just mean ... I've seen that show."

"It would essentially be like that. Most profilers don't travel in a team. I'm not familiar with the individual he's sending – he didn't provide a name – but he'll be here this evening."

"Coming from Detroit?" Chief Terry asked.

Landon shook his head. "This area is too small to have its own profiler. The one they're sending works in the Midwest office in Chicago. I guess he's taking a flight up to Traverse City and then driving here."

I studied his face for signs he was upset. "Are you worried?"

He already had a smile on his face when he turned to me. "Why would I be worried?"

"Because of me."

"I'm always worried about you." He rubbed my back. "Luckily, you're pretty good at taking care of yourself, so some of that fear has dissipated since we hooked up. I'll always be terrified that something could happen to you, though."

It was a good attempt to avoid the question, but there was no way I was letting it go. "That's not what I mean, and you know it. I want to know if you're afraid that this guy will find out what we are."

Landon hesitated and then shrugged. "I'd be lying if I said I wasn't frightened at the prospect of you coming across the wrong person, someone who could hurt you if he found out witches were real. There's no reason to think this guy will be that person."

"Except his entire job description is human behavior. How much do you want to bet Steve arranged for him to stay at The Overlook?"

Obviously that possibility hadn't occurred to Landon, because his face drained of color. "Oh, crap."

"There's nothing you can do about it," Chief Terry said. "You can't very well call Steve and ask him to find different accommodations for this guy. He'll be suspicious because he knows that you and I are at the inn all the time. It makes sense to book the profiler there so we're all close."

"I'm sure that Steve will have told him about Aunt Tillie," I said in an attempt to be helpful. "We can always blame anything strange on her."

"That's all well and good, but Clove is going to give birth any minute," Landon said. "What if she goes into labor when he's there?"

Now I was lost. "Why does that matter?"

"Because you guys are born in swirls of light."

I pursed my lips, confused. "Um ... we are not."

"Um, you are. Do you remember when we were trapped in Aunt Tillie's mind after she was hit in the head? I saw your birth."

I'd forgotten that. In fact, I'd forgotten the part of her memory that involved my birth entirely. "Oh, well ... that was a weird exception. It's not the norm. Clove won't give birth to some swirling bits of light on the dining room floor."

"No?" Landon didn't back down. "Sam has witch in his lineage. That's the reason he came to town. Are you really telling me that there's no chance this kid is going to have a weird birth?"

I didn't know what to say so I simply sat there with my mouth open.

"I think you broke her." Chief Terry waved his hand in front of my face. "She's speechless. It's never happened before."

"I'm not speechless. I'm just ... thinking."

"You hadn't considered a weird birth," Landon mused. "That's kind of funny given the way Clove has been freaking out. How can you guys have overlooked that?"

"Clove is freaking out over the pain," I said. "In case you're not aware, giving birth hurts."

"Oh, I'm aware." Landon's expression darkened. "I heard the story about the watermelon and the orange."

I laughed, some of the weight I'd been carrying since we visited the girls leaving my shoulders. "I'm just saying Clove has had other things on her mind."

"Well, if I were in her position, I'd be worried about what the hospital staff is going to do with a glowing baby."

Landon was right. Sam's lineage could very well push Clove's baby into uncharted territory. Somebody was going to have to raise the issue with her, but it wasn't going to be me. "I'll mention it to my mother and aunts and let them tackle that."

"Good plan. We still have to deal with this profiler. I think we have to warn everybody to be on their best behavior."

That sounded absolutely terrible. "You can tell Aunt Tillie."

He made a face. "Thank you for that."

I laughed again, more of the darkness that had been dragging me down burning away. "I'm sure it will be fine. We've dealt with FBI agents at the inn before."

"But we didn't have Brian and Rosemary to deal with at the time," Landon pointed out. "Speaking of, they just walked through the door."

Chief Terry growled as he turned to look. "Man, is anyone else annoyed that we can't even have lunch without those jerkoffs showing up to ruin it?"

"I'm right there with you." Landon's hand was on my back again. He was constantly rubbing these days because he thought it would alleviate the tension I carried around. I didn't have the heart to tell him that the only thing that would truly make me feel better was Brian and Rosemary leaving town. That was a little too "Aunt Tillie" for my comfort.

"You know, Brian was hanging around that clearing behind the Dragonfly right before the parties ended," I said, my mind drifting back to the night I'd glamoured myself to appear as a teenager and attended one of the gatherings. "Maybe we should ask him if he has any knowledge of what happened to Paisley."

Chief Terry lamented, "There's no way it's him. That would make our lives easier and we all know that's not happening anytime soon."

I did know that. Still ... . "It will make him uncomfortable. I wouldn't mind seeing his reaction."

Landon nodded. "Okay. Let's see if they seat him near us."

"Can I question him?" I asked.

Landon shook his head. "That would take it to an uncomfortable place. Let Chief Terry and me do the questioning."

I blew out a sigh. "Okay, but you'd better grill him like it's a

Scorsese movie."

"I'll do my best."

THE HOSTESS SEATED BRIAN AND ROSEMARY one table over from us. Whether that was by design or coincidence, I couldn't say, but Brian's smug smile led me to believe he'd arranged it that way. I couldn't wait for Landon to wipe it off his face.

"Good afternoon," Brian offered. "It's lovely to see the fine law enforcement officials of Hemlock Cove having a relaxing lunch. I guess that means crime is under control in our fair town."

"I'm pretty sure they have next to zero crime," Rosemary offered.

"You might be surprised." Brian's eyes twinkled as they met mine. "How are you doing, Bay? Excited for your wedding?"

"Of course," I answered. "There's nothing better than marrying the person you love and want to spend the rest of your life with."

"I feel the same way," Rosemary said. "We're already planning for our wedding next summer. We've booked the Hemlock Cove Catholic Church."

"We're not getting married in a church," I said.

Rosemary almost looked disappointed. "I don't understand. Why wouldn't you be getting married in the Catholic Church?"

"I think the better question is why would we be getting married in a church at all," I countered. "We're not exactly pious in our beliefs."

That's when understanding dawned on Rosemary. "Oh." Her smile disappeared. "You're probably having one of those heathen ceremonies."

"We do love a good heathen ceremony," Landon agreed. "I love drinking wine and dancing naked under the full moon."

"Wait ... there's going to be naked dancing?" Chief Terry looked horrified. "I hate that idea."

I took pity on him. "The only naked dancing will likely involve the usual suspects and after Landon and I have retired for the evening."

"So you'll get to chaperone." Landon offered Chief Terry a taunting thumbs-up. "Have fun."

"We're not waiting until next year to get married," I added for Rosemary's benefit. "We're doing it in the next few weeks."

Rosemary was taken aback. "I don't understand why you're doing it so soon."

"Because we can't wait to be married," Landon replied, his gaze landing on Brian. "Speaking of things I can't wait to do, I have a few questions for you, Kelly."

"Oh, yeah?" Brian didn't look bothered by the change of topic. "If this is about how much greater our house is compared to that spit of crappy land you own, I have nothing to say. We're not in the mood to sell our house."

"We're not in the mood to buy it," Landon said. "We're going to build our dream house out there. That's not what I want to question you about."

"Question me?" For the first time, Brian looked mildly concerned. "Is this an official interrogation?"

"Official? No. I'm simply curious if you've been out to the Dragonfly recently."

"Why would I go out there?"

"Last time I checked, you were partying with underage kids in the general vicinity."

Brian shot a furtive look toward Rosemary and then shook his head. "That's a lie. I haven't been hanging out with kids."

Landon continued. "You should know that a body was found in that clearing this morning. A local teenager was killed. We'll be digging deep on answers regarding what's been happening in that party spot."

Brian did his best to remain calm but his cheeks flushed with color. "You'd better have something to back up any allegations you make where I'm concerned. I haven't been hanging out with teenagers. You're just saying that to mess with me."

That was a lie. I saw him when I went undercover. I still didn't know what he'd been doing out there with a bunch of underaged girls and boys, but I knew it couldn't be anything good. "Why would we want to mess with you in that manner?" I blurted out.

"Who knows why you two want to mess with me," Brian shot back. "You've made it your life's mission to ruin me since I came to this stupid town. You took my business, for crying out loud. I have no idea why you do the things you do."

"My grandmother says it's because they're evil," Rosemary offered.

"I never really believed in evil until I met Tillie Winchester," Brian said. "Now I know what abject evil looks like."

"Oh, I wouldn't go there if I were you," Landon warned. "Aunt Tillie may be mouthy, but she's pretty far from evil."

That wasn't the tack I wanted to take. "She idles at evil," I countered. "She's the evilest of evil, and you should keep that in mind if you continue to mess with us," I warned. "Also, I know you were out there with those kids, Brian. I saw you. Keep lying to Rosemary, by all means, but you're not fooling us. I know what I saw."

"I didn't see you," Brian said. "How odd."

"You just said you weren't there," Chief Terry pointed out. "How could you see her if you weren't?"

Brian opened and closed his mouth, and then shook his head. "You're trying to trip me up. You can't railroad me. While we're at it, I *will* get my newspaper back. You may think you've won but I'm nowhere near done."

Landon rested his hand on mine to keep me from leaping over the table and strangling him. "Don't go near Bay," he ordered. "I've warned you before that I won't put up with it. If you go after her, I'll make you pay."

"I'm looking forward to the attempt." Brian was back to smarmy. "May the best man win."

"If I were you, son, I wouldn't be worried about us men," Chief Terry intoned. "The women in these parts can take care of themselves, and they're far more terrifying."

"Definitely," Landon agreed. "Just say the word and we'll let Aunt Tillie off her leash."

Brian swallowed hard. "I'm not afraid of that crazy old bat. She's all talk."

Now it was my turn to smirk. "Famous last words."

6

SIX

Brian refused to engage with us after a few more minutes of traded barbs. That left us to eat our pot pies in peace.

Landon snagged the bill as we were leaving and I stood next to the front door waiting for him, my eyes drifting to the window when something caught my eye. There was a momentary shadow, but it disappeared almost instantly. I narrowed my eyes to look again but saw nothing.

That's when Rosemary exited the bathroom and almost ran directly into me. I tried to move out of her way, but she was having none of it.

"I don't know why you feel the need to fixate on Brian," she said. "He's a good man."

"He is not a good man."

"Who knows him better? I'm pretty sure it's me, and I happen to know he's a great man. I wouldn't have fallen in love with him if he wasn't."

"I have no idea how your relationship works," I said. "I don't really care to know." That wasn't entirely true. I was more than a little curious about how they'd managed to hook up in the first place. I didn't want her to know I was interested, though. It would give her too much power. "As long as you and Brian stay away from my family, I really couldn't care less about your plans."

"We're going to be happy." Rosemary was adamant. "That's all I've ever wanted."

For a moment, my heart went out to her. Her grandmother, Willa, was a tyrant of epic proportions. She made Aunt Tillie look like a fuzzy pet bunny giving nose kisses. Part of me believed Rosemary didn't have a chance of growing up to be a decent human being. Then I reminded myself that Rosemary was an adult capable of being what she wanted to be. She'd chosen to be this way.

"I hope you find the happiness you're looking for," I said. "But I don't want you near me. I don't trust you. As for Brian, I definitely don't trust him. I'm not sure if you believe the lies he's spouting, but he was at that clearing with the local kids."

"Why would he hang out with a bunch of teenagers?" Rosemary demanded. "That makes no sense."

"And yet you think it makes sense for me to make up that lie to drag you away from him."

"You'll say anything to ruin my happiness."

"Why?"

"Because you hate me. You've always hated me."

"I don't even know you."

"You were cruel to me when we were children."

I sputtered. "I wasn't cruel to you. Why would you think that?"

"Because I was there. My grandmother warned me before our visits that you guys would try to cut me out and be mean to me. She was right."

"So your grandmother poisoned you against us before you even met us," I countered. "I wish I could say I was surprised, but that sounds just like Aunt Willa. I've never known her to be anything other than unpleasant."

"That's rich coming from you." Rosemary's lips twisted. "You were raised by that horrible witch Tillie. She molded you into monsters."

Landon, who had finished paying for our meal, sidled over in time to hear the last part. "What did you just say?" he demanded.

Rosemary's eyes snapped to him, and for a moment she looked fearful. She regrouped quickly. "You heard me. Tillie raised Bay, Clove and Thistle to be monsters. She did a good job, too."

"If you believe that, why are you living in this town?" Landon snapped. "If you think that they're so terrible, why would you want to be near them?"

"I don't. That's Brian. He wants his grandfather's newspaper back. You stole it and he can't let it go. I don't blame him. All he has left of his grandfather is that newspaper, and you swindled him out of it."

Anger, hot and fast, flashed over Landon's face. "Nobody swindled him out of anything," he seethed. "He tried to hurt Bay, ruin her livelihood, and steal that newspaper from her."

"It was never hers!"

Landon refused to back down. "William Kelly left Bay in charge of that newspaper for a reason. He knew she would take care of it, nurture it, and make it what it was supposed to be. There's a reason he stipulated in his will that Brian couldn't fire Bay."

"Brian only fired her because she was a murder suspect."

"He fired her because he took advantage of the situation." Landon was furious. "He got what he deserved. The people in this town might not all love Bay, but they know how important the newspaper is. They understand that she's keeping it afloat. Brian would've run it into the ground with his get-rich-quick schemes."

"You take that back!" Rosemary's eyes flashed with fury, but that's not what caught my attention. No, that was the movement in the window behind her. The shadows were back, and this time they were taking form.

"I won't take it back," Landon said. "Brian doesn't want to put in the work. He expected to sit back and collect a bunch of money. He doesn't understand about dedicating himself to a career."

"Brian is an excellent businessman," Rosemary hissed. "Bay just wishes she could be as smart as him."

Landon slid his arm around my waist. "Come on, Bay. This is a fruitless conversation."

I didn't disagree, but I was too focused on the dark figures in the window to give him my full attention. The figures there were evil, dark wisps of smoke flowing off them. I could see right through them.

"Brian is going to get his newspaper back," Rosemary called out to us as Landon shepherded me toward the door. "Just you wait."

"Don't hold your breath." Landon waited until we were outside to speak again. "She is the absolute worst person I've ever met. Like ... the absolute worst."

"Brian is worse," I said, my eyes returning to the window. The shadows were gone. It was as if they'd never been there and I'd imagined them.

"Brian doesn't worry me."

"Does Rosemary?"

"Rosemary worries me only because she knows a lot about your family and could make life difficult if she applied herself. Of course, if she starts spouting nonsense about witches, people are likely to think she's nuts."

I rubbed my cheek, unable to tear my gaze away from the window. I couldn't help but wonder if I'd really seen something.

"Why are you so distracted?" Landon asked.

I turned back to him. "I'm just ... thinking."

"About the profiler? Don't worry about that. I'm sure we'll be able to figure it out."

I smiled because I knew he needed it. "I'm sure we will. Are you heading back to work?"

"That's the plan. What are you going to do?"

"I'm heading to Hypnotic to hang out with Clove and Thistle."

"Are you going to mention my glowing baby concern?"

"No, and neither are you." I extended a warning finger. "Keep that to yourself. Let my mom and aunts deal with it."

Landon kissed me. "Are you sure you're okay?" He looked legitimately concerned.

"I'm fine," I promised. "I just need to think. There has to be a way for us to figure out what's going on."

"Well, I have faith." He graced me with another kiss and then pulled away. "Call me if you figure something out. Otherwise, I'll see you for dinner."

"I'll be in touch."

"That's just the way I like you." He winked and started down the sidewalk, leaving me to stare at the empty window.

CLOVE AND THISTLE WERE IN THEIR usual spots when I entered their store, the wind chimes above the door alerting them to my presence. From her spot on the couch at the center of the store, Clove shot me a happy smile. Thistle glared at me from behind the counter.

"What's going on?" I asked.

"Clove." That's all Thistle said.

"What did you do?" I asked my pregnant cousin, my eyebrows hopping when I realized she was halfway through a box of chocolate-covered cherries. "Where did you get those?"

"Dad gave them to me." Clove popped another one in her mouth. "I mentioned that I'd been craving them and he dug up this box. They're from last Christmas but still surprisingly good."

"Well, bully for you." I glanced between them, debating, and then decided to tell them. "I saw something in the window of the diner a few minutes ago."

"Was it Aunt Tillie?" Thistle scowled. "I told her to go home, but she's probably stalking Mrs. Little."

"It wasn't Aunt Tillie." In halting terms, I told them what I'd seen. When I was finished, Clove whined.

"Oh, I don't want another crisis," she moaned. "Can't we be crisis-free until after the baby is born?"

"I'm planning a wedding, in case you've forgotten."

"She can't see beyond the chocolate," Thistle said. "She doesn't care about anyone but herself."

"That's not true," Clove protested. "It's just ... I'm going to have a baby. I need to focus on that."

"In other words, she has no time for our issues," Thistle muttered.

I pinned Thistle with a suspicious look, debating whether or not I should chase that topic before deciding against it. Something other than Clove's eating habits was bothering Thistle. If I wanted to drag it out of her, I would need privacy.

"I just wanted you guys to know so you're careful," I said. "I'm not sure what I saw. I'm not even sure it was real."

"Oh, it was real." Clove wrinkled her ski-slope nose. "We don't have good luck, so there's no way you're suffering from a brain tumor and seeing things that aren't there."

My mouth dropped open. "Did you just wish a brain tumor on me?"

She shrugged. "Not a life-threatening one. I just would prefer you have one of those little ones that's easy to take out, not cancer or anything. You have to admit that's preferable to fighting window monsters. I mean ... has anybody even heard of those?"

"No, and that's why I stopped by to warn you guys. I'm not sure what they are." I turned to Thistle. "Be careful. If you stumble across anything in one of your books that explains window monsters, I'd appreciate a heads-up."

"I can do some reading," Thistle offered, her earlier annoyance apparently forgotten. "I'm not sure what I'll find. I've never heard of window monsters. Mirror monsters are a thing, though. I guess I can start there."

I bobbed my head. "Good idea. I need to go to the office and then I'm going home. I have a stack of books there I can go through."

"There's also the library at the inn. You might find something there."

"But then I'll have to bring Aunt Tillie in on the research. That's always hit or miss."

"Given what happened with Paisley Gilmore and those runes, it might be the wise choice. She's a crazy old bat, but she's smart when it comes to dark magic."

PRELUDE TO A WITCH

She had a point. "I'll consider it. For now, I have to focus on work. If you find anything, let me know."

Thistle offered up a mock salute. "No problem. I'll work it in between feeding rounds for Clove. That seems to be my main purpose in life these days."

I shot her another look. She was definitely upset about something.

"We'll talk later," I promised. "I need to get some stuff done at The Whistler first."

I SPENT HOURS WORKING ON THE NEXT edition of The Whistler. My neck and back hurt when it was time to go home.

I pulled into the driveway that led to the guesthouse where Landon and I lived, briefly wondering if I had time for a bath before dinner. All thoughts of relaxation fled when I realized who was standing on my front porch.

I gripped my keys as I moved in Aunt Willa's direction. "This is a surprise."

"Yes, I'm a delightful houseguest," Aunt Willa agreed.

"I didn't say it was a good surprise."

The smile that she'd pasted on her face disappeared almost instantaneously. "Listen, Bay, I know you don't like me."

"That's an understatement."

She pretended I hadn't spoken. "I'm still your family."

I gestured toward the inn, the roof visible in the distance. "That's my family. Landon is my family. Chief Terry is my family."

"We share blood."

"Blood doesn't make family." I tried to edge around her to put my key in the lock, but she refused to move. "What is it you want?" I demanded. I was exhausted and she was the last person I wanted to deal with.

"To strike a deal."

"With me?" I couldn't contain my surprise. "Why would you want to strike a deal with me?"

"Because you're really in charge of this family."

I tried to imagine my mother's face if she heard those words escape Aunt Willa's mouth. "Yeah, I think you're mixed up. It doesn't matter, nobody in our family wants to deal with you."

"I don't want to deal with you either. Heck, I don't want to be back in this stupid town. I hate it here."

"And yet ... ." I held out my hands.

"I'm only here because Brian considers this home. He and Rosemary are building a life. I don't want it to be a terrible life."

"And you think I'll somehow ruin it?"

"Not you specifically, but Brian really does seem to hate you. His feelings for your fiancé are even more difficult to untangle."

"There's nothing to untangle. He hates Landon too."

"You're right. But I'm here to propose a deal."

She had to be joking. But she had no sense of humor. "What do you want?"

"I want you and your cousins to leave Rosemary and Brian alone."

"We have no interest in either of them."

"Then why did Rosemary track me down an hour ago crying because you terrorized her?"

"That's not how I remember it going down."

"She feels you're out to get her."

"That's funny, because I can't help but feel she's out to get me."

"That's why we need to strike a deal." Willa was firm. "If you agree to keep your arm of the family away from Brian and Rosemary, I promise to keep them away from you."

"I can't control Aunt Tillie."

"You could if you wanted."

"I don't want to. I don't want you people here. This is my town. You might consider that rude, but I really don't care. I'm not making a deal with you."

Aunt Willa's eyes narrowed to slits. "You should reconsider."

"I want you off my property. I have nothing more to say to you."

"You'll regret this, Bay," she warned. "I came to you with a truce and you threw it back in my face. That's a mistake."

"The mistake was you guys coming back. This is our town. You have no place here. Get out or get out of the way. Those are your choices."

"I think we have a few more choices than that."

"I guess we'll see."

7

SEVEN

Landon arrived home after I'd relaxed in the tub and dried my hair. I was picking out an outfit for dinner when he strolled into the bedroom.

"You didn't text me all day," he announced.

I shifted my gaze away from the blue shirt I was considering to him. "I was with you for half the day."

"Fine. You didn't text me all afternoon."

"So?"

"So, I was worried." He ran his hands over the shoulders of my fuzzy robe. "There's a murderer on the loose, in case you've forgotten."

"It's Hemlock Cove. Isn't there always a murderer on the loose?"

"This is an especially brutal murderer."

"Well, as you can see, I'm fine."

"You don't look fine." His fingers traced under my eyes. "You look tired. Do you want to skip dinner and stay home tonight?"

"Um ... no. We have nothing to eat but Pop-Tarts."

"I can live on Pop-Tarts ... and love."

"I want real food." I shrugged out of my robe and tugged the shirt over my head. "I'm hungry."

"You're upset," he said.

"I'm not upset." I avoided his probing gaze. What was I supposed to say to him? "I'm ... conflicted."

"Tell me what's bothering you." He insisted.

"I ... saw something this afternoon." It came tumbling out. "I know I should've said something then, but I don't even know what it was. I mean ... evil window people? What is that?"

He dropped to the bed, his hand on my waist. "I'm not an expert on this stuff."

"Apparently neither am I because I've never heard of window monsters."

"Do you think they were ghosts? You can see ghosts that nobody else can."

"Aunt Tillie can."

"But you're the one with the advancing powers."

"You've seen ghosts, too," I reminded him.

"I think I've seen ghosts because you can see ghosts."

"I don't think that's scientific. It sounds like a codependency thing."

He barked out a laugh. "Maybe it is. The few times I've managed it have been because you've been in trouble ... or exceedingly happy, like when I gave you the best proposal in the world."

That made me laugh. He was proud of his proposal, and rightfully so. I would never forget it. "It was the best proposal ever." I sat next to him and dropped my hand in his lap so he could hold it. "I was afraid when I saw them."

He didn't immediately respond, and when I turned to look at him, I found sympathy waiting for me. "Did you hear me?"

"Yes." He nodded. "Do you want me to say I'm disappointed? I'm not. You're allowed to be afraid. I'm afraid all the time."

"I've never really been afraid of ghosts. Well, Floyd, but he was a poltergeist. Other than him, I've never been afraid of the dead."

"What about zombies?"

"I've never seen a zombie. They're not real."

"They might not eat brains, but I guarantee they're real."

"Why do you say that?"

"Because you're real." His fingers danced lightly over my cheek. "You're my magical witch. Because of you, I believe that everything is real ... including this." He moved my hand to the spot above his heart. "If you're afraid, sweetie, don't keep it to yourself. Tell me so we can deal with it together."

"I know I should've told you. I was just so confused." I leaned into him as he wrapped his arms around me. "I don't know what to make of any of it."

"Well, I don't either. We'll figure it out. I don't think it was a coincidence that your window monsters showed up the same day we found Paisley's body."

"I don't think so either."

"So, we need to deal with it."

I pressed my eyes shut and let him rub the back of my neck. "Maybe you should deal with it and I'll hide in bed for a week. How does that sound?"

"If I thought you would actually do that, I'd be all for it. We both know you won't run from a problem. You're just ... tired."

That was a fact. "Aunt Willa was here when I got home." I'd left that part out of the story. She didn't seem as important as the window ghosts. "She wanted to make a deal. She said if I could rein in the entire Winchester clan, she would make sure Brian and Rosemary didn't bother us."

"I think I can guess what you said."

"I told her I didn't want them in my town and I wasn't going to do a thing to stop Aunt Tillie from exacting whatever revenge she cooks up."

"That's exactly what I would've told her."

"What if they don't leave? What if they stay here forever and we always have to deal with them?"

"Then we won't let them affect our lives. Bay, they're not important in the grand scheme of things." He turned me so I had no choice but to meet his eyes. "All that's important is us, and our family. They can't hurt us."

"What if they can?" That was the question that had been eating at me since they returned to Hemlock Cove. "Brian hates you. He's going to mess with you, with your job. What if he gets you fired?"

"He doesn't have that power. I've already told Steve what happened when you bought the newspaper. There's nothing Brian can hold over us. My boss was impressed when I told him what I did. He thought it was funny."

"There's one thing Brian can hold over us." I pointed at myself. "He knows we're magical. He hasn't figured it all out, but Aunt Tillie cursed him, like, three times ... including that one time she gave him spots on his you know what."

Landon broke into a grin. "Ah, that was a fun day, wasn't it?"

Now that he mentioned it, that *was* a fun day. "I'm still worried that Brian will do something terrible to you. I don't trust him."

"I don't either, but we clearly have bigger things to worry about. The stuff with Brian and Rosemary will work itself out."

"How can you be sure?"

"Because I've never been happier in my life." He nodded when I frowned. "It's true. I have you, so I have everything. I will not let gnats derail our happiness. That's all that they are. We'll figure out what's going on with them and get them out of our town."

I wanted to believe him. "How can you be sure?"

"I've spent enough time with Aunt Tillie to know she won't stop until she gets her way. She wants them out of Hemlock Cove. They won't be able to stand up to the tidal wave of crap she sends in their direction.

"Are you really going to sit there and tell me that you don't think she's going to torture them until they capitulate and flee town with their tails between their legs?" he continued. "She's your great-aunt. You grew up with her. You know darned well she's going to win."

I did know that. "It could get ugly before it gets better."

"See, I think watching Aunt Tillie torture them sounds fun. Either way, she'll win in the end. That means we'll win."

I pressed my eyes shut for a beat. "We should probably get ready for dinner. Your profiler will most likely be there when we get to the inn."

Landon nodded. "I got a text from Steve. The profiler is en route from the airport right now. You're right. By the time we get there, we're going to have an entirely new problem to grapple with."

"No matter who he is, or what he sees, he'll be better than Willa and Rosemary."

Landon didn't look convinced. "We need to be careful, though."

He was always bolstering me. "I really hope you're right." I gave him a quick kiss and hopped to my feet. "So ... blue?" I waved my hand before the shirt.

"Whatever you want." His grin was devastatingly charming. "Just make sure there aren't a lot of buttons so I can romance the crap out of you when we get home."

I returned his smile. "Blue it is." I paused a beat and then gripped his hand. "I really do love you. I hope you know that."

"I really love you. That's why I know we can get through anything. Nothing can hurt us as long as we're together."

I gave in and embraced the sentiment. I needed him to be right.

WE WALKED TO THE INN, LETTING OURSELVES in through the rear door. Aunt Tillie wasn't in her usual spot on the couch watching *Jeopardy*, which had worry zinging through my stomach.

"I hope she hasn't already found the profiler," I muttered.

Landon smirked. "Listen, I know you're worried that she'll start spouting nonsense, but it's going to be okay. It's likely that a profiler would assume she's senile before believing anything she says. I mean ... she wears a combat helmet and inappropriate leggings to ride her scooter around town."

"She still likes to freak people out."

"This is a town designed around witches," he reminded me. "It's possible this profiler will believe that Aunt Tillie is simply committed to her role."

"That's true." I brightened considerably. "We are known for our dinner theater."

"See." He tapped the side of his head. "Now you're thinking."

We stopped in the kitchen long enough to talk to Mom and Marnie. They were toiling over dinner and mentioned my Aunt Twila was working the front desk. That was also cause for concern, so rather than stop in the library for a drink as we normally would, we headed to the lobby ... and found my worst nightmare taking shape.

Aunt Tillie, her combat helmet firmly in place and her pig Peg at her side, held up what looked to be a cross made from joined sticks — think very rudimentary *Blair Witch Project* artwork — and was facing down a pretty blonde in an expensive suit.

"We don't want any of your Mary Kay," Aunt Tillie announced. "Now, begone, demon!"

For her part, the woman looked more amused than annoyed. Her smile never faltered and she cocked her head as she regarded my great-aunt. "You must be Tillie Winchester."

Aunt Tillie's eyes narrowed. "Who told you that?"

"You're famous in certain circles," the woman said with a laugh.

"I'm so sorry." I held up my hands as I strode into the lobby. I couldn't believe Aunt Tillie was harassing a guest. I expected her to go all out to drive the profiler crazy. What she was pulling now was beyond my scope of understanding. "Are you checking in?" I saw the reception desk was empty. "Where is Twila?"

"Doing something stupid," Aunt Tillie replied, her eyes never leaving the woman's face. "She mentioned something about getting a book from the library."

"How is that stupid?" I asked.

"It's a book on teaching bears to drink from teacups."

She had to be making that up. "Well, fine." I kept my smile in place even though I wanted to pound Aunt Tillie into the dust for making a mockery of Mom's business. "I can check you in." I moved behind the computer. "Your name?"

"Hannah Waters," Landon replied, taking me by surprise.

"How do you know that?" I was confused.

"Landon." The willowy blonde was completely focused on my fiancé. "It's been a long time." She extended her hand. "A very, very long time."

The annoyance I'd been feeling thanks to Aunt Tillie's antics turned into something else. I couldn't give a name to it — or maybe I simply didn't want to — but it felt like a mishmash of jealousy and discomfort. "You two know each other?"

"We do." Landon shook Hannah's hand and then released it, even though I had the sneaking suspicion Hannah would've been fine extending the greeting. "We were in the academy together."

"Oh, well ... ." I didn't know what to say. I'd been expecting a male profiler. "Um ... it's nice to meet you."

"A pleasure." Hannah's blue eyes were bright when they finally met mine. "Do you work here?"

"Not really."

"This is Bay's mother's inn," Landon volunteered, moving behind the counter to join me.

"And you're Bay?" Hannah's composure never cracked. "Do you work with Landon?"

"Sometimes," I said.

"Bay is my fiancée," Landon said.

"Oh, I heard." Hannah bobbed her head. There was no disappointment when she focused on me a second time, although it was clear she was taking my measure. "I had drinks with Tom and Kevin in Chicago about three weeks ago. They mentioned that you'd gotten engaged. I didn't believe it at first, but they swore it was true."

"Who are Tom and Kevin?" I asked.

"Those are code names," Aunt Tillie hissed. "They're rogue Mary Kay sellers who want to infiltrate my inn."

I lightly cuffed the back of her combat helmet. "Stop being weird."

"Who's being weird?"

"You," Landon replied. "But that's nothing new." He shook his head before turning back to Hannah. "You'll have to excuse Aunt Tillie. She's ... an individual who likes attention."

"So I see." Hannah said. "Steve gave me a rundown on what to

PRELUDE TO A WITCH

expect. He suggested I stay here. I wasn't certain why, but now I assume it's because you're often here."

"Actually, I live on the grounds." Landon was doing his best to appear relaxed, but there was tension around the corners of his eyes. He was stressed out and pretending otherwise.

"You live in an inn." Hannah looked to the ceiling. "That's ... interesting."

"Not in the inn. I live in a guesthouse on the property."

"With your fiancée?"

Landon nodded. "Yes."

"Well, that sounds ... like something out of a book." Hannah giggled. "I didn't realize your life had changed so much."

"You can't trust anyone who smiles that much," Aunt Tillie warned me in a low voice. Even her best attempts at being quiet were failures. "That's one of the first lessons I ever taught you. Remember it. Live it." She thumped her hand against her chest. "Also, Mary Kay is crap. Nobody needs half the stuff they sell."

I felt as if I was out of my element, but I refused to let this person — someone Landon clearly wasn't expecting — rock my world. "Please ignore Aunt Tillie. The longer the day goes, the loopier she gets."

Aunt Tillie growled. "And just for that, you're on my list."

Landon perked up. "Let me just say, I love the smell of bacon."

Aunt Tillie had cursed me to smell like bacon as punishment more than once — resulting in half the male members of the town giving chase. He wanted the bacon curse again, but he couldn't admit that in front of Hannah.

"I'm not rewarding you," Aunt Tillie shot back, extending a finger in Hannah's direction. "I will be watching you. If any of my good makeup is replaced with bad makeup, you'll be in a world of hurt."

Hannah's smile never diminished, even when Aunt Tillie turned on her heel and flounced out of the room with Peg giving chase. "This is a unique place."

Landon chuckled and moved his hand to my back. It was normal for him to touch me, but now the simple gesture felt somehow different, as if he was trying to send a message. I recognized the message wasn't for me but for Hannah, which made me suspicious of exactly what their academy days were like.

"They have you down for a room on the third floor," I said, keeping my eyes on the computer screen. "It looks like they've already run a corporate credit card."

"Yes, Steve said he'd taken care of everything with one of the proprietors. Someone named Marnie."

"It looks like everything is settled here." I grabbed a keycard from the stack on the desk and ran it through the machine. "This should work. Room 302."

"Great." Hannah was all smiles as she took the card. "I believe Steve said that I would be in time for dinner."

"Dinner is in fifteen minutes," I confirmed, looking to Landon, who avoided eye contact. "We're looking forward to a fun meal."

"I can't wait to meet the rest of your family," Hannah said.

"Yes, won't that be fun?"

EIGHT

Once Hannah had gone upstairs to her room, I slid my eyes to Landon. I did not, however, say a single word.

"What?" Landon barked after a few seconds, his eyes flashing with annoyance. "If you have something to say, say it."

"I don't have anything to say." I turned away from him and finished filling out the ledger. When I finished, I moved to slide around him. "I'm going to get a drink in the library."

He caught my shoulders before I could escape. "Bay ... ." It was obvious he was bothered by what was happening. Sometimes he was good with words — especially when he wanted to be romantic — but other times he fumbled like a Lions player taking on the Packers on *Monday Night Football*.

"She's your ex-girlfriend," I said.

He studied my face for a long moment and then nodded. "I don't know that 'girlfriend' is the right word. We dated, briefly, in the Academy. That was a long time ago."

"Okay." I patted his arm. "I want something to drink."

He refused to move out of my way. "I was twenty-two years old," he said. "I thought I was a man back then, but I didn't become a man until I met you and realized what it meant to love someone."

"Do you think I'm going to turn into a puddle of insecurity because your ex-girlfriend is here?" I asked.

"I don't want you feeling insecure. I love you more than anything. That will never change."

"Thank you, but I'm okay. The fact that she's your ex-girlfriend might help us. I mean ... she's less likely to report us for being witchy nuts thanks to her ties to you."

"I don't know about that." Landon scratched his chin. "She was always pragmatic. She didn't believe anything she couldn't see with her naked eye. The good news is that I think it's likely she'll chalk up anything she sees as part of the Hemlock Cove mystique. The bad news is ... if she sees actual magic, I think she'll report it."

That wasn't what I wanted to hear. "Then I guess we need to make sure that she doesn't report it."

"That would be preferable." Landon brushed his fingers against my cheek. "We're okay, right, Bay?"

"Of course. Why wouldn't we be?"

"I don't know." He shrugged. "I just ... this feels weird."

"Why?"

"She's a part of my old life. I broke up with her and she might still have a crush on me. It's just ... odd all around."

"We'll get through it." I squeezed his hand. "I know you love me. I refuse to be jealous of a woman you dated eight years ago."

"That's good, because you have nothing to be jealous about. Not only do I love you more than anything, I'm pretty sure I love you more than anybody has ever loved anybody else in the entire history of the world."

I couldn't contain my smile. "You are the competitive sort."

"This is just an added layer of crap we shouldn't have to deal with. Between Brian Kelly and a murderer, she's just a little too much extra to take."

"It's fine." I wasn't jealous as much as worried. What I didn't say to Landon was that my greatest fear regarding Hannah's possible continued interest in him revolved around her watching us a little too closely. "I'm not insecure about this. It's weird, but we've been through much worse."

He pulled me to him, hugging me tight as he rested his cheek on my head. "I'm still sorry. This is something we shouldn't have to deal with."

"We'll survive." I was certain of that.

HANNAH WAS UPSTAIRS TEN MINUTES, and by the time she came downstairs, Landon and I had cocktails and were completely put together.

Er, well, completely put together for us. We would never be the sort of couple that didn't say moronic things and follow up the words with stupid actions.

"This inn is beautiful," Hannah said as we led her to the dining room. "Will you inherit it eventually?"

I shrugged. "I haven't really thought about it. The women in my family live a long time. They'll be here to keep the inn in good running order for a number of years yet."

"Still, it would be cool to own your own business one day," Hannah pressed.

"Bay already owns her own business," Landon said. "She owns the town newspaper."

Hannah's expression reflected confusion. "You're engaged to a reporter? That seems ... weird."

"Why is that weird?" I asked.

"Because at the academy, Landon always used to say that the only good reporter was a dead one."

Landon pulled up short. "I did not say that."

"You did. We were having that discussion on whether or not the media have the right to hold law enforcement accountable if there's a screw up. We all agreed that it shouldn't be allowed."

Landon looked to me. "I did not say that."

Hannah refused to back down. "I remember very distinctly

because I was the only one who thought the press performed an important job."

Landon glared at her. "I think Bay performs a very important job. I see how hard she works and respect her all the more for it."

Before he could get up a full head of steam, I grabbed his wrist and gave it a squeeze. "It's okay if you've thought better of ideas you had when you were younger and unevolved," I pointed out. "I used to think a lot of weird things. It's not the end of the world."

He didn't look convinced. "I never really wished reporters dead," he said finally, shooting Hannah an annoyed look. "She's making that up."

Hannah's laugh told me she was having a good time. "I see you're still the same protective guy you always were. He's always been a gentleman," she said to me.

"I don't know that I would call him a gentleman," I hedged, thinking back to three nights before, when he conned my mother into making him an entire plate of bacon for a bedtime snack and then proceeded to eat it in bed while trying to get me naked.

Landon's eyes lit with flirty energy when I locked gazes with him. It was as if he could read my mind.

"I'm a total gentleman," Landon countered as he held the dining room door for Hannah and me. "See. Would someone who wasn't a gentleman do that?"

I smirked as I shook my head and followed Hannah into the dining room. Everyone else was already seated and waiting.

"You're late," Mom snapped as she slid a platter of pot roast and potatoes toward the center of the table.

"Ooh, yum." Landon danced around me and took his regular seat next to Aunt Tillie. "I love pot roast night."

Mom shot him a fond smile. "I cooked with you in mind this evening."

"And that's why you're going to be the best mother-in-law ever."

Before I could sit, Hannah took my usual chair, settling between Landon and Chief Terry. "It smells good," she said.

PRELUDE TO A WITCH

I stood where I was, rooted to my spot, and stared at the back of her head.

"What's happening?" Thistle asked from the far end of the table. "Who is that chick sitting in Bay's spot?"

Hannah glanced around the table, her cheeks coloring when she realized Thistle was talking about her. "I'm so sorry." She immediately got to her feet. "I should've realized that was your spot."

Landon already had a dinner roll stuffed in his mouth as he glanced between us.

"It's fine," I reassured her. "It's not a big deal. We just ... eat together a lot."

"And have regular seats," Hannah said. "I get it. Am I okay sitting on the other side of ... this fine gentleman?" She shot Chief Terry a bright smile.

"Of course," I replied. "If you want to sit here ... ." I trailed off and helplessly gestured at my normal chair.

"No, that's not necessary," she said. "I'm fine here." She smiled again for Chief Terry's benefit. "Everything looks lovely."

"There's nothing better than pot roast," Thistle agreed. "Who the heck are you?"

It was only then that I realized I hadn't made introductions. "I'm sorry, this is Hannah Waters. She's an FBI profiler from Chicago and she will be in Hemlock Cove working on the Paisley Gilmore case with Landon and Chief Terry. I put her in the third-floor room you had earmarked for her in the computer, by the way."

Mom nodded. "I'm sorry you had to do that. I thought Twila was at the desk." She shot her flame-haired sister a pointed look. "Which begs the question, if you weren't handling the front desk like you said you would, what were you doing?"

Twila was the picture of innocence. "What do you mean? I was in the lobby."

"Bay just said she had to check in the FBI agent."

"Hannah," I corrected.

"Hannah." Mom gave a smile that didn't make it all the way to her eyes. "What were you doing, Twila?"

"Yes, what were you doing that was so important you couldn't help with dinner?" Marnie drawled.

Sensing trouble, I cleared my throat to shut up my mother and aunts and then focused on Hannah. "I should probably do introductions." I introduced everyone around the table. She lingered on Clove for a moment, seemingly entranced by her huge belly, and then focused on Chief Terry.

"You have a good reputation in law enforcement circles," Hannah offered. "I didn't know that you lived here. I guess I was ... misinformed."

"I don't live here," Chief Terry said, shifting on his chair. "I just ... ."

"He shacks up with my niece," Aunt Tillie blurted, ignoring the death glare my mother beamed at her. "He has a house, but given the hours Winnie works, he's almost always here. Plus, the food is better here, and he's motivated by his tastebuds and libido more than anything else."

"Well, that's nice." Hannah added one slab of meat, one potato and four carrots to her plate from the roast platter. "Do you eat together often?"

She was digging. As a profiler, she wanted to break things down so she could wrap her mind around our family dynamics. I understood her curiosity, but I didn't want her digging too deep. "Landon and I eat about ten meals here a week," I replied. "Clove and Thistle don't live on the family property, so they eat here three or four times a week."

"Still, that's a lot for adults," Hannah said. "And ten times a week?" Her eyebrows migrated up her forehead. "That's ... a lot."

Landon didn't appear bothered about being psychoanalyzed. "It's really not," he said. "We don't cook."

"He means Bay doesn't cook," Thistle sniped.

"I mean that *we* don't cook," Landon shot back. He had a heaping mound of food on his plate and seemed to be over the awkwardness. "We don't need to. Winnie is the best cook in the world and we can walk here in five minutes. Why would we cook under those circumstances?"

"Well, the ease of the meals is definitely a consideration, but it points toward a co-dependent family dynamic," Hannah said. "I'm not judging you. I simply find it interesting."

Landon rolled his eyes. "Please. You're trying to shrink us because that's what you do. Let me save you some time, okay? We're definitely codependent. That's not just Bay and her mother. That's Bay and me ... and Bay and Chief Terry ... and Bay and Thistle."

Now it was my turn to frown. "I think you've said enough."

"Yeah, you've said that Bay is codependent with everyone in her life," Thistle agreed. "And, for the record, Bay and I are not codependent."

Landon shot Thistle a quelling look. "That came out wrong. What I meant to say is that we're all codependent. Bay isn't the only one. I'm just as codependent as everybody else."

"I don't think I understand what's going on here," Twila said in a stage whisper as she leaned closer to Marnie.

"That's not unusual," Marnie said.

"It's not that difficult to understand," Aunt Tillie insisted. "The FBI called in a profiler, like on television. That's her." She waved her fork at Hannah. "What makes everything so weird is that the new profiler used to let this one give her an extra side of bacon every morning when they were in the academy together." She jabbed the fork at Landon.

I pressed my lips together and stared at the ceiling as Landon slid me an incredulous look. Aunt Tillie's take on the subject was pretty accurate.

"Should it be side of bacon or sausage?" Aunt Tillie mused. "Personally, I think sausage is more phallic so it fits the sexual undertones of the statement better. But ... it's bacon, and we all know how 'The Man' feels about bacon."

"You'll have to excuse us," Clove volunteered for Hannah's benefit. "In addition to being codependent, we also don't think before we speak."

"Not even a little," Thistle agreed as she looked Hannah up and down with fresh eyes. "So, you dated Landon back in the day, huh?"

Her expression was hard to read. I'd known her long enough to understand what she was thinking, though ... and it wasn't good. She was debating how we would take out Hannah if it became necessary. I knew because Thistle's mind always went that route.

"I still think it's nice." Hannah never faltered. She was apparently determined to keep things friendly despite ... well ... my family. "You're all close. Landon and Bay live on the property. I wouldn't have thought that was something the Landon I knew at the academy would do, but he's obviously adjusted to a new reality. It's ... fascinating."

Landon reached for more pot roast. Hannah's presence hadn't stopped him from eating his weight in beef and potatoes. "Bay and I are building our dream house on a lake near here. We already bought the property. We need to save up a bit until we can start construction."

"AND LIVING in the guesthouse isn't like living in the inn," Clove added. "It really is a separate house, and our mothers only visit when they're feeling particularly invasive."

"Or have cookies," Landon added, tapping the side of my plate. "Why aren't you eating, sweetie? You've had a big day, what with coming out to the scene and all that other stuff."

Hannah's forehead creased. "Scene? She was at the murder scene?"

Landon appeared to catch himself, and he didn't look happy. "Oh, well ... ."

"I needed Bay there," Chief Terry interjected. "I recognized the dead girl, but that whole little group Paisley is a part of melts together in my head. I knew Bay would recognize the girl, so I asked her to come so that we didn't have to wait for fingerprints to notify the family."

"I see." Hannah gripped her fork and knife and cocked her head. "My understanding is that the girl was killed in the woods, but on property owned by three single men."

I straightened in my chair. "They're not guilty."

"How can you be sure? Statistics indicate that it would likely be those men. It's odd for single adult men to live and work together like that."

Landon finally pulled away from his dinner and cleared his throat to draw Hannah's attention. "The Dragonfly is owned by three men we know. They just happen to be the fathers of Bay, Clove and Thistle."

Hannah's expression turned serious. "That's awkward."

"It is," Landon agreed. "I agree they're not guilty. They've been having problems with kids partying in the woods for several weeks. We were made aware of those problems long before Paisley Gilmore was killed."

"Still, we're talking about single men of a certain age."

"No, we're talking about our fathers," I argued, annoyance bubbling up. "They're not murderers."

"I would expect you to believe that."

I opened my mouth to argue further but Landon gripped my wrist and shook his head. Pushing Hannah would get us nowhere. We had to be smart and act strategically. That was the only thing that would get us out of this mess.

"The food is delicious, Mrs. Winchester," Hannah said as she beamed at Mom. "Are you a trained chef?"

"Self-trained," Mom replied, her eyes landing on me. It was clear she didn't like where this conversation was heading. "Our mother was a masterful cook. She taught us everything she knew."

"Oh, that's lovely." Hannah smiled and turned to Aunt Tillie. "Are you also a masterful cook?"

Aunt Tillie's mood matched a crockpot of rancid split-pea soup. "The only thing I like cooking up is trouble. While we're on that subject, Mary Kay, we need to set some ground rules. The first of which is, you're to stay out of my business. What I have brewing on this property is none of your concern."

Hannah's lips twitched but she remained impassive. "Okay."

"Secondly, if you see me in town, you're to pretend you don't know me," Aunt Tillie continued. "I do not want to be associated with 'The Man.' I have business associates who will balk at seeing me with

'The Man.' You're a woman, but you're still technically 'The Man.'" Aunt Tillie turned to Landon. "Why couldn't they send us Shemar Moore?"

Landon held out his hands. "Probably because Shemar Moore is an actor and not a profiler."

"He would still have been preferable to her." Aunt Tillie glanced back at Hannah. "Finally, if you don't stop saying passive-aggressive things to my family I'm going to have to put you on my list. That might not mean much to you, but it's important you stay off my list.

"This might be a confusing visit for you," she continued. "You might want to psychoanalyze us and write a book or something. Well, we're above your pay grade. Just stick to finding Paisley Gilmore's killer and ignore the rest of us."

"I only care about finding the killer," Hannah reassured her.

"Good. Then we won't have a problem." Aunt Tillie snagged her glass of wine and shifted her gaze to me. "And that is how you do it." Her smile slipped. "Where did we land on sausage versus bacon again? I'm still confused which was funnier."

"Definitely the bacon for Landon," I replied. "The sausage would've been funnier for anybody else."

"Good analysis. I knew I nailed that joke."

"You always do."

NINE

I slept well, despite the upheaval of the meal, and found Landon already awake the next morning when I opened my eyes.

"Hey." He leaned in and kissed me before I could respond. "Did you sleep okay?"

I nodded as I rubbed my face. I was not on my game when I first woke up, something he knew well. That's when he tried to get me to promise things like staying out of trouble and ridiculous sex pledges that he found funny. I had no intention of making that promise today ... although I wasn't necessarily opposed to one of his pledges. "I slept hard. How about you?"

"I always sleep hard."

That was true. "It's probably because you ate your weight in beef and potatoes last night."

"Hey, pot roast is good."

I thought back to the dinner, which seemed to last forever. "What do you think about Hannah?"

"We talked about this last night," he moaned. "I love you."

"Not that. I know you love me."

"The proposal to end all proposals proved that."

I couldn't swallow my smile. "It did, but I knew before that."

"Good. I wasn't with Hannah very long."

"How long?"

He shrugged. "A couple months, on and off. Believe it or not, I was dedicated to being a good agent. I didn't have much time for personal stuff. We dated, but we weren't devoted to one another. It wasn't like that."

"Are you saying we're devoted to one another?"

"I'm completely devoted to you and will be forever."

"Oh, that's kind of sweet." I kissed his cheek. "I'm devoted to you too."

"I know. I'm handsome, make a good living and give the best proposals in the world. I'm a catch."

I laughed again, as I knew he'd intended. Then I sobered. "She's going to be a problem, Landon." I didn't want him dwelling on it all day, but it had to be addressed. "She might be over you, but she's still curious about how you ended up here."

"Anybody who knew me back then would be curious about that."

"Why?"

"I had intense plans back then to end up in a huge office in a big city."

"And instead you settled for Hemlock Cove."

"I didn't settle," he argued. "I found you. I fell in love ... with you and this town. I don't want to be anywhere else. We've talked about this."

"The old you would look at the new you and be disgusted," I mused.

"I don't know that I would've been disgusted. I would've been confused. Old me — and I'm still young and hot so we need to come up with a different way to phrase that — would've taken young me aside and explained about true love and how it makes everything perfect."

I stared at his stubbled profile. "Okay, you've got me. You don't have to say schmaltzy stuff like that *all* the time."

"Maybe I like the schmaltz." He dug his fingers into my side and tickled, causing me to gasp. "Don't worry about Hannah," he said after a few seconds, turning serious. "She might try to shrink us all because that's her way, but this is hardly the first time we've protected ourselves from law enforcement invaders. We'll be fine."

I hoped he was right. "We should probably get dressed and head to the inn for breakfast," I said as I glanced at the clock. "Hannah will be there, and I don't want to risk her sitting through an entire meal with Aunt Tillie alone."

"Good idea. We could probably go faster if we showered together."

I shot him a dubious look. "Yeah, I'm thinking showering together will take longer."

"Yet I'm willing to risk it. What does that say about me?"

"It says that you're a pervert. If you want to shower together, we definitely need to get moving."

HANNAH WAS IN THE DINING ROOM POURING juice when we joined her. We drove to the inn parking lot to be prepared for whatever the day would bring, so we entered through the front door rather than the back.

"Good morning." Hannah greeted us with a bright smile. "Looks like it's going to be a beautiful day."

Landon moved around me and broke into a huge grin before I could answer. "There's my girl!"

For a moment, I was confused — and a little horrified — but then I realized who he was talking to.

Snort. Snort.

Peg, dressed in a camouflage sweater, appeared from beneath the table and headed straight for Landon. She wriggled in ecstasy as he dropped to the floor and showered her with attention.

"I thought this conversation was going to take a weird turn," Hannah admitted as she watched the show. "I'm both relieved and ... baffled. Is that a pig?"

"Peg," I answered with a nod and grabbed the tomato juice carafe. "She belongs to Aunt Tillie. Landon loves her beyond reason."

"What's not to love?" Landon demanded as Peg jumped all over hm. "She's my little lover."

I watched them a moment and then shook my head. "You'll have to excuse Landon. It's come to my attention that he might be starved for love from an animal. I'm thinking of getting him a dog for Christmas this year."

"Nobody needs a dog," Landon countered as he scratched Peg's flank. "We have Peg ... who we don't have to take care of because she belongs to someone else. We work too much for a dog."

"I could take a dog to the newspaper office with me."

He stilled. "You know, that's not a bad idea. We should adopt a really big guard dog. Then I wouldn't have to worry about Brian Kelly showing up at the newspaper to mess with you. He would crap his pants if you had a hell hound to protect you."

Hannah's expression reflected curiosity. "I think I'm behind. First ... Peg the pig?" She appeared to be battling back laughter.

"She named the pig after her arch nemesis," Landon volunteered. "Margaret Little. They've been trying to kill one another for eighty years."

"More like seventy years," I corrected.

"Ah." Hannah's smile widened. "That's kind of cute."

I could think of other words to describe it. "It's ... just how we live our lives. Aunt Tillie is feisty. She likes messing with the neighbors. It is who she is."

"That explains a few things. Who is Brian Kelly? Is he one of her enemies?"

"Yes," I answered.

"He's Bay's enemy, which makes him Aunt Tillie's enemy," Landon replied.

"You have an enemy?" Hannah looked impressed. "Why is that?"

"Oh, well ... ." What could I say?

"Brian Kelly owned the newspaper before Bay did," Landon volunteered. "His grandfather left it to him. There was a stipulation in his will that Bay be kept on as a reporter. Brian broke that stipulation and tried to fire her because he's a douche. The town rallied behind Bay and she bought the newspaper after an advertising boycott."

Hannah's eyes sparkled in such a way that I knew she actually found joy in the story. "I thought small towns were boring, but apparently not."

"Not Hemlock Cove," I agreed as I hunkered down to look at Landon, who had shifted under the table to play with Peg. "Orange juice?"

"Yes, please." He shot me a pleased grin. "I kind of want to talk about this dog idea at some point. I don't need a dog, but I think you having one is a good idea."

"A dog won't stop Brian if he really wants to get me," I replied. "But I'm willing to talk about a dog. I was considering one for your Christmas gift."

"Maybe we should pick out a dog together and do something else for Christmas." Landon, now serious, crawled out from under the table. "I still want you to be careful around Kelly. I know you think he's a schmuck, but that doesn't mean he's not dangerous."

"Who's dangerous?" Aunt Tillie demanded as she strolled into the room from the opposite direction I would've expected her. On a normal morning she enjoyed sitting in the kitchen and annoying my mother and aunts as they prepared breakfast. One look at her outfit told me why she hadn't gone that route this morning.

"Has Mom seen those leggings?" I demanded as I cocked my head to figure out what she was wearing. "Is that a ... ?" I couldn't finish the question.

"Penis," Landon supplied, making a face. "It's from that David statue. I saw those leggings advertised online a few weeks ago and knew Aunt Tillie would end up with them."

I was caught between amusement and horror. "Mom will not let you leave the house wearing those," I said. "She'll melt down."

"Your mother is not the boss of me," Aunt Tillie countered, and when she moved past me, I found that the butt crack of the leggings didn't match up correctly on her small frame.

"Oh, no way."

Landon tilted his head to see what I was looking at and burst out laughing.

"It's not funny," I groaned. "Mrs. Little will take one look at her in those leggings and then track down Chief Terry to arrest her for indecency."

"Hey!" Aunt Tillie jabbed a finger in my direction. "This is art."

"If you say so." I'd listened to Aunt Tillie's arguments enough to know that the more attention she got because of the leggings, the less likely she was to change her outfit. "Mom won't like them."

"Well, she can suck it up." Aunt Tillie plopped down in her normal chair. She was without her combat helmet and whistle this morning, but I had no doubt they would join the ensemble before she left the house. "What's the plan of attack today?"

The question caught me off guard. "What do you mean?"

"A teenager was murdered in our town, and in ritualistic fashion. We have to do something."

I looked to Hannah, momentarily worried, and then shrugged. "We're not investigators."

Aunt Tillie snorted. "Right."

"We're not," I insisted. "This is Landon's case. Oh, and Hannah's case."

"They're not witches," Aunt Tillie pointed out. "Only witches can solve this case."

My stomach constricted and I lowered my juice to the table, my appetite vacating in an instant. "Listen ... ."

"It's okay," Hannah said hurriedly, perhaps picking up on my distress. "I'd be interested in hearing a witch's take on this case. I've looked over the photos of the dead girl and they're ... troubling. I'm especially interested in the runes that were painted in blood on the trees. I can't believe you thought to check the trees, Landon. That was good investigative work."

Landon slid his eyes to me and I could tell what he was thinking. He didn't want to take credit for my discovery. He also didn't want Hannah becoming suspicious of me. Unfortunately, he didn't get a chance to decide what he wanted to say in response because Aunt Tillie, as was her way, took control of the conversation.

"He didn't find those runes. Bay did." Aunt Tillie jerked her thumb at me. "She's the master investigator on this one."

"Bay?" Hannah's eyebrows drew together as she regarded me. "I guess I didn't understand the extent of your involvement."

"It was a trick of the sun," I lied. "It hit in just the right manner and I saw something on one of the trees. Landon called for the evidence technicians to use luminol on all the trees."

"Yes, Landon is a virtual wonder," Aunt Tillie drawled. "We're all amazed at the way his brain works."

I shot her a warning look. "Stop being you," I hissed.

"Um, no." She shook her head. "You have to understand, Agent Mary Kay, we're often involved in Landon's cases. We're the reason he's closed so many of them."

I wanted to crawl in a hole and die.

"So, you work cases with your girlfriend regularly?" Hannah asked Landon.

"Bay is my fiancée, and she's helped more times than I can count." Landon's tone was even. He didn't look uncomfortable in the least. "You have to understand something. Hemlock Cove is not a normal town. Weird things happen all the time. Bay grew up here. She knows all the players. She's been an invaluable source during my time here."

Hannah didn't look convinced. "She's a civilian. She's not supposed to be involved in cases. It's against the rules."

Terror rippled through me. Would she report Landon? I didn't know her well, but she seemed a stickler when it came to rules. Clove, the tattler of our group, reminded me of Hannah ... only less whiny, something I could never say in front of Clove because it would result in a meltdown.

"Then I guess it's good Landon doesn't invite Bay into cases," Chief Terry announced as he joined us. I had never been so happy to see anybody in my life. "I invite Bay in. This is my town, after all."

"Of course." Hannah nodded once. "I wasn't saying anything untoward about Ms. Winchester. I'm just curious about why a civilian is involved in murder cases."

"This is in my town. I make the decisions on who is and isn't involved in investigations in my town." Chief Terry shot me a wink as he headed for the juice carafes. "I've known Bay her whole life. She spent a lot of time with me when she was a teenager."

"Because she was interested in law enforcement?"

"Something like that." Chief Terry poured a glass of orange juice. "Bay's father was not in Hemlock Cove when she was younger. Tillie often had the girls and would involve them in ... games. I regularly got called to the scene of those games and had to instill a few life lessons. Bay developed an interest in law enforcement then."

That was as good of a lie as I'd ever heard him tell. "It's true," I said. "I like to solve mysteries."

"I guess that makes sense," Hannah said. "You became a reporter, so naturally you like to put the pieces together."

"Yes." I forced a smile I didn't feel. "I love puzzles."

Landon slipped his arm around my waist and tugged me toward my chair. "My Bay is a genius at puzzling things out. I'm always glad when Terry involves her."

"Well, if it's okay to discuss the case in front of civilians, I spent a lot of time looking at the photographs of the scene last night," Hannah said. "I was hoping to go out there this morning for a better look. There's something about it that feels familiar."

I was taken aback. "Seriously?"

She nodded. "I'm almost positive I saw something like those runes when I was on a case in Salem two years ago."

"Salem, Massachusetts?"

"Yes."

I slid my eyes to Aunt Tillie. She looked as interested in the new tidbit as I was.

"There are witches in Salem," Landon noted as he sat next to me.

"This town's decision to turn itself into a fake paranormal haven makes me think that somebody wants the populace to believe that witches are killing people," Hannah said,

"I assume you don't believe in witches," I asked.

"I guess that depends on your definition." Hannah said. "Wicca is a real religion and the practitioners are real people. Their religion is far removed from the stuff of Hollywood. They don't capture children and sacrifice them to gods. That sort of witchcraft is nonsense."

"I don't know," Aunt Tillie said dryly. "When they were younger, there were times I wanted to sacrifice Bay and her cousins, especially Thistle. There's all different kinds of magic."

"People find magic in small, everyday things," Hannah said. "Some might look at Bay and Landon and assign magical qualities to the fact that they found each other and fell in love."

"You don't assign magical qualities to that?" I asked.

She shook her head. "I'm what would be considered ruthlessly pragmatic," she said. "I don't believe in soulmates. That idea is straight out of romance books. I don't believe in destiny. Life is a series of actions and reactions.

"You and Landon, for example, found each other at a time when you were open to a relationship," she continued. "It was about the timing, nothing more."

I pressed my lips together and glanced at Landon, who was frowning. "Well, I believe in destiny."

"As do I," Landon interjected. "Bay is my soulmate and I believe we were always destined to find one another."

"What if you hadn't?" Hannah was serious. "What if you two had never crossed paths? Would you still be soulmates?"

Landon rested his hand on my knee under the table. "I think if you're meant to find each other, you do. Bay and I were always meant to find one another."

"It's a sweet thought, but I can't get behind it in practice."

"That's sad for you." Landon squeezed my knee. "As for the scene, we can take you there." He flicked his eyes to me. "It's probably best if you go and smooth the way with your father."

"Absolutely. I kind of want to get another look around the area."

10

TEN

Dad, apparently hearing the vehicles pull up, met us in the driveway of the Dragonfly. He seemed confused when Chief Terry introduced Hannah.

"A profiler? Here?"

I slipped my arm through his, tugging him toward the inn. "I'll tell you all about it and then I'll meet you guys at the scene," I said, casting a pointed look my fiancé.

Landon looked as if he wanted to argue the point, but he simply nodded.

I dragged Dad into the inn, waiting until the door was shut to speak. "I don't have much time. She's a profiler. She used to date Landon when they were at the academy. She's starting to really bug me, but I have to pretend otherwise because it's undignified not to like your fiancé's former girlfriend simply because she speaks her mind."

Dad chuckled. "That's a lot to unpack. For the record, Landon often bugs me, but I don't doubt for a second that he loves you. I'm certain he doesn't harbor any feelings for this Hannah."

"I'm not worried about that," I said. "He's as irritated with her as I am. I just need you to know that she might be hanging around. Don't mention any of the witch stuff. She doesn't believe in witches, but she's sharing a roof with Aunt Tillie, so that's going to lead to problems. I should probably get out there now."

"Because you're worried she's hitting on Landon?"

"Because she doesn't believe in witches and there's clearly something otherworldly going on here."

I cut through the inn and exited the rear door. I was about twenty feet from the inn when I glanced over my shoulder, my gaze instinctively going to the windowed laundry room ... and my heart lodged in my throat.

The ghosts — what else was I supposed to call them? — were back, hovering in the glass. Their reflections were dark, their eyes bright with hatred, and the glass appeared to ripple as they stared at me.

"Who are you?" I asked. "What do you want?"

The reflections didn't answer. Perhaps they couldn't.

"If you have something to tell me, now would be the time," I groused. "I mean ... if you're going to keep showing up, there must be a reason. You need to tell me if you expect me to help ... or do something else."

Still nothing.

"I could smite you if that's what you prefer," I offered.

The reflections began to dissolve and were gone within seconds. This time I was certain I'd seen them. Were they following me? Was it something else?

I checked the windows three more times before reaching the tree line. The shapes didn't return, so I forced them out of my mind as I traipsed through the woods in search of Landon, Chief Terry and Hannah. I found them within a few minutes.

Hannah stood in the center of the clearing, staring down at the spot where Paisley's body was found. Chief Terry and Landon were positioned outside the circle, and Landon's gaze immediately sought out mine when he heard me.

"Is your father okay?"

I nodded as I moved closer to him. "He is. He was confused ... but now he's not."

"Hannah is getting a feel for the area." He studied my face. "You're pale." He pressed his hand to my forehead. "Like ... really, really pale."

"I'm fine," I reassured him, flashing a look toward Hannah and cringing when I realized she was staring at us. "It's just hot out."

Landon waited a moment longer and then nodded. It was obvious he didn't believe my "hot" excuse, but he knew better than to question me in front of Hannah. "What's your plan for the day?"

"I have work to do at the office."

"Keep the doors locked when you're in there."

"Brian wouldn't be stupid enough to come there in the middle of the day," I scoffed.

"Keep the doors locked," he said. "I installed that security system for a reason."

"Fine." I didn't bother to hide my eye roll. "I'll probably spend some time in Hypnotic too. Well, that is if Clove isn't being annoying. She's seriously driving me nuts these days."

"Have some sympathy for her. She's uncomfortable with the changes in her body. It doesn't help that you guys keep freaking her out by telling her she'll never lose the baby weight. That just makes her eat more."

"She won't lose the weight if she keeps eating the way she does."

"Does that matter?"

"Wouldn't you be upset if I didn't take off the baby weight after I popped out our first kid?"

He chuckled at the way I'd phrased it. "I would not. I'm the sort of man who loves a person and not a body type."

"Oh, whatever."

"It's true. You need to leave Clove alone."

"Fine." I shifted my gaze back to the tree that had the rune on it yesterday. Hannah was staring at it now, likely trying to pretend she couldn't hear us. "I should probably head to town." I tugged on Landon's shirt sleeve. "Do you want to walk me to the lot?"

He answered without hesitation. "Absolutely. Terry, can you stick with Hannah? I'll be right back after I walk Bay to her car."

Chief Terry was well aware what we were really doing and

nodded. "No problem. It's smart to walk her back when there's a killer on the loose."

"My thoughts exactly." Landon linked his fingers with mine as we headed back, waiting until we emerged from the woods to ask the obvious question. "What is it?"

"I saw those ghost things in the window of the Dragonfly," I whispered. "They were watching me when I headed out to meet you guys."

"And?"

"I tried to communicate with them. They didn't respond. Then they disappeared. They're gone now."

"What do you think they are?"

"I don't know, but I think they're connected to what happened to Paisley."

"Obviously." He rubbed the back of his neck. "I'm not keen on you running around on your own when these things are out there."

"I don't see that we have much choice," I said. "You cannot spend all your time checking in with a civilian. Hannah is already suspicious."

"I don't know that she's suspicious," he hedged. "She is curious. She finds our entire relationship odd."

"Which means your relationship with her was nothing like what we share."

"I believe I already told you that." He stroked his hand down the back of my head and then tilted it to meet his insistent gaze. "We flirted and ... did other things. I didn't want anything bad to happen to her, but what I felt for her wasn't even a shadow against what I feel for you."

"I'm not being insecure," I reassured him. "I know you love me. But I don't understand how you could have fallen for her in the first place. She's boring. Other than the hair, we have nothing in common."

"Well, believe it or not, baby, the only type I had before I fell in love with you was beautiful blondes. In that respect, you are my type."

My cheeks colored. "I'm not beautiful. I'm ... cute."

"You're beautiful. You don't want to argue with me about that. You're right about Hannah, though. She does not believe in the paranormal. She'll be looking for an explanation on everything that happens between now and then ... human explanations."

"That's a pretty tall order in the Winchester house."

"I guess it's good she can't see ghosts staring back at us from the windows."

I blew out a sigh. "I can't be around her. I need to use my magic to dig."

"You're only telling me that because you think it means keeping a safe distance from me, too. I'll figure out a way for you and me to get time together."

"Private time or investigative time?"

"Both." He was firm. "I'm going to figure this out. Hannah doesn't need to be with us every moment of every day. She'll go off on her own eventually. She has a process."

"That means she'll wander around on her own. That's probably not good."

"It's not," he agreed. "We have to deal with it. Speaking of that, what are you really going to do now that you're separating from us?"

"I'm going to research that Salem thing she mentioned. There's probably more to it than even she knows."

"Okay. Be careful and keep in touch."

"Don't I always?"

He growled and leaned in for a kiss. "You do what you want and run off willy-nilly. You give me ulcers and nightmares."

"And I'm guessing that's not fun for you."

"Not even a little. We're in a weird spot right now. We have to be careful and trust one another."

"I trust you more than anyone. That thing you said about destiny and soulmates, I believe that. No matter what, I was always meant to find you."

"Of course you were. I'm a catch. I believe I've pointed that out multiple times."

I laughed. "I'll get in touch if I find anything in the research that can help."

He gave me another kiss and then released me, waiting until I was halfway to the front of the inn to call out. "I love you, Bay."

I smiled. "As much as Peg?"

"Don't push it."

"That's what I thought."

I LOCKED THE FRONT DOOR OF THE office as Landon demanded, but only because I wanted quiet time to myself. Given Aunt Tillie's leggings, I had a feeling she was going to be looking for some place to shelter.

I booted my computer after taking a lap around the office. Viola, the resident ghost, was nowhere to be found. Unlike the ghost who lived in the office before her, Viola enjoyed gallivanting around town.

I searched for "Salem" and "runes" and came up with so many matches that I had to winnow it further. I added murder to the mix. Hannah had mentioned the incident was two years ago, which made finding what I was looking for all the easier.

"What are you looking at?" a voice asked as I settled in to read a news article from back then.

I found Aunt Tillie staring at me from across the desk. "How did you get in here? I locked the door and set the security system."

She snorted. "Security systems can't stop me. You know that."

"Yes, well ... ." I looked down. "What happened to your inappropriate leggings?"

"I decided to change."

"You mean Mom made you change."

Her scowl took up half her face. "Your mother is horrible," she said, whipping out another pair of leggings from the backpack she wore. "I knew she would be a pain and bought more than one pair."

Even I had to admit that was mildly genius. "By wearing the leggings this morning and putting up a fight when she tried to take them away, you set the stage for getting away with the second pair. If you'd given in easily, she would've known something was up. Well done."

"I'm a genius," she agreed. "Seriously, what are you looking at?"

"You heard Hannah at breakfast this morning. She said a similar incident happened in Salem two years ago."

"She's not a believer, so I don't really care what she says. She doesn't know anything."

"She knows about human behavior."

"I hate to break it to you, but I don't think she's very good at her job. She's no Shemar Moore."

"Is anybody?"

"No. That man is beautiful and I want to rub myself all over him."

I made a face. "That's a bit of an overshare."

"I have to watch you and Landon pet each other like puppies at a stroking contest so I don't really care what you think."

"Fair enough."

"I'm serious about that. She watches you and Landon as if there's some sort of trick being played on her. Be careful."

"I'm not afraid of her where Landon is concerned. They dated a long time ago and it wasn't serious."

"I'm not saying you should have anything to fear romantically. Her interest in your relationship could lead to interest in other things. We really don't need her digging into our family."

"What do you suggest I do to fix things?"

"I have no idea. I have bigger things to deal with. Namely Willa. I'll come up with a way to get her out of town if it's the last thing I do."

I went back to staring at the story on the computer screen. "This says a teenager was killed in the woods outside Salem. Her blood was used to paint runes on the trees. The runes were believed to be tied to the four elements."

Aunt Tillie straightened. "You mean the four corners."

"I think that's what they're getting at."

Aunt Tillie tugged her lower lip. "Anything else?"

"There is something that Hannah left out," I said. "The murder in Salem was tied to a similar murder, also in Salem, that happened twenty years before."

"The same circumstances?"

"Yeah. What do you think that means?"

"I have no idea. I'm not much of a researcher."

I was quiet a moment. "Thistle has been busy with other things and can't really do research for me right now. Any suggestions on who might be able to help?"

"Ignore Thistle. Her nose is out of joint because Clove is having a baby and you're getting married. She's the only one who hasn't moved forward. She'll get over it on Christmas."

"What happens on Christmas?"

"That's when Marcus will propose."

"Are you sure?"

"I know all and see all."

She was full of it, but if she was so determined about the date I figured she had inside information. She and Marcus were tight. He helped her with her pot field, so maybe he'd confided in her.

"I'm happy for them," I said. "He's good for Thistle."

"He's way too good for her." She pressed her lips together. "You know who knows a lot about Salem?"

"No. Who?"

"Helen Archer."

I was taken aback. "Stormy's great-grandmother?" Stormy was a witch from the neighboring town we'd met several weeks before. She was just coming into her powers and her great-grandmother, an old acquaintance of Aunt Tillie's, was in town to give her a helping hand.

"Do you think she would know about these murders?"

"It couldn't hurt to ask."

"I guess that means I'm heading to Shadow Hills." I stood and grabbed my purse. "Do you want to come with me?"

"Are you kidding? I'm torturing Willa today. Nothing short of wild hell hounds or Shemar Moore and a box of candy could tear me away from that."

"Okay, but be careful. You could get arrested in those leggings if you come across the wrong uniform."

"Oh, I'm counting on it." She winked at me. "I'll make sure to drive

Margaret and Willa insane before I let them nab me and call your mother."

That's when the final piece slid into place. "You're going for all three of them today. It's like the torture hat trick."

"You're smarter than you look."

ELEVEN

It was hard for me to admit as I drove toward Shadow Hills, but I would've preferred Aunt Tillie had come with me. She was a badass witch. Sure, she spent most of her time using her powers to torture her enemies, but she was also good in a pinch when the battle got serious.

Seeing the ghosts in the window made me think the battle was going to get serious ... and fast.

The thing is, most people were starting to look at me as the badass witch of the family because of my growing necromancer powers. It wasn't sitting well with Aunt Tillie, though she didn't come right out and say it. I was slowly taking over as the magical center of the Winchester family, a fact that frightened me while also bolstering my ego.

That meant it was up to me to figure out what was going on. I appeared to be the only one seeing the ghosts. It had to be a byproduct of my necromancer powers. But how?

My phone rang as I parked in the lot of Two Broomsticks Gas & Grill. The quaint restaurant was a throwback to a time long forgotten. Charles Archer, the owner, had decided that modernizing wasn't necessary. He relied on good food and an outlandish attitude to draw people in. The regulars were happy with what he had to offer and he did a brisk business.

I'd been to the restaurant once or twice, so I took a moment to scan it when I walked through the door. To my relief, Stormy was delivering food to one of the tables. She primarily worked morning shifts, so I was hopeful she was almost done. I wanted her with me when I talked to her great-grandmother.

"Hey." A friendly male voice drew my attention to the right and I found Hunter Ryan, Stormy's boyfriend and Chief Terry's protégé, sitting at the counter nursing a mug of coffee.

"Hey." I returned his smile and climbed onto a stool next to him. "Are you here for Stormy?"

He smiled and nodded, sheepish. "Always. What about you?"

"Actually, I was hoping she would take me to visit her great-grandmother."

Confusion washed across Hunter's features. He was tall — a good two inches taller than Landon — and lean. His hair was close-cropped and neat, and he was always friendly. I liked him a great deal even though I'd only recently started to spend time with him thanks to my association with Stormy.

"Why do you want to talk to her?" Hunter looked horrified at the thought. "You know she's ... difficult."

The way he said the word had me battling back laughter. "I've met her," I reminded him. "She was at the inn a couple of days ago with Aunt Tillie. They spent the entire afternoon in the greenhouse with Aunt Tillie's wine."

Hunter's expression darkened. "I remember. Stormy had to drive her home and basically carry her into her grandparents' house. She's a lot of work."

"Yeah, until you've spent a week with Aunt Tillie when she's on a revenge kick against Mrs. Little, you don't know what real work is. Stormy's great-grandmother is the Junior League compared to my great-aunt."

"That's probably true." Hunter looked me up and down. "Does Landon know you're here?"

I knew what he was asking and it grated. "Yes, but he's not my keeper. I texted him before I drove over."

"I heard you guys had a murder." Hunter was a police officer in Shadow Hills. He hadn't tackled nearly as many wacky cases as we had in Hemlock Cove, but he understood about magic and murder colliding. That was good as far as I was concerned. Another ally couldn't possibly hurt.

"It was one of the girls," I said.

Hunter's expression was blank. "What girls?"

"The ones I told Stormy about. The ones who were stealing the magic fragments from Hollow Creek and using them against people. They faked a kidnapping in an attempt to get money to run away."

"Ah." He sipped his coffee and nodded. "Landon and Terry mentioned that. They were worried because you made the decision to alter memories."

"I'm still wondering if that was a mistake." I rubbed my cheek and forced a grin as Stormy slipped behind the counter. She was all smiles as she regarded me.

"This is a surprise," she chirped, automatically reaching for the coffee pot. "Caffeine?"

I nodded. "Are you always so cheerful after working a morning shift?" I asked.

She nodded and Hunter made a face.

"She's not cheerful in the morning," he assured me. "She has decided to stay on the morning shift with her grandfather because it's better for us when we want to spend time together. If she takes an afternoon or evening shift, it cuts short our quality time. But she's not happy when her alarm goes off in the morning."

I smiled at the way Stormy glared at Hunter. They were cute. They'd known each other from childhood, so their relationship differed from the one Landon and I shared. We fell in love as adults and had to learn to navigate life together. They fell in love as kids, separated for an extended period when Stormy moved away, and then had to learn how love was different when hormones weren't leading the way. I found watching them rediscover one another to be fascinating.

"I need to talk to your great-grandmother."

If Stormy was surprised by the declaration, she didn't show it. "May I ask why?"

"Aunt Tillie says she's done a lot of research over the years — Goddess knows Aunt Tillie isn't willing to do the work, so she makes friends with others who will do it for her — and I have a unique situation in Hemlock Cove."

"I'm almost afraid to ask," Hunter murmured. "What unique situation?"

I hesitated and then barreled forward, keeping my voice low so nobody at the surrounding tables could hear. "I've seen things."

"Like werewolves?" Hunter asked, frowning when Stormy shot him a weird look. "What? The body was found in the woods and she was stabbed multiple times. It's possible it was werewolves."

I had to laugh. "I see you've kept up on the story."

"We're only twenty minutes away," Hunter reminded me. "If you have a killer there, it wouldn't take much energy for him or her to drive here and kill someone else."

"It's not a werewolf. Twice now I've seen reflections in windows, people who aren't really there and yet they seem to be watching me."

Stormy's eyebrows drew together. "I don't understand."

That made two of us. "They're evil entities. At least, they look like evil entities. I would call them ghosts but I've never seen ghosts trapped in reflections like that."

"Sounds odd." Stormy looked legitimately concerned. "Why do you think my great-grandmother can help?"

"I don't know that she can," I admitted. "But she's my best shot. Aunt Tillie suggested your great-grandmother might have answers, something about her knowing a great deal of information about Salem."

"Okay. That's good enough for me." Stormy smiled. "I have twenty minutes left on my shift. Are you okay hanging here?"

I nodded. "I'm fine. I'm going to bug your boyfriend about information on FBI profilers."

Hunter's eyebrows hopped. "Wait ... you have a profiler in town?"

"Yup, and she dated Landon when they were together at the academy."

"You don't think Landon still has feelings for her?" Stormy looked appalled at the thought. "I've seen you together. He's completely in love with you."

"I don't. He thinks she might have feelings for him, although it feels somehow ... different than that. I don't know how to explain it.

"I'm not worried about her having feelings for Landon," I continued. "I'm worried about her being so intrigued by us that she starts digging and sees something she shouldn't."

"Oh, right." Stormy bobbed her head. "That's my greatest fear too."

"You live in a town that's supposed to be populated by witches," Hunter pointed out. "Don't you think that you can get away with almost anything, profiler or not?"

"No. We need to be careful. This woman ... she could blow our world out of the water."

Hunter didn't look happy with the response. "What are you going to do?"

"I honestly have no idea."

ONCE STORMY FINISHED HER SHIFT, she bolted upstairs long enough to change clothes and then met me behind the restaurant. She volunteered to drive the three blocks to her grandparents' house, and I was more than happy to have her navigate the Shadow Hills streets.

"It's quiet here," I noted. "Hemlock Cove is quiet most of the time ... until Aunt Tillie decides to go on a rampage."

"I just love her," Stormy enthused.

"Then you should borrow her a couple days a week. I'm sure she would love to have an impressionable new mind to bend to her will. When Belinda and Annie were living in the inn, she took Annie under her wing. Now that they're out on their own she's had more time to fill, and I think she would love to fill it with you."

"No way." Stormy was fervent as she shook her head. "My family is even kookier than your family. There's no way I'm falling for that."

"There's no way your family is kookier than my family."

"Um ... it totally is."

"We have Aunt Tillie."

"I have an uncle named Brad who believes the government has been overrun by aliens. He believes if you rip their skin off that they're lizards underneath and they're trying to take over the entire population."

I had to bite back a smile. "He sounds ... fun."

"I also have a cousin who prefers working at the gas station to the restaurant because he can wave around the gas nozzles and present them as phallic symbols to pick up women."

"That sounds immature but normal for guys of a certain age."

"He's almost thirty."

"Well ... ." I broke off and laughed. "Fine. We both have nutty families. Aunt Tillie is an unbelievable amount of work, though."

"Oh, I don't doubt it, but you have fun with her. You can't pretend otherwise with me. I see it."

"She's not often fun."

Stormy didn't look convinced. "About a week and a half ago I was with you in Hemlock Cove when she made that woman with the porcelain unicorns so angry she started throwing them at her. I believe it revolved around making her store smell like a giant rotten egg."

I smiled at the memory. "That was kind of fun. It was also loud."

"There's nothing wrong with loud." Stormy parked in front of a nice house that boasted a pool, tennis court and an old-school trampoline that didn't have a net to catch flying kids. "Wow. This is nice."

Stormy slid her eyes to me as she pocketed her keys. "Yes, my grandparents built a wonderland here because they wanted all of us to hang out together. They thought this would keep us close."

"Did it?"

She hesitated and then held out her hands. "I'm close with some of my cousins. There are a few that I would rather run over with my car than talk to. I think that's normal of every family."

I thought about Clove and Thistle. "Not my family."

"Yes, but you have two cousins and were raised under the same roof. I have fifteen blood cousins and a few that were added by marriage. I know I shouldn't segregate them, but it's impossible not to because there's an invisible line between the ones who came in later and the ones I grew up with. Those of us who were raised together know exactly what buttons to push to drive each other crazy."

"That's how it is with Clove, Thistle and me," I said. "We all know exactly how to drive each other crazy."

"And you probably enjoy it."

"Yeah."

"I enjoy messing with my cousins, too." She gestured toward the garage. "Come on. My great-grandmother is probably on the patio. That's where she's been hanging out of late."

I followed her through the garage, smiling at the huge rose garden she led me through at the back of the house. It was absolutely beautiful, and whoever was caring for it had put in a lot of time.

"This is my grandmother's pride and joy," Stormy explained. "She's been taking care of these rose bushes forever."

"They're lovely."

"The thorns hurt when you're screwing around as a kid and accidentally run into them."

"I hadn't considered that."

"I still have scars on my arms."

"We all have scars like that."

She nodded in agreement. "We most definitely do."

Helen Archer was indeed sitting at the patio table. She was reading a book, a glass of iced tea at hand. She looked up when she heard us and smiled.

"This is a pleasant surprise." She nodded at me as a greeting. "How are you, Bay?"

I decided to get right to the heart of matters. "We're dealing with something in Hemlock Cove and Aunt Tillie thought you might be able to help."

Surprise rushed over Helen's features. "Tell me about it."

I did just that, leaving nothing out. When I finished, she looked perplexed.

"You said they look like ghosts in the windows?"

I nodded. "That's what it looked like to me. I've never seen anything like it. That's why I'm searching for answers. I don't think the appearance of the images in the glass can be a coincidence. It has to be tied to what happened to Paisley Gilmore."

"I would think," Helen agreed, thoughtful as she rocked in her chair. "And you saw the reflections in two different locations?"

"Yeah. Once was at the diner in town. The other time was at the inn my father runs with my uncles."

"Which means they're not trapped in one specific location."

"Do you know what they are?" Stormy asked.

"I can't be certain without seeing them — and since I can't see ghosts, that seems unlikely — but they sound like shades."

I was familiar with the word. I'd come across it and them a few times. "I've seen a few shades here and there," I said. "They were different."

"That's because all shades are different."

"I don't understand," Stormy said. She was still learning about magic and was always brimming with questions. "What's a shade?"

"It's a ghost that's been anchored by something," I replied. "I mean, that's the best way I can explain it."

"It's a rather broad description, but it does the job," Helen agreed. "Shades are ghosts that have been enslaved by other magical beings, or tied to a talisman, or even cursed to walk the land for eternity. They're not normal ghosts."

I thought back to the images I'd seen in the window. "These ghosts definitely didn't look happy. They also didn't look like true ghosts. They weren't wandering around. Why can I only see them in glass reflections?"

"That I can't answer. I have to think it's some sort of spell or curse.

I'm not an expert on shades. I don't know why Tillie thought I could help you."

"You *have* helped me," I reassured her. "Aunt Tillie had no idea what we were dealing with. She's too busy messing with Mrs. Little and Aunt Willa to care about anything else right now, and that includes shades. I hadn't really given the possibility much thought, but now that you mention it, shades sound as likely as anything else."

"You need to figure out who is controlling them," Helen said. "They're ... dangerous ... in their current form. They may appear to be trapped in the glass, but that's likely not true. You might only be able to see them in the glass for some reason."

That was a sobering thought. "Maybe someone made them invisible and I can only see them in the glass because of that, some weird glitch of the spell."

"Anything is possible." Helen looked worried. "Be careful. Your necromancer powers make you an appealing target. If someone did cast a spell to hide these ghosts, they know what you are."

"And if they know my weakness, they'll likely know Aunt Tillie's as well," I mused.

"According to Tillie, she doesn't have any weaknesses."

"Her biggest weakness is that she's full of crap," I said as I got to my feet. "I thank you for your time. You've given me something to think about."

"What are you going to do?"

"I'm going to do what I always do. Figure it out and then wing it."

She smiled. "You have a great deal of your Aunt Tillie in you. It's lovely."

I frowned at her. "I think that's the meanest thing anyone has ever said to me."

"I meant it as a compliment."

"Well, try better next time."

TWELVE

Once back in Hemlock Cove, I headed for the inn's extensive library. I needed to bone up on shades. If Helen was right, we were dealing with an enemy who knew us. That made things dicier.

I heard my mother and aunts in the kitchen sniping at one another, which was their way. More guests would start rolling in for the weekend this afternoon, and even more tomorrow. They had a lot on their plates when it came to running the inn and I had no intention of interrupting them.

I selected several books from the shelves and sat on the couch, glancing over at my phone when it started buzzing. Landon's name scrolled across the screen.

"Is anything wrong?" I asked as I answered.

"Sometimes I just like to call my future wife to hear her voice," he said. "I don't only call when something is wrong."

"True, but we're in the middle of a murder investigation, so I figured it was a possibility."

"I just wanted to check on you." His voice was soft. "Are you still in Shadow Hills?"

"No. I'm at the inn."

"Doing what?"

"Researching." I told him about my conversation with Helen. "I don't know if it's shades but it's as likely an explanation as anything else," I said. "Helen suggested that the shades could've been spelled to be invisible so I couldn't see them."

Landon was quiet a beat, and when he spoke again his tone was sharper. "You specifically?"

I hesitated. The last thing I wanted to do was frighten him, but now wasn't the time to hold back information. "Maybe. I honestly don't know."

"Well, I don't like that," he groused. "If someone cast a spell so these shades are invisible that means they know what you're capable of."

"I don't disagree."

"Bay ... ."

I waited for him to continue. When he didn't, I decided to take control of the conversation. "I'm being safe, Landon. I'm researching shades to figure out what I can do to make them visible. I'm not out running toward danger without backup."

"And what good will that do?"

"At least if I can see them, I'll know how many I'm dealing with. I also might be able to control them."

"Have you tried to control them so far?"

"No."

"Why not?"

"You know why."

His sigh was long and drawn out. "You don't like enslaving souls. It makes you feel icky."

"While I would hate you using the word 'icky' under different circumstances, it feels like the correct word now."

He laughed. "Sweetie, I know you feel as if you're stripping free will from the ghosts when you call on them, but that's going to be necessary under certain circumstances. You need to get used to it."

"I've been doing it."

"Only as a last resort."

"Which is exactly how it should be." I refused to back down. "I don't want to be some all-powerful oracle who uses ghosts whenever the mood strikes. That leads to bad witches."

"I don't think you could ever turn bad, but I'm not going to argue with you. I love you and know you'll do what's right. I just wanted to check on you. Terry and I are heading out with the search teams looking for Richard and Anna Gilmore. We've had no luck so far, but we're hitting the woods. My cell phone might not get service out there and I didn't want you to worry."

That was so Landon. He always thought ahead on issues like that. "Well, I appreciate the call. Is Hannah with you?"

"No. She's doing her own thing. She says she needs to get a feel for the town if she's going to profile the sort of person who would carry out a murder like this in our neck of the woods."

"Do you believe her?"

"Why wouldn't I?"

I shrugged. "I don't know. I can't decide how I feel about her."

"No matter what you say, I think you're feeling a bit of jealousy because she's clearly still carrying a torch for me."

"I don't feel jealous," I countered. "I know you love me. There's no reason for me to feel jealous."

"I agree."

"So why do you keep circling back to that? Do you want me to be jealous?"

"Absolutely not." I could practically see the emphatic headshake he was likely putting on display on the other end of the call. "I want you to always feel secure where I'm concerned, Bay. It's normal human behavior to feel a bit of jealousy when an old girlfriend shows up. Your place in my heart is secure. Forever."

"I know."

"She never got the proposal to end all proposals, did she?"

That made me laugh. "You're going to throw that proposal in my face for the rest of our lives, aren't you?"

"That was my moment."

"And you nailed it."

"I did. I just wanted to make you aware that I might be out of phone contact for a few hours. With Hannah running around town, I want you to be careful."

"I'm not even sure I'll be heading to town. I've got my research books and am comfortable here."

"That's good. You're safe there. Nothing will get past Aunt Tillie."

"I'm pretty sure she's in town torturing Mrs. Little. She stopped in at the newspaper office this morning. She needed a place to change into her leggings after Mom confiscated the first pair."

"Ah. She's shopping in bulk now."

"Mom should stop complaining about the leggings and then Aunt Tillie will stop trying to outdo herself with each subsequent pair. Trying to control her just gives her more power when she's in a mood."

"That's a Winchester family trait. I have to go. I love you. I'm looking forward to learning more about shades when I see you tonight."

"And I look forward to telling you."

I DUG DEEP INTO THE BOOKS, JOTTING notes on a legal pad I'd found in the drawer. It was like being back in school and cramming for a test, but this time the stakes were much higher. I was so lost in thought I didn't realize that somebody was hovering by the door until I heard a soft throat-clearing. When I glanced up, I found Hannah watching me.

"I don't want to intrude," she said.

"It's fine." I closed the book because I didn't want her curiosity getting the better of her. "I'm just ... reading."

"It looks like you're researching." She sat in one of the chairs across from me, her eyes going to the legal pad. "May I ask what you're researching?"

I wasn't sure how to answer. "Oh, well ... ."

"This town is interesting," Hannah noted when I didn't continue. "It should be a case study for a psychology journal. I've been walking around for a few hours and I've seen any number of strange things."

"Aunt Tillie?"

"Your great-aunt could definitely be studied. She has a few diagnosable personality quirks."

Oh, well, I didn't mind this conversation. "Which quirks?"

"Well, for starters, I think she has ADHD and could use some medication."

"She would say her wine is medication enough." And the pot field that was strategically hidden from prying law enforcement eyes on the back property, I silently added.

"She has trouble focusing on one thing," Hannah mused. "She clearly enjoys torturing people."

"That makes her sound evil. She only likes torturing *some* people. If you're not on her list, you're perfectly safe."

"Have you been on her list?"

"Yup."

"And what sort of punishment has she doled out to you?"

"Most of it was minor, kid stuff." I couldn't answer that without mentioning the big family secret. All of Aunt Tillie's punishments involved curses and spells.

Hannah studied me for a long moment. "You don't trust me."

"I don't know you."

"Would it help if I told you I'm not interested in Landon?"

I liked that she was straightforward. "I don't think you're interested in Landon," I assured her. "I do think you're intrigued about how Landon ended up here."

"That's a very astute observation. The man I knew, who was then more of a boy really, had big dreams. They involved city hopping until he got to a big metropolis. He started in Traverse City and was expected to jump to the Detroit office. It never happened."

"He was offered a position in Detroit," I explained. "He decided to stay here."

"With you."

"You think I held him back." It was a statement, not a question. "It's okay. You can say it."

"Actually, I think you balance him out," Hannah corrected. "Holding him back is something you're worried about. I should point out that nobody else here is worried about that, including Landon. That's all internal, coming from you."

"Is this your psychology degree at work?"

"Yes, and I know it drives people crazy. That's a failure of mine."

"I don't think you're a failure."

"No?" She arched an eyebrow. "I do have a few bad personality quirks. Analyzing people is one of them. Yours is occasional bouts of insecurity.

"I like watching you and Landon together," she continued. "It's obvious you love one another. He's vastly changed from the man I knew at the academy. The job is no longer his only reason for being. Now you're his main reason for being."

My cheeks burned under her studied gaze. "I don't think that's true."

"But it is. He loves you with his whole heart. It's written all over his face when he looks at you."

"Are you bothered by that?"

"No. Landon was nothing more than a passing phase when I was young and trying to figure things out. You needn't worry. I've since figured things out. I'm not the same person he knew back then either."

"You're not?"

"Nope. I'm involved, too."

I tried to decide if that was a relief. I didn't look at Hannah as a threat — despite Landon's insistence that she was likely still crushing on him — so I was happy for her. "That's nice."

"Her name is Adrian."

"Oh." Realization dawned. "Oh."

Hannah laughed at my response. "It's okay. I didn't realize when I was dating Landon. We didn't connect, and part of that was because he was looking for a fling. I was trying to figure out who I was at the time. I wasn't looking for a connection either.

"The thing is, at the time, I assumed Landon would spend fifteen to twenty years focused on his job," she continued. "Then I thought he would find some pretty young thing to marry and have children with. He did the exact opposite."

My nose wrinkled.

"Not that you're not pretty," Hannah offered with a laugh. "That came out wrong. You're definitely pretty. I simply thought he would opt for an empty-headed woman because the job was going to be his driving force. He went the other way, though. He went for a woman of substance ... and he's completely infatuated with you."

"We're happy," I said. "I don't know that he's infatuated with me."

"You associate that word with the negative when it's not necessary," Hannah said. "He is infatuated with you. He's constantly touching you, whether it be a stroke of the hair or his fingers brushing against your arm. He's also constantly looking at you. That's infatuation."

"We're newly-engaged. It's a hormonal thing."

"I don't think so, and there's no need to sell yourself short." Hannah graced me with a kind smile. "You changed Landon's life. You worry that you won't be enough for him, but you're wrong. He loves the life you've built together. I've never seen him more fulfilled."

"I guess that's good." I dragged a hand through my hair. "You know, he's going to be really upset when he figures out you no longer have a crush on him. That was boosting his ego."

She laughed. "Something tells me he'll survive. You're all he really cares about."

"That's not true. He cares about his job. This murder is giving him fits."

"It's giving us all fits." Hannah leaned back in her chair and flicked her eyes toward the window. "Part of my job is to read a community. That's what I've been trying to do while hanging around Hemlock Cove today. Do you know what I found when I tried to read Hemlock Cove?"

"Schizophrenia?"

"Kind of, and it makes me laugh that you also see it. My understanding is that you left Hemlock Cove for a few years and moved to Detroit."

I froze. Had she been checking on my background? "Who told you that?"

"Landon. We had lunch at the diner before he took off with Chief Davenport. He mentioned that you'd only been back in Hemlock Cove a few months when you two met."

I was intrigued. "What else did he say?"

"It wasn't so much what he said but how he said it. He always smiles when your name comes up. So does Chief Davenport."

"Chief Terry helped raise us. Aunt Tillie was our primary caregiver sometimes when we were kids. She would drag us around when she was in the mood to torture Mrs. Little. Sometimes Chief Terry would have to get us out of trouble."

"He's your father figure."

I pressed the tip of my tongue to the roof of my mouth and considered the statement. "I have a father. I love him."

"Yes, but Chief Davenport is the father of your heart."

"I love them both." I would never say otherwise. "In some ways I'm closer to Chief Terry."

"He loves you dearly." Hannah's smile turned enigmatic. "He's also determined to cover for the fact that there's real magic in this town."

All of the oxygen whooshed out of my lungs and I had to tamp down my panic. "W-what?"

"You look surprised." Hannah's chuckle was light. "I'm a pragmatic woman, Bay, but I'm not so pragmatic that I'm incapable of believing in the fantastical."

I chose my words carefully. "What is it you think you believe?"

"I believe that there's real magic hidden under the fake witch stuff in Hemlock Cove. I also believe your family is at the heart of that. It's okay if you don't want to admit it. I can't imagine being in your position."

I fervently wished Aunt Tillie would interrupt us, something I never thought I would wish for. "We're just a normal family."

"You're not, but that's none of my business. If you choose to trust me going forward, I'll be grateful. If you don't, I'll understand. I'm here to solve a murder, and I would be lying if I said the blood runes on the trees don't give me reason for concern."

"I researched the case you mentioned in Salem," I said. "Did you know there was another case twenty years before that?"

She nodded. "I did. Unfortunately, the evidence in the older case wasn't filed correctly and has since been lost. There are only two vague reports. The case from two years ago has a lot of the hallmarks of this case. However, it's difficult for me to believe that someone came from Salem to Hemlock Cove to commit ritual murder."

"Then what do you believe?" I asked.

"I believe there's something significant about the runes," she replied. "It's some sort of magical ritual. The similarities are because someone is looking for a specific outcome. We need to figure out what that outcome is."

"Yeah." I blew out a sigh. "I don't know what the runes signify."

"Is that what you're doing here? Researching the runes."

"Oh, um ... ." I watched as Hannah took the book from my lap and flipped it to the page where I'd placed a pen to keep my place.

"Shades?"

"I'm thinking of writing a book," I lied.

She immediately dismissed the lie. "You think this has something to do with evil ghosts."

Despite her interest in magic – which she'd hidden pretty well during our ride to the scene hours earlier – she obviously didn't understand what we were dealing with. Still, I liked her a great deal more than I did at breakfast. She was a woman trying to find her place in the world. That didn't make her evil.

"I'm just reading," I said. Despite her amiable nature, I didn't feel comfortable admitting the truth about my family. "It's nothing more than that."

Hannah nodded and handed the book back. She looked tired when she got to her feet. "You don't trust me. It's okay. I've given you no reason to trust me."

"I'm just reading," I insisted.

"Then I'll leave you to your reading. If you find anything important, I'm sure you'll tell Landon. He obviously knows the truth about you."

My stomach did an uncomfortable flip. "The only truth about me is that I love him and my family is nuts."

"Keep protecting yourself, Bay. Your instincts are good. But I'm not the enemy. When you do know something, I'm sure we'll all be able to work together to figure it out. Until then, I'll keep doing what I do best and assume you'll do the same." She didn't wait for an answer before heading for the door. "Good luck," she called out before disappearing.

I started rubbing my forehead. Things had just gotten more complicated, and I wasn't sure that was even possible.

THIRTEEN

I worked all afternoon in the library, which is where Landon found me when he showed up for dinner.

"Have you been home at all?" He tipped up my chin and kissed me before settling on the couch next to me.

I shook my head. "There's a lot of information here on shades."

"And?" He looked hopeful.

"And none of the information is the same. I mean ... none of it. Nobody seems to agree on why they are what they are, or why they can do what they can do. Speaking of the things they can do, it varies and is all over the place. Some think they're enslaved ghosts. Others think they're different entirely."

"Okay, so what do we do?"

"I don't know. I think I'm going to have to try to communicate with them."

"What if they don't want to be communicated with? What if they want to kill you?"

"If movies and television have taught me anything, they definitely want to kill me. They have that look."

He managed a smile, but it didn't touch his eyes. The worry lurked there. "Maybe you should bring the whole team in on this."

"Clove can't be brought in on anything right now."

"Then bring in Aunt Tillie and Thistle. At least then I wouldn't be as worried."

"I can't bring them in until I know what I'm dealing with. I ... ." The sound of wheels on the hardwood floor drew my attention to the hallway, where Aunt Tillie was zooming up and down on her scooter, Peg following.

Snort. Snort.

"What is she doing?" Landon asked, allowing himself to be momentarily distracted.

"Mom vetoed the second set of leggings about an hour ago. She demanded Aunt Tillie hand them over or eat liver for dinner."

Landon made a face. "Oh, please tell we're not having liver for dinner?" He looked horrified at the prospect. "Let's go to the diner."

I laughed. "It's Mexican night. They made burritos, tacos and quesadillas. The only one who would be eating liver in that scenario is Aunt Tillie."

"That sounds fun."

"Then I'm telling the story wrong. Aunt Tillie has been ranting since she got home."

"Is she still wearing the leggings?"

As if on cue, Aunt Tillie zoomed by again, Peg's hooves echoing on the floor as she chased her.

Snort. Snort.

"So, the leggings are still on," Landon confirmed. "I guess Aunt Tillie isn't taking the threat seriously."

"It'll bubble over once we all sit down to dinner together."

"Hey, we've had some quiet dinners. We're due for some fun." He leaned in and kissed my temple. "You seem tired. We could order pizza and go home if that appeals to you more."

"I kind of want tacos."

"They are delightful."

"How did your search go?"

"We found absolutely nothing. The state police brought in dogs and an evidence team for the house. We have nothing but a dead teenager."

"And three other teenagers who might be considered suspicious."

"I can't really share that information with the state police. Marcus's attack went down as an accident in the books and Amelia's disappearance was recorded as 'teenage misadventure.'" He used the appropriate air quotes. "I can't tell them the truth."

"No." I rubbed my chin. "We have to figure out how it all fits together."

"Any ideas?"

"No."

"Have you seen Hannah?" He looked to the hallway when Aunt Tillie sped by again. "She added her cape."

Snort. Snort.

I laughed. "She's been steadily adding components. She didn't start out with the hat or the shoes. She was barefoot. Mom insisted that if she was going to terrorize the house she wear shoes so she wouldn't accidentally slide off and break a hip."

"Good plan."

"Yes, it's delightful." I stretched my arms over my head. "Hannah showed up here a few hours ago."

Surprise lit Landon's handsome features. "What did she say?"

"She stopped in to visit me, mentioned that you were different from the way you used to be when you guys were involved, and then went on her merry way."

"I *am* different."

"Were you not a bacon glutton back then?"

"Oh, I was always a bacon glutton. Back then I was a bacon glutton boy. Now I'm a man who embraces his bacon gluttony."

He was so serious I had to tilt my head to study him. "You've been a man as long as I've known you."

"Not really. Back on that first case, I was giddy about being undercover. I took my job seriously but didn't consider the ramifications for anybody else. Then you came out of that maze, white as a sheet, and I felt this ... tug."

"That sounds serious."

His lips curved. "It was. The tug I felt was for you. I didn't like that you were unhappy. I didn't like that you were afraid. Er, well, at least I thought you were afraid. I didn't realize you had magic backing you up. I thought you were some poor, demure flower who needed me to protect her."

"And how long did that last?"

He shrugged. "Probably until I saw your entire family wearing matching track suits in a cornfield."

"Hey, Clove, Thistle and I were not wearing those track suits."

"In my memory you were because that makes it funnier."

"It didn't end funny. You got shot."

"I survived. That's when I started thinking hard. That's when I started growing up."

"What did you think about?"

"The prettiest woman in the world."

"Am I supposed to believe that's me?"

"Yup. I fell in love with you right away, Bay. I might not have realized it, but you changed me right from the start. Hannah isn't wrong about that. Even if she is still harboring a crush on me, I couldn't become a man for her. You were the only one who could make that happen."

I considered telling him about Adrian. Ultimately, I decided that was Hannah's business. If Landon got puffed up thinking that Hannah still had a crush on him, there was no harm in it. He might've been a man, but he still liked his ego stroked.

"Well, I happen to love the man you've become." I pressed a kiss to his cheek. "He might be a glutton, but he's loyal, funny and gives the best proposals in the world."

"Don't forget sexy."

"You're definitely sexy."

. . .

WE GATHERED IN the dining room for dinner thirty minutes later. Hannah joined us, her smile broad and pleasant, seemingly delighted by the food on the table.

"I love Mexican food," she enthused. "This looks amazing." Her smile slipped when she saw Marnie walk out of the kitchen with a plate piled high with liver and onions.

"Don't worry." Marnie's smile was evil when it landed on Aunt Tillie. "Only one person will be eating this tonight."

Aunt Tillie's gaze was dark as it landed on Marnie. "I'm not eating that."

"Then give me the leggings," Mom instructed in her harshest voice.

"No. They're my leggings."

"Well, this is my Mexican feast," Mom shot back. "I get to decide who eats what, and you get liver this evening."

"I don't like liver."

"Tough." Mom watched as Marnie slid the plate in front of Aunt Tillie and then folded her arms across her chest, practically daring Aunt Tillie to reach for a taco.

Rather than acknowledge my mother's power over her, Aunt Tillie shifted her attention to me. "Can you believe this?"

I held her gaze for a moment and then reached for a burrito. "I'm going to stay out of this one."

"That's wise," Mom intoned, her gaze never leaving Aunt Tillie. "Eat it."

Landon was taken aback as he sat next to me. "Wow. That's an evil face. I've never seen her make that expression before."

"That's her 'You're going to do what I say whether you like it or not' face," I offered.

"No, I've seen that face. It's frightening, but this is way worse."

"She has two of those faces," Chief Terry volunteered as he settled next to me. "One is vastly more terrifying."

"Have you seen this one before?" Landon appeared to be mesmerized by my mother. "I mean ... if I had to see that face when I was trying to sleep I'd have nightmares."

"Thank you, Landon," Mom hissed.

"You're welcome."

"Eat your burrito, Landon," Mom ordered.

"Yes, ma'am." Landon shuddered and then smiled at me. "I hope you didn't inherit that face," he whispered.

"Why? Will that make you want to call off the wedding?" I asked.

"Nothing will make me want to call off the wedding, but I need to be prepared. That face is just ... wow. You know that doll that everyone wants to kill in those movies?"

"Chucky," I said.

"Yeah. Your mother reminds me of that doll right now."

I had to swallow my laugh. My mother remained rooted to her spot, glaring at Aunt Tillie. They were locked in a battle of wills and I was curious which of them would come out the winner.

"Did you find anything during your search?" Hannah asked, wisely changing the subject. Her plate was heaped with quesadilla pieces and tacos. "I didn't get an update, so I assumed that you didn't find anything."

"You assumed right." Landon's expression slipped. "We have nothing to show for our efforts. I mean ... absolutely nothing."

"I'm sorry." Hannah looked genuinely contrite. "I'm still trying to piece together a picture of our perpetrator. I don't have much to go on, but Hemlock Cove is a fascinating town."

"Fascinating?" Landon flicked a quick look toward me but kept his face impassive. "What do you mean?"

"Well, the entire identity of this town shifted when it became Hemlock Cove. Before, it was a struggling small town with no industrial base. Now it's a thriving tourist destination with paranormal undertones."

"You mean the witch stuff. I thought this place was nuts when I first visited. Now I'm used to it."

"The witch stuff is smart," Hannah said. "I've been to Salem. They've based their entire economy on a tragedy from hundreds of years ago. They've modernized it over the years, but the witch history drives their economy. Now it's known as a Halloween town year-round, and that allows them to thrive.

"Hemlock Cove did the same thing, but didn't have a tragic history to build on," she continued. "I don't know who came up with the idea of populating a small Michigan town with witches, but whoever it was should receive an award."

"Actually, that was a conversation that spanned a full year," Mom offered as she sat down. She was still watching Aunt Tillie to make sure she didn't try to steal a taco but seemed engaged in the conversation. "We knew we had to save Hemlock Cove. Some of the other communities around us had based their economies on leaf tours and lake visits. We don't have a water feature besides the cove out by the lighthouse — well, other than Hollow Creek, which isn't really a draw — so we needed to do something to stand out."

"I was part of those discussions," Chief Terry said. "I thought those suggesting the witch theme were crazy, but when things started to come together, I saw how it would work. We needed a gimmick, and that's what we ended up with."

"I've read up on the town," Hannah said. "There were a few hiccups at first, but things caught on quickly. This town is uniquely situated for small inns and bed and breakfasts."

"We are," Chief Terry agreed.

"Also, this family has taken on mythic proportions in some online forums," she added.

I froze, my taco halfway to my mouth. I should've known she would broach the subject again.

"Mythic proportions?" Mom's forehead wrinkled. "What does that mean?"

"I think she means our dinner theater," I volunteered weakly.

"Oh, the dinner theater here is revered," Hannah agreed. "Your former guests rave about it online."

"What dinner theater?" Aunt Tillie demanded, her hand snaking around the plate of liver and heading for the burritos. "We don't do dinner theater."

Thwack!

Mom pulled a wooden spoon out from Goddess knows where and viciously smacked Aunt Tillie's hand.

"Ow!" Aunt Tillie pulled back her hand and cradled it, glaring murderous holes into my mother. "What was that?"

"It's liver or nothing," Mom insisted. "If you're going to insist on wearing those leggings, then you'll eat what we see fit."

"Tomorrow it's split pea soup," Marnie warned.

"Oh, I hate split pea soup," Aunt Tillie moaned. "It looks like green diarrhea."

"And thank you for that," Landon drawled. "You're going to ruin my appetite. Oh, wait, it's still good. I'll just stay away from the green salsa."

"This would be an example of the dinner theater," Hannah explained. "People love it. They think it's an act and don't realize it's authentic."

"That's because they don't want to admit that my supposedly sweet-as-pie nieces are really torturers of the highest order," Aunt Tillie muttered. "I'm not eating this liver!" Her voice echoed throughout the room, causing me to look up.

My heart did a long, slow roll when I saw the movement in the window at the far end of the room. "Crap." My mouth went dry.

"What's wrong?" Landon was almost completely focused on his dinner. "Don't eat the green salsa if you've still got what Aunt Tillie said in your head. Save it for later."

I kept my gaze on the window, frowning when the shades began to grow in number. What started out as two had grown to five in the blink of an eye.

"Your family's history is amazing," Hannah continued, oblivious to what was happening behind her. "You've owned this property for years and people online swear this is the most magical place in town."

Landon stiffened next to me. "What do you mean?"

"Something about the bluff," Hannah replied, making a face and glancing over her shoulder, probably to see what I was staring at. "What is it, Bay? Is something wrong?"

Landon finally tore himself from his feast and moved his hands to my face. "Sweetie, you're really pale. Are you sick?"

"I'll have her food." Aunt Tillie reached for my plate.

Thwack!

"I said no," Mom barked. "You're eating the liver or giving me those leggings. Those are your only two choices."

"You're not the boss of me," Aunt Tillie railed. "You can't decide what I eat."

"I'm the cook, so I most definitely can."

The number of shades in the window had grown too large to count. I was about to suggest that we get Hannah out of the room when the lights flickered, followed by a huge bolt of lightning outside. The low roll of thunder followed less than a second later.

Hannah practically jumped out of her seat. "Wow. That storm came out of nowhere."

Did it? Did the shades bring it?

Another flash of lightning lit the room, and as the thunder rolled, the power went out.

I jumped to my feet.

"It's okay," Mom intoned. "The generator will kick on in a minute."

"Oh, that's good." Hannah sounded relieved.

I sensed the shades moving even though the darkness wouldn't allow me to see them.

"Stop," I ordered when the shadows began encroaching on Hannah.

The shades froze.

"Stop what?" Hannah asked, confused.

Next to me, Landon's hand landed on my hip. "What is it?" he asked in a low voice. "Is it them?"

"What's happening down there?" Hannah asked. "I can't make out what you're saying."

"You're not supposed to be here," I warned the shades. I felt them filling the room. Whatever was going on, whatever spell they were under, the darkness made them bolder. "You can't be here."

"Are you talking to me?" Hannah sounded upset. "I'm not trying to make you uncomfortable. Honestly, I find this town fascinating."

"She's not talking to you," Landon said.

"The lights should be back on any second." Mom's voice was laced with nerves. "Bay ... ."

She didn't get a chance to finish what she was going to say. The lights flared to life at the exact moment the shades attacked. I didn't have time to react.

The nearest two, the ones I'd seen every time they appeared in the glass, had their ghostly hands on me a split-second before the lights flared. They threw me into the wall on the opposite side of the room with enough force that my bones rattled.

"Bay!" Landon raced to me, his face flushed.

The blow knocked the wind out of me, but the return of the lights had the shades retreating. They were gone in an instant.

"What was that?" Hannah asked, her eyes wide. "Is that more of your dinner theater?"

"Yes," Mom automatically answered as she scurried from her spot at the table to kneel next to me. "We're nothing if not diligent about our theater."

"Bay." Landon drew my eyes to him. "Are you okay?"

I nodded because I still hadn't caught my breath.

"Apparently Bay is the one spoiling for attention this evening," Aunt Tillie said around a mouth full of food. She'd snagged my plate when the room went dark. "It's because Clove isn't here. She would be the kvetch if she were here."

"What are you doing?" Mom demanded when she realized Aunt Tillie was eating. "What did I say?"

Thwack!

"Stop that!" Aunt Tillie was irate. "I'll put you all on my list if you don't stop that right now!"

Landon ignored the hoopla behind him and kept his eyes on me. "Shades?" he asked under his breath.

I nodded.

"Bay, this is serious," he whispered. "We have to deal with them as a group whether you like it or not. We need the entire team."

FOURTEEN

"**T**ell me what hurts."

Landon gave the appearance of calm as he looked me over, but it was obvious he felt anything but calm. There was a storm brewing in the depths of his eyes and he looked as if he wanted to fight.

"I'm okay." I grunted as I tried to stand. His arms were around me almost instantly. "I'm not hurt ... mostly."

His expression was dubious. "I'm getting you home." He lifted me from the floor, his gaze immediately snapping to the door at the sound of footsteps. If I thought he was in a bad mood before, it was nothing compared to the expression on his face when Aunt Willa appeared. "What are you doing here?" he snarled.

Willa barely blinked at his greeting. She was used to people hating her — or at least that's how I rationalized it — so she wasn't surprised at Landon's vitriol. "I'm here to discuss how things are going to be moving forward."

Aunt Tillie, still smarting from Mom stealing the tacos from her, glared at her half-sister. "You want to discuss how things are going to be?" She was incredulous.

"That's right." Willa bobbed her head. "I'm living in this town, too, at least for now. I won't be leaving anytime soon, so you're going to have to adjust."

"Yeah, I don't adjust." Aunt Tillie glared at Mom. "Give me those tacos."

"No." Mom's eyes flashed with annoyance, but even though she wasn't in the mood to deal with Aunt Tillie she looked anything but thrilled by Willa's appearance. "As for you, Aunt Willa, I don't believe we invited you into our home."

"I don't have to be invited. This is a business."

"That's not true," Landon countered as he pulled me against him. He was shielding me, protecting me from Willa. "It doesn't matter if this is a place of business or not. It's not a public building. We can refuse service to anyone we want, including you."

Mom's grin was wide until it landed on Landon, and then she looked conflicted. "I'm with Landon." She shuffled closer, giving him a wary look, and then pressed her hand to my forehead. "How do you feel?"

"I'm confused," Hannah said from the other side of the table. "I thought this was all part of the dinner theater."

"It was," Landon replied. "Bay just hurt herself because she was too enthusiastic with the performance."

"Yes," I agreed dryly. "I love good dinner theater. Sometimes I love it so much I get overenthusiastic." Aches and pains were beginning to make themselves known but I held it together. "I'm fine."

Hannah didn't look convinced, but she said nothing.

"I'm taking Bay home," Landon insisted to Mom. "I'm going to get her in a warm bath and ... just talk to her about how she doesn't need to get so enthusiastic with her performances."

Mom could read between the lines. "I think that's a fine idea. I can send some food home with you."

Landon hesitated and then glanced at me. He wasn't one to turn up his nose at food. "I'm not all that hungry," he said.

I made a face. "I killed your appetite. I always thought that was impossible."

He shot me an amused look. "You didn't kill my appetite. You simply postponed it until tomorrow morning. Unless ... are you hungry? I can take food home for you."

I wasn't hungry. I knew his appetite would eventually return, though, and there was nothing for him to eat in the guesthouse. "Maybe take a few burritos home to heat up just in case." I forced a smile.

"Good idea." Landon watched as Mom placed four burritos into a plastic bag, all the while keeping one ear on Aunt Willa and Aunt Tillie as they sniped at one another behind his back. His expression darkened as he regarded them. "Don't come back here, Willa," he ordered as he slipped his arm around my waist. "There's no reason for you to be here. You don't have a claim to this property. The owners don't want you here. You've officially been warned. I'll arrest you if you come back."

Aunt Willa's eyes filled with fire. "You wouldn't dare!"

"I would and I will." Landon was firm. "I'm not the only one." He inclined his head toward Chief Terry. "You don't belong here, Willa." He led me toward the door, pausing long enough to pin her with a glare. "The only reason you came back to Hemlock Cove was to torture your family because you think you've been cheated."

"I *have* been cheated," Aunt Willa insisted. "I grew up on this property, too. I was cut out of the will."

"The property went through the matriarchal lines. You weren't Caroline Winchester's daughter."

"I was cheated," Aunt Willa insisted louder. "You all banded together to cheat me."

"As long as you take no responsibility for your part in this, we're at an impasse." Landon's voice was chilly with resolve. "Nobody wants you here. And, yes, I'm talking about Hemlock Cove, not just this inn.

"You've joined with an individual who also wants payback, and it doesn't take a genius to figure out that you've decided to work together because you somehow think that will help you win," he continued. "I have news for you. Brian is not going to win."

"You stole his grandfather's newspaper," Aunt Willa insisted.

"No, he tried to hurt Bay and the town banded together to stop him," Landon shot back. "He did this to himself. You're doing it to yourself right now. I don't want to hear a single word when this blows up in your face."

Aunt Willa worked her jaw. "I think there should be ground rules for what's to come. That's the only fair thing in a civilized society."

"Oh, no." Landon made a tsking sound with his tongue as he wagged a finger. "You've done this to yourself. If you wanted ground rules, you should've stayed away. Instead, you invaded our turf."

"That's a little dramatic," I noted in a low voice.

He ignored me. "Now you're on your own, against Aunt Tillie." He mock shuddered. "May the Goddess have mercy on your soul." He accepted the bag of burritos from Mom and shepherded me to the door. "We're going home. We'll be back for breakfast. I'm sure my appetite will have returned by then."

"I'll have the bacon waiting," Mom promised.

"Great." Landon cast one more look toward Aunt Willa. "Quit while you're ahead. You can't beat Aunt Tillie. If you leave town now, you can save face."

"I won't ever lose to that woman again," Aunt Willa insisted.

"Then you deserve whatever she dishes out."

Aunt Tillie's smile was a little too "cat that ate the canary" for my liking when I risked a glance at her. "You'd better start running now, Willa." She reached over to snag a taco, clearly riding high on the threat.

Thwack.

"Stop it," Aunt Tillie demanded, fury filling the room. "I need my strength if you want me to take Willa down."

"Then change your leggings," Mom growled.

"I'll die in these leggings," Aunt Tillie warned. "You're just making me more determined."

"Then you'll die extremely thin," Mom shot back.

"I hate this family," Aunt Tillie muttered.

"Join the club," Willa fired back.

I pushed the argument out of my head as I let Landon drag me through the inn, my eyes drifting to the windows as we passed. The shades — if that's what they were — seemed to be able to do what they wanted in darkness. The light drove them back. Was that important? Was it a coincidence?

"Do you want to eat burritos in the bathtub with me when we get home?" I asked.

Landon's lips curved. "Actually, I want to dote on you and act like a mother hen."

The fact that he could admit it was progress, although it didn't sound all that entertaining. "I prefer the burrito and bath therapy."

"Maybe we can figure out a way to split the difference," he said.

"Compromise." I bobbed my head, groaning when an ache went up my spine. "We're getting good at that."

"We are." He helped me into the passenger seat of his truck. Apparently we were leaving my car in the lot overnight. All I really wanted to do was soak away the aches and pains. He stood at the open truck door and studied my face. I understood what he was thinking.

"It's okay," I reassured him. "There's no reason to get worked up. I'm fine."

"That's not what I was thinking."

"What were you thinking?"

"I love you."

I waited for him to expand, add a "but" somewhere at the end. When he didn't, I traced my finger down his cheek. "I love you. I really am okay."

"No, you're achy and in pain, and I need to take care of you. That's only part of it."

"What's the other part?" I asked.

He grasped my hand tightly in his. "I can't live without you, Bay."

"I guess it's good you don't have to."

"I just need you to remember that." He rubbed his finger over my engagement ring. "It's you and me forever."

"I know."

"And probably Aunt Tillie because she'll likely outlive us all."

"Mostly us, though." I flashed a smile.

"We need to fix this. You obviously can't control these ghosts like you do all the others."

I shook my head. "I don't think so."

"Then we'll figure it out." He leaned forward and pressed a firm, lingering kiss to my forehead. "I'm going to take care of you the rest of the night and I don't want to hear a single complaint about it."

"I can manage that."

"Good. Then we're going to bed. We'll start strategizing in the morning."

LANDON GOT IN THE BATHTUB WITH me for a bit and then left me to soak. There were no burritos, which meant he wasn't hungry, almost unheard of for him. I filled the tub twice to keep the water hot before drying off and climbing into fuzzy sleep pants and an oversized T-shirt. Upon exiting the bathroom, I heard voices in the living room.

"I don't know what you're talking about," Landon insisted. "You're talking crazy."

Who was he talking to? Then I heard the other voice and froze.

"She's magical, Landon," Hannah insisted. "You can deny it, but I know you know. It's not as if she's the type of person who would keep something like that from you."

My heart lodged in my throat. I recognized in the library that Hannah was suspicious, but I didn't think she would go this far. She'd come to our home and put Landon on the defensive. That wouldn't end well.

"It's a town of fake witches," Landon said. "I can't believe you're actually suggesting this."

"Are you really going to sit there and lie to my face?" Hannah demanded. "I'm not an idiot. There's no way she flew against that wall with the force she did without magical intervention."

"You should hear how you sound."

I licked my lips, debating, and then walked out of the bathroom.

Landon stood about five feet from the front door, his arms folded across his chest. The look on his face could've set the world ablaze.

For her part, Hannah was calm. She hadn't adopted an aggressive stance, but the set of her shoulders told me she wasn't going to let this go.

It was time to take a leap of faith.

"I'm a witch," I announced.

Landon growled as he turned to face me. "Why aren't you in bed?"

"Because I just got out of the tub and heard voices."

"Bay ... ." He looked caught. It was rare he didn't know what to do. It might've been funny under different circumstances, but I hated the fear etched across his face.

"I'm pretty sure she already knew, Landon." I padded into the room and fixed Hannah with a curious look. "You were trying to get me to admit it in the library."

Hannah nodded. "You weren't ready. After what happened during dinner, I figured I couldn't just let it go. What's going on here?"

I gestured to the chairs. "You should sit. I know I'm going to. My back hurts."

Landon immediately moved between us, taking his place at my side. His hands were on my back, rubbing, before I finished sitting. "This is a bad idea, Bay," he muttered. "A really bad idea."

He was likely right, but there was nothing I could do about it. Denying what I was would only further Hannah's suspicions. We needed her on our side. "She knows. We have to deal with it."

"We do." Hannah flicked a curious look to Landon. "I'll be honest here. I never thought you'd end up with a witch."

"Love is love," Landon replied, his hands busy on my back. "I don't care what she is. She's ... Bay. I had no choice but to fall in love with her."

Hannah's smile was warm. "That's really sweet. I was just telling Bay this afternoon that you'd grown quite a bit since last we met."

"I don't know about growing," Landon hedged. "I'm a different man than I was before meeting her. She made me a better man."

"I think you were always a good man. She's definitely made you more observant and accepting. I applaud that."

"I love Bay," Landon said. "I know you still have a crush on me, but it doesn't matter. She's it for me."

I pressed my lips together and stared at the ceiling. His ego was out of control sometimes.

"I think I'll survive," Hannah said dryly.

"She's a lesbian," I whispered to him, shaking my head as his eyebrows drew together. "Her girlfriend's name is Adrian ... and you're coming across like an idiot."

Landon frowned. "You're a lesbian?"

Hannah nodded. "I am. Still, if I was going to have a crush on a man at this point in my life, I guess it might be you. I hope that helps."

"Not really." Landon slid his eyes to me. "I can't believe you didn't tell me."

"You seemed to like the fact that you thought she had a crush on you. I didn't want to ruin things for you."

"You could never ruin things, but I do feel like a bit of an ass."

I patted his knee. "Welcome to the family." Now that the Hannah's purported crush had been put to rest, I focused on her. "Are you going to tell the higher-ups at the FBI what I am? If so, I'll deny it."

"I'm not telling anyone," Hannah reassured me. "It's nobody's business. Besides, the odds of them believing me seem slim."

"What are you going to do?" Landon asked. "I mean ... this changes things from your perspective."

"It does," Hannah readily agreed. "It makes things easier. Bay can help me. I figured there was something odd here when I saw the runes. The fact that there are real witches hiding amongst fake witches explains a lot."

"We don't know what's going on," I said. "We don't have the answers you're looking for."

"We can work together to find them." Hannah cocked her head. "What did you see tonight?"

"I don't know what they are."

"You were researching shades in the library."

"That's our best guess. We don't know that we're right."

"Well, it gives us a place to start looking." Hannah slowly got to her feet. "You two obviously need some time alone to ... regroup. You're going to want to talk about the fact that I know. I want you to know that I would never tell your secret. You're not the first witch I've come across, though I'm careful who I acknowledge that to because I don't want to look like a loon."

Now I was curious. "Where have you met another witch?"

"Just like I won't tell your secret, I won't tell hers. Just suffice it to say that I'm more open to the paranormal world than you might guess. We need to compare notes, but it's late and you've had a rough night. I'll leave you two to each other. We can talk tomorrow."

I nodded. "I'd like that."

"We'll talk," Landon agreed. "You should know, I'll die to protect Bay. If you're lying about keeping her secret ... ." He trailed off.

Hannah said, "I know trust has to be earned. You can trust me."

"I guess we'll see."

15

FIFTEEN

I moved with hesitancy upon waking the next morning. My back ached a bit, but the bath salts I'd thrown into the tub had done their job and I wasn't feeling nearly as rough as I feared.

"Take a minute," Landon murmured, stirring next to me. His fingers lightly trailed over my back. "How do you feel?"

"I've been through way worse than last night."

"That wasn't what I asked."

"I'm okay, a little sore. Nothing to worry about."

"Oh, right." He let loose a raspy chuckle. "If only that were true." He placed a gentle kiss on my forehead. "Be honest with me. Do you think you would do better if you stayed in bed all day?"

"Are you staying with me?"

"If I thought that would work, I would call in sick."

"No, you wouldn't." That was laughable. "You would never rest during a murder investigation. Frankly, I'm insulted you'd try to run that nonsense on me."

He rubbed his jaw with the hand that wasn't working on my back. "You're right. But you can spend the day in bed. I'll even pick up breakfast and lunch for you like a good husband-to-be."

"You're already a good husband-to-be." I carefully rolled on to my back and stretched my arms over my head. I did feel better than I expected. "I can't back away from this any more than you can."

"Fine."

"I'm not trying to upset you."

"I said it was fine. I didn't really expect you to stay in bed, but one of these days I'm going to get my way on this."

"Once this is behind us, we can both schedule a day to stay in bed. I'll even cook for you so neither of us have to leave the guesthouse."

"Don't threaten me."

I propped myself up on one elbow to stare down at him. "I can cook."

He snorted.

"I can," I insisted. "Just because I choose not to cook, doesn't mean I can't. I grew up watching my mother and aunts cook."

"You have many fine qualities, including beauty, sweetness and a keen mind. But you burn toast."

I was offended. "Maybe I like dark toast."

"Burnt. Not dark, burnt."

"I still maintain our toaster is faulty," I grumbled, studying the ceiling. "What are we going to do about Hannah?"

"You opened that door. I was perfectly content pretending that you weren't a witch."

"She knew."

"She suspected. She didn't know until you admitted it."

"I think we'll do better working with her."

"Then that's what we'll do." He turned to his side and rested his hand on my stomach. "I'm not upset you told her, I just ... think we should talk about these things before they happen. You didn't mention that she was digging as hard as she was."

"That's because she was only circling the subject in the library. I knew she was suspicious, but I couldn't believe she'd just jump to that conclusion. I mean ... who does that?"

"Someone who has crossed paths with the paranormal before."

"Yeah, I'm curious about that."

"As am I. Her not telling us about it is a good sign, though."

"I agree. She's not the first one to find out the truth about us."

"No, but I still think we should have protocol for situations like this."

I grinned. "That's so you. I love how you want to establish protocol. That's such a man thing."

"It's the smart thing."

"I think it'll work out."

"I hope you're right, and not just because our lives could drastically change if the wrong person finds out."

I'd been worried about the same thing, so I could hardly chastise him for saying it out loud. "I'll do my best not to ruin your life."

"Don't say things like that. The only thing that would ruin my life is losing you. We'll deal. I trust Hannah."

"Even though she doesn't have a crush on you?"

He scowled. "I'll never live that down, will I?"

"No. It's too cute."

He sighed. "Honestly, thinking back, it makes sense. There were ... *hints* ... that she wasn't as into me as most women are."

"Ah, a way to boost your ego even in the face of defeat."

"Ha, ha." He started tickling my abdomen, causing me to squirm. "The only person I want to have a crush on me is you. As for Hannah, I never had reason to think she wasn't trustworthy. I have hope that she'll work with us. Is that what you need to hear?"

"Pretty much. I'd hate to be the one who opened my big mouth and put my family at risk. I always assumed that would be Aunt Tillie."

He laughed. "I'm right there with you." He nipped in for a kiss and then pushed his unruly hair from his face. "I'm starving. My stomach is about to lodge a formal complaint. Let's head to the inn early so we can talk to Terry. It's best he knows that the witch is out of the bag, so to speak."

"He'll probably be angry."

"I don't think so. He loves you too much. He'll be worried, but he needs to know."

I nodded. "I have to tell Mom and the others too. I only outed myself, but Hannah isn't an idiot. She'll figure out that the entire family is involved."

"She will. I'm sure they'll be fine."

I figured otherwise, but there was only one way to find out.

CHIEF TERRY WAS AT THE TABLE WITH Aunt Tillie when we entered the dining room. I couldn't help but notice Aunt Tillie had opted for standard blue leggings today instead of her usual loud ones. That likely meant she was hungry.

"Something happened last night." Landon didn't stand on preamble, but he did dart a look toward the door to make sure Hannah wasn't approaching. "You're not going to like this." He laid it all out for Chief Terry, who frowned throughout the entire tale.

"Well, that's just great," Chief Terry rumbled. He didn't yell, but I could tell he wanted to. "That doesn't sound very smart."

I shrugged. "She knew."

"She *suspected*," Landon corrected. "It's done now. We have to deal with it. I just wanted you to be aware before she comes down."

"It will be fine," Aunt Tillie waved away his concern. "She's not evil."

"How can you be sure of that?" Chief Terry challenged.

"Because I'm me. I know things." She tapped the side of her head. "You guys need to stop getting worked up about things like this. Worry about the big stuff."

Landon, from his spot by the door, swiped his hand across his throat to silence Aunt Tillie. It didn't work.

"Is that a gang symbol?" Aunt Tillie demanded. "Did he just gang signal me?"

"No." I shook my head. "He just wants you to stop being you."

"Fat chance." The smile Aunt Tillie pasted on her face when Hannah appeared was straight out of a horror movie. "Welcome to the wonderful world of witches. If you open your big, fat mouth, we'll curse you to within an inch of your life. We're having bacon for breakfast, though, so there's that to look forward to. If you want some, you'll have to get in there fast before the glutton steals it all."

I briefly shut my eyes. Only Aunt Tillie would think that was appropriate.

Landon cleared his throat, discomfort rolling off him in waves. "Ignore her."

"I don't think that's wise." Hannah returned Aunt Tillie's smile. "I see everybody is caught up on where we stand."

"Not everybody," I said, shooting a worried look toward the kitchen. My mother's reaction was yet to come. "We thought it best to tell Chief Terry, though."

Hannah poured herself a glass of juice and focused on Chief Terry. "And how long have you known?"

"Since ... forever." Chief Terry's expression didn't change. "She's always been my little sweetheart. Even though she's an adult now, that hasn't changed. It won't ever change."

"And you want me to be aware that you'll be working against me if I blab," Hannah surmised.

"He doesn't think you're going to blab," I offered awkwardly. "He's just ... ." What? How could I explain it?

"He's her second father," Landon volunteered. "In some ways, he's her first father. Everybody here will go to the mat for everybody else. You should be aware of that."

"I'm aware." Hannah took a seat at the table. "I have no interest in ruining this family. Everybody is delightful."

"Have you met Aunt Tillie?" I pointed to the woman in question. "And what about Aunt Willa? She's not delightful at all."

"Well, I guess she's not delightful." Hannah smirked. "She is, however, a concern. What does she know about your family?"

"Not enough to matter," Aunt Tillie replied. "We grew up together, but she was always separate. That was her choice. My mother tried to include her, but it never went well. Willa was always ... Willa."

"She knows you're a witch."

"She knows I'm the queen of witches," Aunt Tillie snorted. "I'm the super witch of super witches. Don't worry about Willa. I have plans for her."

Hannah's eyebrows hopped. "That sounds ominous."

"Oh, you have no idea." Aunt Tillie's lips curved. "Willa isn't a concern for us."

"Well, she's somewhat of a concern," I hedged. "Her association with Brian isn't good."

"And what's the deal with him?" Hannah asked. "I assume you told me only part of that story."

"He's a schmuck," Aunt Tillie replied. "That's all you need to know about him. He's not a concern either."

"He *is* a concern," I countered. "He knows enough about us to cause trouble if anybody bothered to believe him."

"He knows very little," Landon said. "He believes Aunt Tillie cursed him."

"I made his tiny man parts itch ... and turn green ... and there might've been some puss balls," Aunt Tillie said.

Hannah wrinkled her nose. "Well ... that's lovely."

"I'm good with a curse," Aunt Tillie said. "Just ask these guys." She jerked her thumb at Landon and me."

"You've been cursed?" Hannah sipped her juice. "Do tell."

"Some curses are worse than others," I explained.

"And some are delightful," Landon added. "There's this bacon curse that makes me warm and tingly all over." He took on a far-off expression.

Hannah pressed her lips together, her eyes dancing with delight. "You like smelling like bacon, do you?"

"Oh, not me. Aunt Tillie curses Bay to smell like bacon. That's like Christmas for me."

"Yes, and I attract every derelict man in town," I said. "Not so fun for me."

"It's tons of fun for me," Aunt Tillie said. "Just out of curiosity, you don't seem surprised that we're witches. Why is that?"

"I've met a witch or two in my time," Hannah replied. "I'm careful who I admit that to for obvious reasons. You're not the only witches I've crossed paths with."

"We're the strongest." Aunt Tillie sounded so sure of herself, all I could do was smile.

"We have a certain reputation," I explained at Hannah's quizzical expression. "I'm sure you'll figure it out going forward."

Hannah turned serious. "We need to talk. You're obviously holding things back. I can't help if I don't know everything."

"As I told you last night, we don't know anything."

"I know that you've seen things."

"Images in windows." I flicked my eyes to the dining room window. It was empty. "I don't know why I can't see them anyplace else."

"Can you see ghosts regularly?"

I hesitated.

"It's okay." Hannah prodded. "I know that some witches can communicate with the dead. One of the other witches I've crossed paths with explained it. She said it's a rare gift, passed down in families. Can all of you see and talk to ghosts?"

"Just me."

"Um, and me," Aunt Tillie said. "I'm a master at talking to ghosts."

"You rarely do," I shot back.

"I don't feel the need. If people were stupid in life, they're going to be stupid in death. That's simply how it is ... and you can tell that idiot Viola I said so."

"Who is Viola?" Hannah asked.

"She's the ghost that lives at the newspaper office," I said. "She can't help with this."

"Because she's an idiot," Aunt Tillie reiterated.

"Because she's outside of this," I corrected. "I don't know that any ghosts can help us. If I can't see the enemy, they might not be able to either."

"You could still try," Landon suggested as he sat in his chair and collected my hand. "I know you're uncomfortable bossing them around, but it's worth a shot."

"I don't think I understand," Hannah said, glancing between us. "What do you want her to do?"

Landon held my gaze rather than respond.

"I'm more than a witch," I replied. "My ghostly abilities are ... enhanced."

"Enhanced how?"

"She's a necromancer," Aunt Tillie said. "She can control ghosts. She wasn't always able to — or maybe she was and didn't realize it — but now she can amass a ghost army to fight for us. It has come in handy."

"For what?"

"We like to fight." Aunt Tillie sent her a wink. "That's a conversation for another time, though. If you want stories, I've got them."

"And she's good at telling them," Landon said. "Some of them are even true."

"Keep it up," Aunt Tillie warned. "I'll put you on my list."

"If you make me smell like bacon, it's not a hardship. Then I'll just molest myself."

Aunt Tillie rolled her eyes. "I'll make you smell like liver and onions. Then Bay won't come within twenty feet of you."

"Yeah, I don't want that."

"I'LL HIT you up for the stories later," Hannah promised. "For now, we need to talk about what we're going to do today."

"What did you have in mind?" Landon asked as he pushed my glass of tomato juice toward me.

"You're part of the team," Chief Terry said. "Now that Agent Waters is in on the big secret, there's no reason you can't openly help us."

"I was pretty sure there was something weird going on when you took her back to the scene with us yesterday," Hannah said. "I've never known an FBI agent to take his girlfriend to a crime scene. I was curious enough that I read through some of Landon's field reports from the last two years. Do you know how many times Bay's name is mentioned?"

Landon shrugged. "It's better to include her than get caught in a lie. Besides, it's a small town and she's a newspaper reporter. She's with me all the time."

"And she actually helps you," Hannah agreed. "I don't have a problem with it. A smart agent uses the weapons at his disposal. It sounds like Bay is a weapon."

"She is," Landon agreed. "She's more than that, though. She's my heart. I'm glad you're on board, but I'll still protect her with everything I have."

"You won't need to. I have no intention of hurting her."

"That's good."

"It is," Aunt Tillie agreed. "What's the plan to figure out who's doing this? We have to put our heads together if we want answers."

"We?" Landon shot her a dubious look. "Since when are you part of the team?"

"Since I don't want to be around Winnie the Whiner today. The best way to punish her is to deprive her of my company."

I very much doubted my mother would consider that punishment. "You should stay out of it. You have revenge to dole out to Aunt Willa and Mrs. Little. Focus on that."

"I can multitask. Besides, you might need me."

I pressed my lips together, debating, and then nodded. "Okay, but only because I still don't know what we're dealing with."

"Do you really think she can help?" Chief Terry asked.

"*She* is sitting right here," Aunt Tillie snapped.

I ignored her. "She's been around the block a few times. She can't possibly hurt anything."

"I believe the entire course of my career proves that wrong," Chief Terry said dryly. "Still, if you want her on the team, given what happened last night ... ." He trailed off.

"What happened last night coincided with the storm. They could only attack when it turned dark. I don't know why, but that has to be at the top of our list of things to figure out. Until we do, we're stuck."

"Then she's in." Chief Terry smiled for my benefit. "If we can stop you from getting hurt, that's good enough for me."

"And me." Landon rubbed my back and focused on Aunt Tillie. "You have to do what you're told for a change."

"Yeah, yeah, yeah." Aunt Tillie leaned to her left far enough that her bottom came off the cushion. That's when I realized the leggings weren't as harmless as I originally thought.

"Is that a clown's face on your butt?" I asked.

She quickly sat back down and extended a finger in my direction. "Don't even think about telling your mother."

"But ... ."

"Don't bother," Landon said. "She's going to do what she wants. If she wears those leggings, we'll just tell anybody she weirds out that she's senile. The leggings will sell it."

He had a point. "Mom is still going to kill you when she finds out," I warned.

Aunt Tillie's smile was sly. "I'm actually looking forward to that."

SIXTEEN

"I want to talk to Paisley's friends," Hannah said from her spot next to me in the backseat of Chief Terry's vehicle. We'd gorged on eggs, hash browns and bacon, and were ready to hit the investigation hard.

"I don't have a problem with that," Chief Terry said. "I don't know that they can offer anything." He met my eyes in the rearview mirror. We hadn't told Hannah about our previous run-in with the girls. It wasn't by design, but her mentioning wanting to talk to them made me uncomfortable.

"Teenagers usually confide in friends, not parents. If Paisley really did have a boyfriend, it's likely the girls know more than they told you the first go-around. I've been trained in how to talk to teenagers."

I shifted on my seat but said nothing.

"These girls have been mentioned in two case files in the past few weeks," Hannah noted. "One of them was kidnapped, correct?"

"Actually, that's not correct," Landon replied. "The girl who disappeared showed up after a few days. It was all a plan that they cooked up together because they wanted Amelia's parents to pay a ransom so they could run away together."

"All the more reason to question them," Hannah insisted. "If they were plotting that, maybe something else happened. Maybe they had another plan and it somehow went wrong."

"That's possible," I said, "but I don't know how probable it is. They don't really remember their last plan, other than the basics."

"Why is that?"

"I modified their memories."

"I helped," Aunt Tillie added. "In fact, I wanted to saddle them with a few nightmares along the way as payback, but Bay vetoed that."

"You modified their memories?" Hannah looked perplexed. "May I ask why you did that?"

"They were collecting magic fragments from Hollow Creek and using them against us," Aunt Tillie replied. "It was all borrowed magic, nothing to frighten us, but they could've terrorized the town with it."

"That wasn't in the report." Hannah stared at her legs and shook her head. "How many of the cases Bay is mentioned in have magical ties, Landon?"

"Almost all of them," Landon said. "Does it matter?"

"I'm just curious. It seems that Hemlock Cove is more magical than I realized."

"Hemlock Cove is crawling with magic," Aunt Tillie agreed.

"I wonder why."

"Because we're here."

"The magic is attracted to you?"

"Magical beings are drawn to other magical beings. Bay's abilities draw in ghosts. It's not a big deal."

"It feels like a big deal," Hannah insisted. "You modified four teenagers' memories."

"And a perverted kissing booth owner," I added.

"What?"

Landon sighed. "Thank you, Bay. I hadn't included that part in my report."

Whoops. "I ... didn't know that."

He glanced over his shoulder and offered me a half-smile. "It's not the end of the world. All sorts of truths are coming out here."

"Apparently so." Hannah folded her arms across her chest. "Who is the perverted guy? And what is a kissing booth?"

Landon perked up markedly. "A kissing booth is the greatest invention this side of bacon. They have it at all the festivals. You get to take your significant other into a dark booth that smells like cinnamon rolls and make out with her."

"That's ... lovely. What do you do after that?"

"Get snacks," Landon replied. "After you work up an appetite in the kissing booth you need to bolster yourself with elephant ears and chocolate."

"Todd Lipscomb runs the kissing booth in Hemlock Cove," I explained. "He was working with the girls on their plan."

"Because he's a pervert?"

"And he wanted money."

"His part in the plot was harder to explain away," Landon said. "That's why I didn't mention him in my report."

"But he's still running free," Hannah prodded. "That can't be safe with teenaged girls running around."

"Oh, don't worry about that." Aunt Tillie was back to looking smug. "Bay did let me give him nightmares. If he even thinks about an underaged girl, he has dreams about giant spiders eating his sausage link."

I shrugged when Hannah turned her questioning expression to me. "I don't feel guilty about it, if that's what you're wondering. He had it coming. He claimed the girls terrorized him into helping, but I didn't believe him."

"Nobody believed him," Landon said as we pulled into the driveway of Amelia's house. "If you want to talk to the girls, they're likely all here. Just be forewarned, they don't remember everything that happened a few weeks ago. Bay left some of their memories purposely fuzzy."

"Okay, well, I guess we'll take it one step at a time."

"These girls are manipulative," I warned as Hannah unfastened her seatbelt. "They might not remember everything that happened — we wanted to carve the magical memories out of their heads and leave as much of the rest as possible — but that doesn't mean they won't try to bamboozle you."

"I've dealt with teenagers before," Hannah reassured me. "Once we're done talking to the girls, I wouldn't mind seeing this spot with the magical fragments you mentioned."

"Sure." Landon opened my door and helped me out. "I don't know how Hollow Creek can help us on this case, but I'm willing to try anything at this point."

AMELIA, SOPHIE AND EMMA WERE GATHERED around the television. Tina showed us into the living room and then left, which I found strange. She hadn't even asked why we wanted to talk to the girls this time. One look at Hannah told me she found it equally interesting.

"Girls, this is Agent Hannah Waters," Chief Terry began. "She's with the FBI. She's here to help us with Paisley's case."

"Another FBI agent?" Emma's eyes widened. "I didn't know two could be on the same case."

"I'm a different type of FBI agent," Hannah explained as she sat at the table across from them. "I'm a profiler. Do you know what that is?"

"It's like that show," Amelia replied, her eyes glued to the television. Some reality show I didn't recognize was airing, and she seemed completely disinterested in the conversation. "That one with the hot guy on it."

"Shemar Moore," I supplied.

Amelia shrugged. "If you say so."

Chief Terry leaned over and snagged the remote from Amelia before she could protest and killed the television. "Focus on Agent Waters," he ordered. "She's a professional here to help us figure out who murdered your friend. Show some respect."

If he'd pinned me with that same look when I was the girls' age I would've burst into tears and begged his forgiveness. Amelia and her cohorts were different.

"You're not my father," Amelia challenged. "This is my house."

"Paisley is dead," Chief Terry shot back. "Don't you want to help us figure out who killed her?"

"We don't know who killed her," Sophie insisted. She, at least, showed a modicum of emotion. I had a feeling, however, that the person she was feeling sorry for was herself.

"We already told you that," Emma added. "How would we know who killed her?"

"You're her friends," Hannah said in a soft voice. "It's your job to protect her, even in death. There's a predator out there. He might not stop with Paisley. We want to make sure you're protected."

Amelia snorted. "We're not in any danger."

I jerked my eyes to her. "How do you know?" I asked. "Unless you know who killed Paisley, you can't possibly know that."

"I don't know who killed Paisley, but I know we're safe," Amelia replied. "We haven't done anything to deserve being killed, so why would anybody want to kill us?"

"Why do you think Paisley deserved to be killed?" Hannah asked.

"I didn't say she did."

"You indicated that you hadn't done anything worth being killed over. That seems to suggest you believe Paisley did something to earn her death."

"I didn't say that." Annoyance burned bright in Amelia's eyes. "Why are you putting words in my mouth? I would never say Paisley deserved what happened to her."

Hannah regarded Amelia for a moment. "Okay, let's start over. I fear we've gotten off on the wrong foot."

"Or you could just go," Amelia suggested. "We don't have anything to talk to you about."

Hannah ignored her. "What did you feel when you heard your friend was dead?"

"What do you mean?" Sophia asked. "How were we supposed to feel?"

"There is no right or wrong answer to the question."

"I felt sad," Emma volunteered, her bottom lip quivering. "I kept thinking about all the stuff we would never get to do together."

"That's quite normal," Hannah encouraged, her eyes drifting to Sophia. "And you?"

"I didn't really believe it," Sophia said. "I mean ... it made no sense. We'd just seen her. I still don't know that I really believe she's dead."

"Maybe you should go to the funeral home and take a look at her body," Amelia suggested. "That will make you believe."

"Is that what you did?" Hannah asked.

Amelia shrugged.

"Is it?" Hannah persisted.

"I might've gone down there last night," Amelia replied. "They were just getting her body in. They didn't want to show me, but I made them."

"And what did you think about what you saw?"

"That her hair was a mess. She would've hated people seeing her with her hair looking like that."

"The funeral home will make sure her hair is okay," Hannah reassured her. "What else did you think?"

"That she looked like wax."

"Is that the first time you've seen a dead body?"

Amelia shrugged again, noncommittal. "I saw my grandmother in the funeral home two years ago. She looked like wax, too, but a different kind of wax."

"Paisley hasn't been treated yet by the funeral home," Hannah explained. "She'll look more natural next time you see her."

"That's a weird thing to say." Amelia let loose a derisive snort. "She's dead and somehow that's not natural. They're going to pump chemicals into her and you think that will make her look natural. I don't think that's the case."

Hannah pressed. "You don't show much emotion, Amelia. None of you really do, but you're being purposely cold. Why do you think that is?"

For the first time since we'd walked through the door, Amelia showed an actual emotion. Sure, it was annoyance, but it was a genuine feeling. For some reason, I was relieved to see it.

"What is it that you want me to feel?" Amelia demanded. "What emotion will make you feel better about our friend dying?"

"There's no right emotion." Hannah remained calm. "You don't have to feel a specific way. That's not the problem."

"Then what is the problem?" Sophie asked. "If we're not supposed to react in a specific way, why are you giving us crap?"

"Because your friend is dead. She was killed in brutal fashion. Friends care about one another. I would expect sadness ... or even anger. I would expect confusion. I might even expect disbelief."

"Well ... I guess you should arrest us then," Amelia drawled. "We're going to feel what we want to feel and there's nothing you can do to change that."

"Fair enough." Hannah straightened and glanced between the girls one more time. "Am I to assume you still don't know anything about what happened to her?"

"We know she was an idiot who brought this on herself," Amelia replied. "If she'd been with us, this never would've happened. She took off on her own. She was messing with some guy she wouldn't tell us about. That's on her."

"I see." Hannah stood. "I'm sorry for your loss, girls. Whether you believe it or not, you're going to have feelings about this eventually. I urge you to talk to a professional when those feelings bubble up."

"Yeah. We'll get right on that." Amelia held out her hand to Chief Terry. "My remote please."

Chief Terry slapped the device into her palm. "We're not done here, girls," he warned. "We will be back."

"Next time leave the blondes and the old lady behind," Amelia suggested. "Actually, you don't have to come either. Send the hot FBI agent and we'll be happy."

Emma's eyes sparkled. "So, so happy."

Chief Terry grunted and then motioned us to the front door. I was almost out of the room before I realized Aunt Tillie had remained rooted to her spot. She hadn't moved a muscle, staring at the girls.

"What are you doing?" I asked when I returned to her side.

"It's like a movie," Aunt Tillie noted, not caring in the least that she was talking loudly enough for the girls to hear. "They're like Stepford teenagers."

It wasn't a bad description. "They're grieving," I said. "Nobody grieves the same."

"I don't know what they're doing, but it's not grieving." Aunt Tillie met Amelia's defiant stare for another few seconds and then moved with me toward the door. "That's not grief, Bay. It's something else."

I waited until we were outside. "Well, now what? They're not going to help us."

"Definitely not," Hannah agreed. She stood in the middle of the yard and stared at the house. "Those are the most emotionally vacant girls I've ever come across. If teenagers could be profiled as sociopaths under the auspices of the law, I would diagnose them right now."

It was a sobering thought, one I wasn't quite willing to embrace. "What if I did that to them?"

Hannah flicked her eyes to me. "What do you mean?"

"What if I'm the reason they're like that?" I persisted.

"Why would you say that?" Landon asked. "You're not responsible for them."

"No, but I messed with their minds. They weren't like that before I shuffled their memories. They might've been lying to us last time, but they showed emotion. It's as if I drained that out of them."

"They were putting on an act last time," Landon argued. "Maybe they're really not capable of emotion. All that crap they put out there for us to absorb last time was fake. It could be that they're only capable of being fake."

"Maybe, but what are the odds of four legitimate sociopaths finding one another in their teens in one small town?" I challenged. "Think about it. True sociopaths are rare. How would we get four of them?"

"Bay is right," Hannah interjected. "True sociopaths lack a

conscious. They can't feel guilt. They don't have the ability to make and keep friends."

"Unless they're covering," Landon said. "If they all need friends to appear normal maybe this is their way of covering what they really are."

"We don't have firm numbers on this because most sociopaths don't get diagnosed, but it's believed that three to five percent of the population are sociopaths. For those four girls to all be sociopaths and find one another, well, the odds would be astronomical."

"Then what else could it be?" Landon demanded.

Hannah turned her gaze to me. There was worry there. "Is it possible Bay changed their personalities when she modified their memories?"

"Bay didn't do that alone," Aunt Tillie argued. "I was there with her. I've modified memories before. She didn't do anything out of the ordinary."

"Then maybe it's something else."

"Like what?" I asked. "What else could it be?"

"I'm not sure. Those girls were completely devoid of emotion. The only time any of them reacted with something akin to a genuine feeling was when Amelia yelled at us. Even that didn't feel as vehement as it should have."

"So what do we do?" Landon asked. "How do we break them down?"

"I don't know that we can." Hannah dragged a restless hand through her hair. "I'm not sure those girls have anything to do with what's going on, but if we're going to talk to them again, we're going to need a different approach."

"I guess that means Hollow Creek," Landon said. "You wanted to visit there."

Hannah agreed. "I need to see where all of this started. At the very least, it might give me a few ideas."

I didn't know how that was possible, but she was in charge of our investigative course. We had to follow where she led ... at least for now.

17

SEVENTEEN

Landon ceded his spot in the front to Hannah and climbed in the backseat with me for the ride to Hollow Creek.

"I'm fine," I said when he plucked my hand off my lap and studied my palm.

"Did I say you weren't fine?" He kept his voice low. Aunt Tillie shared the back bench with us. "Maybe I just want to sit next to my future wife. Have you ever considered that?"

"Not really."

Aunt Tillie stirred. "You need to get over it," she instructed Landon. "She's berating herself and she won't stop any time soon. You'll spoil her by doting on her this way."

Landon turned to her. "What do you suggest I do, oh wise oracle?"

"Let her stew. She'll get over herself eventually. She always does."

"I'm not feeling sorry for myself," I insisted. "I'm just ... thinking."

"Right." Aunt Tillie stretched her legs out. "I happen to know what you're thinking, and it's a waste of time."

I wasn't in the mood to kowtow to her nonsense and yet I was curious. "What am I thinking?"

"That you somehow altered those girls."

"Well ... what else is there to think? It's statistically impossible for three sociopaths to find one another at that age."

"No, it's not. It's rare, but not impossible. For all we know, these girls were drawn to each other because they are sociopaths."

"Paisley too?" Landon asked.

Aunt Tillie nodded. "There's no way she would be the only normal one in that group."

"So you didn't do this to them, Bay," Landon pressed. "You can't blame yourself."

"They weren't like this before," I insisted.

"We don't know that. They were acting when we crossed paths with them the first time. Nothing they said or did can be considered true."

I wasn't convinced, but I didn't want to argue. "Okay." I leaned back and closed my eyes.

"Bay." Landon slipped his arm around my back, fighting his seatbelt so he could cuddle closer. "This is my least favorite thing about you," he said. "You constantly blame yourself for things you can't control. You're a martyr."

I shot him a dirty look. "I am not a martyr."

"You are." He brushed my hair from my eyes. "You can't blame yourself for what's going on. It's not on you. None of it is. Those girls did this."

"Unless they didn't."

"Stop it." He was firm. "We didn't have many options. We couldn't put them in jail because of the magic. We couldn't kill them because ... well, you know. What did that leave? You came up with the only option you could."

I knew he was right, but it still bothered me. "I'm not a martyr," I muttered.

He laughed. "I love you." He pressed a kiss to my cheek.

"I'm not a martyr," I repeated.

"You're a total martyr," Aunt Tillie shot back. "You're the biggest martyr I know."

I rested my head on Landon's shoulder. "I'm not a martyr."

"You're my angel," Landon whispered, his lips so close to my ear I shuddered. "I'm going to take you to heaven later if your back is better."

"My back is fine."

"Then heaven it is."

Aunt Tillie leaned forward and hit Chief Terry's arm. "I'm gonna need a barf bag back here," she announced.

"Stop being a pain," Chief Terry barked.

"I can't control my urge to regurgitate around these two idiots." She jerked her thumb at Landon and me. "They're disgusting and I hate them."

"Well, maybe we can add that to our list of fun activities for the evening," Landon whispered. "How long do you think it will take to push Aunt Tillie over the edge?"

"Not long."

"Something to look forward to."

"Yeah." I tried to force myself out of my funk. Landon was right. I wasn't responsible for what happened to the girls. Still, I couldn't shake the feeling that something very big was happening to them ... and I was at least partially to blame.

HOLLOW CREEK WAS QUIET. Unfortunately, it was not still.

"Look at this." I was dumbfounded as I stepped to the bank and surveyed the magical fragments flying around. Not only were there more than before, they were also bigger.

"This is bad," Aunt Tillie intoned, glancing around. "This is really, really bad."

"What do you see?" Hannah asked, her forehead creased in frustration as she tried to follow our gazes. "There's nothing out here."

"Oh, there's something." My stomach rolled as I looked to Landon. "This place is getting out of control again. There's magic everywhere. We're going to have another situation just like before if we don't get this under control."

"Any suggestions?" Landon couldn't see the magical shards flying about, but he trusted me enough to know they were there.

"I ... don't know." I reached out to one of the magical shards. It flew away from me, as if coasting on a warm breeze, and collided with another shard. Several splinters flew off and began growing their own shards.

"This place will turn into a magical bomb if we don't do something about it," Aunt Tillie insisted. "It's feeding off the energy of anybody who comes here."

"I don't understand any of this," Hannah admitted.

"This place is a mess," Aunt Tillie replied.

Hannah's gaze was beseeching when it landed on me. I searched for the proper way to make her understand.

"Um ... it's hard to explain. In a nutshell, we've used our magic in this spot multiple times. It hasn't always been good magic. On more than one occasion, we've had to take an enemy down here."

Hannah's expression didn't change. "That doesn't explain what you're looking at now."

"The remnants of magic we've used here have been building," I said. "They're ... hanging in the air. You can't see them because you're not magical. Several weeks ago, the girls came out here and found the shards. They managed to use them to give themselves magical abilities. That's how all of this started."

"Okay." Hannah flicked her eyes to Landon, but he was completely focused on me. "If I can't see the shards because I'm not magical, why could the girls see them? Are they're magical?"

I held out my hands. "Maybe. If they are, the lines that run through their families are weak."

"What's the option if they're not magical?"

"Their age," Aunt Tillie replied. "Children are more open to believing. There's a reason I was more than happy to run around with Bay, Clove and Thistle when they were younger. They believed anything I told them. That made them more powerful, even as children.

"I knew my little girls were magical," she continued. "These other girls might not have been magical, but their age and the town they grew up in allowed them to believe enough that they could see the shards ... and decide to use them."

"You have to understand," I said. "The magic the four girls were using didn't belong to them. They were burning through it fast. They didn't realize the ramifications and what that might do to their bodies. They only cared that they were suddenly magical."

Hannah seemed lost in thought. "So what do we do?"

"I'm not entirely certain. It's dangerous for kids to be out here, but this is a party spot." I looked to Aunt Tillie. "Can you ward it like you do your pot field?"

Aunt Tillie's eyes went wide and she made a series of slashes across her throat. "*Utshay ouryay outhmay*," she hissed.

Hannah's face lit with amusement. "I haven't heard pig Latin since I was a kid."

Landon interjected. "Hannah doesn't care about your pot field. She's a profiler."

"I love pot," Hannah said. "I don't remember seeing a pot field anywhere on the property, though."

"That's because she has it warded," I explained. "Any law enforcement type who wants to find it will get a severe case of diarrhea instead. Plus, it's invisible."

"Wow." Hannah's eyes went wide. "That is ... diabolical."

Aunt Tillie gave a satisfied grin. "Thank you."

"We need something similar for this place," I insisted. "We have to keep the kids out of here until we can figure out what to do with these shards. The circus people tried to help us but obviously it didn't work."

"Obviously," Aunt Tillie agreed. "We need bigger witches."

"Bigger witches than us?" I was confused.

"Or witches who are already working together and know how to combine their magic. I heard about a group in Hawthorne Hollow. I've heard whispers about them several times over the years. They're making magical waves these days because they have a new member."

"The witches ride motorcycles," I said.

Aunt Tillie nodded. "I'm thinking maybe they can help with this. I'll reach out when we have this behind us."

"Can you ward it until then?"

"I can, but I would really like to know what's been going on down here." She planted her hands on her hips. "It was nowhere near this busy with shedded magic when we took down those girls the first time. I would really like to know how this happened."

I could think of only one way to do that. "You start the wards," I suggested. "Don't make them specific for teenagers. We need to close off this space from everybody but ourselves until we can fix this."

"Yeah, yeah, yeah." Aunt Tillie rolled her eyes. "This isn't my first ward."

"What are you going to do?" Landon asked as he followed me away from the water. "How are you going to figure out what happened down here?"

"There's only one way I can think of." I was grim. "Remember I told you about the two ghosts I managed to call to me here, the ones who had been sort of forgotten?"

He nodded. "You were going to interview them for that series you have planned for The Whistler."

"Yes, and I still plan to do that. I haven't been back down here since the girls went nuts and wanted to kill us. I've been busy with other stuff. They're still down here."

"Ah." He nodded. "They'll know if anybody else has been here."

"In theory. They're sort of detached from this world, which is why I want to get their stories and help them move on. But they should know something."

Landon rubbed his hand up and down my back. "Let's see what they know and go from there."

I WAS NERVOUS PUTTING MY abilities on display. I had to wipe my sweaty palms on my jeans as I prepared.

"It's okay," Landon said as he stood in front of me. "You don't have to put on a show."

"No, but from Hannah's perspective I'll be talking to thin air. It's nerve-wracking."

He sighed. "It doesn't matter what she thinks, because I know you're amazing. Just do your thing like you normally do. Everybody else here believes in you."

I cocked an eyebrow. "Aunt Tillie?"

"Well, maybe not Aunt Tillie." He grinned and then leaned close. "She believes in you more than anybody." His voice was low. "She's a Winchester, so she can't admit it. If she does, she'll look soft."

I shook my hands at my sides. "You're right. I need to do this. Just ... keep everybody behind me."

"I will." He gave me a kiss. "Do your thing." I watched him retreat toward the others, deftly reaching out his arm to catch Aunt Tillie around the waist as she tried to cut around him. "Where do you think you're going?"

"To help," Aunt Tillie replied. "That's what I do."

"Since when?"

"Um ... since before you were born, Sparky."

"We should let Bay do this on her own. She's the one in control here."

"I'm in control. In fact, if there was a job for people who simply had control of everything, I would be the queen."

"Yes, you could do it professionally." Landon refused to let her go. "You're sticking with me."

Aunt Tillie didn't put up much of a struggle. She positioned herself between Landon and Chief Terry and waited. That was as good as a declaration of love from her.

"Okay," I murmured to myself as I closed my eyes. I knew who I was calling to this time. I wasn't casting a net. There were two specific souls in this vicinity. Carol Umber and Carter Culpepper. They'd both died years ago. I planned to get their stories for a series I was going to run in the newspaper and then set them free.

Carol.

Carter.

I whispered their names in my head over and over again. They weren't "present" ghosts. They spent most of their days drifting. Unlike the first time I'd called them, there was no reticence. They showed up right away.

"I knew you would be back." Carol's eyes sparkled as she looked me up and down. "Is it time for us to go?"

"Soon." I felt guilty for ignoring her as long as I had. "It won't take long," I promised. "I have some questions first."

"She always has questions," Carter grumbled. "So many questions. Typical woman. That's what she is."

"If you ask my husband-to-be, I'm not typical at all," I argued.

"Definitely not," Landon agreed. "That's one of the best things about you."

"Has anyone been out here?"

Carol's face was blank. "You're out here right now."

"I mean before now."

"You've been out here before," she said.

"Yes, but ... I'm talking about between the time I was here before and now. You saw us that night, the big group of us, and we were working against some younger girls. Do you remember that?"

Carol nodded. "You said they were evil."

"She didn't say they were evil," Carter countered. "She said they were consumed by magic. There's a difference. I just found them to be mouthy females. There's always a lot of mouthy females out here."

I studied him a moment, considering. "Have those girls been back here?"

"Not that I've seen." Carter was blasé. "But I haven't been looking."

"What did they say?" Hannah asked.

"Shh." Landon admonished her with a whisper. "Let her work. She'll fill us in when she's done."

I appreciated that he'd taken control of Hannah. That allowed me to deal with my ghosts. "What about you, Carol?" I asked. "Have you seen them here again?"

"I ... don't ... know." Carol appeared conflicted. "I know they've been here, but I have trouble marking time. I've told you that."

"You *have*," I agreed. "You're floating a lot of the time because

AMANDA M. LEE

nothing really anchors you here any longer. This is important. I need you to remember."

"I can't really remember." Carol held out her ghostly hands. "All of it is ... jumbled. It doesn't help that the dark ghosts have been here. I don't like them, so I hide when they come. I don't want them to find me."

My heart skipped a beat. "The dark ghosts?"

She looked around. "They're like us." She gestured between herself and Carter. "They're no longer in this world yet they stay. But they're different in some ways."

"More mouthy females," Carter groused. "They talk and talk and talk. They never shut up."

"What do they talk about?" I asked. "What do they say?"

"They have dark plans."

Carol agreed. "They want the power that they say is floating around Hollow Creek. They want to take it and use it."

"For what?"

"I don't know. They talk about a lot of things."

"They must have mentioned specifics," I insisted.

"There is one thing." She spared a glance for Carter. "You tell her. I don't want to be the bearer of bad news."

Carter rolled his eyes. He was a cranky bastard when he wanted to be ... which was apparently all the time. "They want to take out you," he said.

"Me?"

"Yes. They want to take out the rest of your family, too. They said something about a baby."

I thought I might fall over. "A baby?"

Landon was suddenly by my side. "What are they saying?"

"THEY SAY that dark ghosts have been here, that they want the magic fragments that we can't seem to get rid of. They've specifically mentioned me ... and a baby."

"Clove's baby?"

"I don't know of another."

He looked to Chief Terry. "Do they know how to stop the dark ghosts?"

Carol emphatically shook her head. She was too fearful to have any ideas regarding a takedown. Carter was more difficult to read.

"Do you know how to end them?" I asked.

"You're the expert," he said. "You should know."

"Maybe you should tell me."

"Like I said, you're the expert. You need to take on the mouthy females. That's your battle. I just want to be left alone." With that, he disappeared.

"What did he say?" Landon demanded.

"He doesn't know. He said it's up to me."

"Well, that's just great." Landon rolled his neck. "Have I mentioned I hate it when things take a turn like this?"

I managed a weak chuckle. "You might've mentioned it a few times."

18

EIGHTEEN

Landon was quiet after the ghosts departed. Chief Terry suggested lunch. We went to the diner and sat at our usual table. I wasn't hungry but ordered soup because I wanted something to do with my hands.

"So what do we do?" Chief Terry asked when I hadn't spoken in several minutes.

I shrugged and went back to playing with my napkin. "I don't know."

"I'll tell you what we do, we make a shade trap and blast those things into the next century." Aunt Tillie, unlike me, wasn't having trouble talking. "I'll make the trap."

Landon turned to study her. "Can you do that?"

"I can do anything."

"Let me rephrase that. Have you done it before?"

"Of course."

That stirred me. "You have not. Stop telling tall tales."

Her look was dark. "Do you want to be on my list?" she challenged.

Landon coughed one word into his hand. "*Bacon.*" Then he smiled at me. "I can tell you're upset about what the ghosts told you, Bay, but as you like to remind me, we've been through this kind of thing before. We'll figure it out."

"I'm not upset," I argued, surprised at how vehement I sounded. My annoyance was on full display, and I wasn't proud of it. "I'm just thinking."

"Well, think out loud." Landon patted my hand. "I'm going to find the waitress and add a grilled cheese to your order."

I watched him go to the front counter. He was determined when he wanted to be and there was no chance of talking him down now. He couldn't fight ghosts for me, or control whatever was to come. He could, however, force me to eat a sandwich with my soup.

"He loves you a great deal," Hannah noted as she watched me.

"He does. He's just really bossy when he wants to be."

"He's also a glutton," Aunt Tillie added. "He thinks food solves every problem."

I thought about the way he'd ignored the burritos in favor of a bath the previous evening. "Actually, he doesn't think that. He just needs to feel as if he's doing something."

"I agree with your assessment." Hannah's smile was easy. "Landon is the sort of person who hates when those around him are unhappy. While he could live with other members of your family being unhappy, you're a different story. When you feel pain, he feels pain."

"Without a doubt," I agreed. "He's feeling pain right now."

"Then let's fix it." Hannah dug inside the bag she'd carried into the restaurant. I'd seen her hitch it over her shoulder when we exited Chief Terry's vehicle. She pulled out a thick folder.

"What is that?" Aunt Tillie asked, leaning forward. "Is that your list?"

Hannah chuckled. "I don't have a list. Maybe I should start keeping one. You seem to find true joy in your list."

"I do." Aunt Tillie beamed at her. "Do you want to know who's on my list right now?"

Hannah nodded at the same time I shook my head.

"She doesn't care about your list," I said.

"On the contrary." Hannah's smile never wavered. I could see why she was so good at her job. "I find stuff like this fascinating. Your great-aunt's list will tell me a lot about her, and I find her to be an open book in some respects but an enigma in others. Who is at the top of your list, Ms. Winchester?"

"Call me Tillie or you'll be on the list," Aunt Tillie warned. "Willa is at the top of it right now. Usually it would be Margaret — she lives at the top — but I've moved her down a spot for the time being."

"So you moved Willa to the top of your list because you consider her a threat," Hannah prodded.

"I'm better than her," Aunt Tillie insisted. "She's no threat to me."

"Then why did you move her to the top of your list? If you don't fear her, there must be another reason."

"There is. I hate her."

"No." Hannah shook her head. "There's another reason."

"Are you a shrink on top of being a profiler?" Aunt Tillie demanded. "I hate it when people try to shrink me."

"And yet it's so much fun." Hannah winked at her. "I believe you moved Willa to the top because you think she's a genuine threat, although not to you. You can handle anything. In fact, I'd wager that you *have* handled almost everything for your family for a long time.

"For example, where is your other sister?" she continued. "Where is your nieces' mother?"

Aunt Tillie frowned. "Ginger died when they were younger."

"So you raised them."

Aunt Tillie hesitated. "I was always around when they were little. My husband and I didn't have children. We helped raise Winnie, Marnie and Twila. They were like our children anyway."

Hannah leaned back in her chair. "Were Winnie, Marnie and Twila adults when their mother died?"

"Winnie was. Marnie was close enough. Twila was still technically a minor for a few years."

"And what happened then?"

Aunt Tillie didn't respond, so I did.

"Willa wanted Twila," I explained. "She didn't want her to raise and love, though. She wanted her because she thought that would grant her access to the family land."

"Willa wanted to do the worst possible thing in your view," Hannah said to Aunt Tillie. "She tried to break up your family."

"That was never going to happen," Aunt Tillie insisted. "I told Willa that right from the start. I would've killed her before I let her separate those girls."

Hannah's eyebrows hopped. "You would've killed her?"

"I said it, and I meant it. Screw Willa. She doesn't care about anybody but herself."

"I don't think that's entirely true," I argued. "She seems to care about Rosemary. I mean ... why else would she be here?"

"To screw with us," Aunt Tillie snapped. "She only cares about Rosemary enough to use her as a weapon against us."

I wasn't certain I believed that. "I think she genuinely cares about Rosemary."

"And what do you think of Willa?" Hannah asked me.

"I don't think much of her. We didn't grow up knowing her. She was this relative way out there we never saw." I waved my hand for emphasis. "We knew she was Aunt Tillie's sister, but she wasn't part of our family."

"So she's an outsider who is trying to invade your family."

"That sounds a bit dramatic."

Hannah laughed. "Maybe, but Tillie believes she's an outsider. Did you always believe that? Were you always aware she wasn't a full sister?"

Aunt Tillie held out her hands. "I knew there was something different about her. Ginger and I were close. Willa and I were not. I always hated Willa."

"Did your mother treat her differently?"

"My mother raised her," Aunt Tillie insisted.

"Yes, but did she treat her differently?"

Aunt Tillie worked her jaw. "I didn't think so at the time," she said finally, taking me by surprise with her honesty. "But now ... I think she was colder with Willa. There was an invisible wall."

"And you picked up on it," Hannah surmised.

"Probably. It doesn't matter. Willa is the devil."

"Willa probably picked up on the fact that she was an outsider and hated you for it," Hannah said. "You're right about her not being here for Rosemary. Er, well, she's not entirely here for Rosemary. Payback against you is her primary motivation. That's why she came to the inn the way she did last night.

"You obviously didn't invite her, and any sane person would realize that going to the inn wouldn't accomplish anything," she continued. "She went anyway. I can only conclude that was to push buttons, something she managed to achieve."

"Why would she do that?" I asked.

"It could be that she feeds off negative attention like Tillie, but it could also be that she wanted to serve as some sort of distraction. Perhaps Rosemary was doing something and she wanted to make sure that you were distracted enough not to figure it out."

"That's diabolical," I muttered as Hannah laughed.

"We have other things to worry about," Chief Terry interjected. "Willa is an issue — she's always an issue when she comes to town — but Tillie will take care of her as she always does. She's an annoyance but she can't be our primary concern. Those shade things that hurt Bay last night are our primary concern."

"That's why I brought this." Hannah tapped the folder on the table. "This is the case file from Salem. I had it messengered to me and it arrived this morning. I thought maybe Bay might want to take a look. I would like her opinion."

"Why?" Landon asked as he returned to the table. "What good will that do?"

"I think the cases are similar. If they are, we might find answers in the first case. If they're not, we can eliminate that right away."

"I can look at it." I accepted the file from her. "This is the case from two years ago?"

"Yes. The case from twenty years ago does not have complete information."

"Why is that?" Landon asked.

"I'm not a hundred percent certain. I could chalk it up to lazy police work, or at the very least lazy filing. It's likely a multitude of things."

"But?" Landon prodded.

"But the pages of the file that are missing feel a little too strategic," Hannah said. "I think someone purposely removed them."

"Why?"

"Because there was a paranormal element," I said. "Whoever hid it didn't want people to read that part."

Hannah nodded and brightened. "I like that I don't have to explain myself. Anyway, I'll let you look at this and explain a bit to the others while you do."

I flipped the file open. I'd read case files with Landon. Still, it was slow going.

"Two years ago in Salem, I was called in because their regular profiler was on paternity leave," Hannah started. "The initial case I was called in on involved three men. Their bodies were found on the second floor of a downtown business. They had long rap sheets, mostly for petty crimes, but there were some other disturbing allegations.

"One of them had twice been accused of rape," she continued. "The women who accused him recanted at some point. The case notes explained that the women were terrified and the officers investigating believed that this man had intimidated them. But they could not prove it."

"Okay." Landon rubbed his hand over my neck as I read the file. "You're talking about general dirtbags. How did they die?"

"There was discoloration around their necks, but there were no other obvious marks on the bodies. This happened two months before I was called to Salem. It only came up because of what I'm going to tell you next.

"The first individual who died in Salem was Maggie Masters," she continued. "She was sixteen, beautiful, and her family owned an Irish pub. Maggie did not work there because she wasn't old enough, but she came in to visit her parents from time to time. The men who died visited the pub often. They were fans of the atmosphere because it didn't involve kitschy drinks. It was more like a standard pub."

Landon nodded as he stroked his chin. "Okay, but Maggie died two months after these men died."

"Yes. Her body was found in the same downtown building. Her parents said she had no reason to be there. Maggie was a good girl who never gave them a lick of trouble."

"But trouble found her," Chief Terry mused.

Hannah continued. "Maggie was stabbed multiple times. Someone used her blood to draw runes on the around the scene. Much like Paisley Gilmore, almost three-quarters of her blood was removed from her body and not found at the scene."

I jerked up my head and looked at Landon. "You didn't mention that."

"We just got the report this morning," he replied calmly. "I was going to tell you ... when it felt like the right time."

"And when was that going to be?"

He arched an eyebrow at my challenging tone. "When you weren't dealing with ghosts explaining that you're a target. Believe it or not, I don't like to add to the weight you already carry."

Chief Terry extended his hand to stop us. "Let's not turn this into a thing," he said. "You know I don't like when you two go at each other."

Landon held my gaze a moment longer and then backed down. "I wasn't keeping it from you, Bay. I was going to tell you. You were already aware that I didn't feel all the blood was left at the scene. I just didn't get into the specifics with you."

"I'm sorry." I held up my hands. "I didn't mean to go all crazy on you, but that's a big detail."

"Someone is performing blood rituals," Aunt Tillie said. "The runes — which I still feel I know but can't place — are a sign that this differs from a normal murder. The blood, though ... ." She trailed off.

"Why is the blood important?" Hannah asked.

"Blood is always important," I replied. "It's ... life, right? It's the symbol of life. If your blood stops flowing, you die. When it's taken in this manner, it's being used for something else. Given where we are — a witch town — the blood holds significance."

"Was Maggie the only one to die in Salem?" Landon asked. "How many murders are we talking about?"

"Three," Hannah said. "Maggie was the first. Two other girls followed. Their manner of death was similar to Maggie's, but they were both killed in some woods."

"Three is symbolic in the witch world," Aunt Tillie said to me. "The power of three."

"I believe that's from the show you hate," I argued. *Charmed.*

"They're not real witches."

My lips curved. "They're not," I agreed. "You're not wrong about the symbolism of the number three. Three is a powerful number in the witch world, as is four."

"Is that why there are three witches in each generation of your family?" Hannah asked.

"What?" I flicked my eyes to her. "What do you mean?"

"You, Thistle and Clove are one generation. Winnie, Marnie and Twila are another. Then there's Tillie, Willa and Ginger."

"Yeah, but Willa wasn't born from their mother," Landon argued. "That's where the witch genes come from. She's not a witch."

"No, but there was another baby," Aunt Tillie volunteered. "My mother gave birth to a stillborn after Ginger. Nobody talks about it because that was common in those days. There would've actually been three of us."

I went back to looking at the file. "You have an idea, Hannah. I would love to know what it is."

"I was hoping to hear your hunch first."

I hesitated.

"Bay, she wants to hear it," Landon said in a soft voice. "So do I. You're the smartest person I know."

"Hey!" Aunt Tillie made a face. "Did you forget someone?"

Landon shook his head. "I did not. Bay is far smarter than you."

"Oh, I hate you sometimes," Aunt Tillie groused.

"You'll survive." Landon kept his eyes on me. "What is it?"

"Hannah is leading me to her idea, but she doesn't have to," I said. "The answers are all there. The three men who originally died were dirtbags, as you put it. That means they likely knew they were in trouble. They decided to embrace the paranormal to escape. They purposely turned themselves into shades."

"There's more," I continued when Landon furrowed his brow. "I'm assuming they got their hands on a book, something that told them what to do. Their bodies weren't emptied of blood?"

Hannah shook her head. "They were not."

"They turned themselves into shades. Nobody did it for them. They won't die that way, at least not their souls. They won't suffer. They still need to feed, though, because they're not real ghosts. To sustain themselves, they have to drain others."

"Oh, gross." Landon screwed up his face. "They drink blood."

I nodded. "It makes sense." I turned to Hannah. "What happened in Salem? What's not in this file? The killings wouldn't have stopped unless someone stopped the shades."

Hannah's grin widened. "You really are on top of things. You're right. Something didn't make that file and yet you figured it out. A local coven stepped in and trapped the souls of the shades."

"I told you we needed to trap them," Aunt Tillie said smugly.

I ignored her. "How did they trap them?"

"Poppets."

I nodded, thoughtful. "Do the souls have to be trapped in physical items?" I directed the question to Aunt Tillie.

"You can't cut them loose because they're already loose," she said. "You have to trap them in a place they can't do any harm."

"Which means poppets ... or other magically-imbued items."

"Pretty much." Aunt Tillie was grim. "How many shades have you seen?"

"A lot. Like, ten of them."

"Ten?" Hannah looked horrified at the prospect. "How is that possible?"

"I can't say. Maybe they're trapping the souls of their victims upon death as a way to enslave them or something. I mean ... Paisley wasn't hanging around the spot where she died. Maybe that's because they absorbed her into their group."

"Why have we only had one murder?" Chief Terry demanded. "If these things kill to feed, why haven't we seen more murders?"

"Because we're at the beginning," I replied. "This is the start of the cycle. If we want to stop them, we have to do it before they get a foothold in the community. The more they feed, the more dangerous they'll get."

"Then let's get some poppets and trap them," Chief Terry said.

"That's the plan," I said. "I need to go to Hypnotic. We're going to need Thistle to make poppets for us."

"Lunch first," Landon insisted, his hand on top of mine. "You need to eat and keep up your strength. You can go to Thistle for the poppets after."

I thought about arguing, but found I was hungry. "Okay." I leaned in and laid my head on his shoulder, smiling when he kissed my forehead. "Lunch ... and then we'll start working a plan."

"I would like to point out that we'll be working the exact plan I suggested twenty minutes ago," Aunt Tillie said. "We're going to build a trap. That's what I said to do."

"You're wonderful and wise," Landon drawled. "We're all in awe of you. Is that what you want to hear?"

Aunt Tillie didn't miss a beat. "Yes. I would like a crown, too."

"I'll get right on that."

19

NINETEEN

I ate my soup and sandwich — there was little joy to be found in it — and then headed outside. Aunt Tillie had excused herself after eating, explaining she would find her own way home, and then disappeared. I figured that wasn't a good sign, but as long as she wasn't my responsibility, it didn't matter.

"What are you thinking?" Landon asked when he found me sitting on a bench outside the diner.

"I'm thinking you ate two BLTs for lunch, both of them slathered with mayonnaise, and if we want you to live a long and happy life, we need to start watching your food intake," I answered.

"Don't torture me," he warned with a grin, laughing when I glared at him. "I'll switch to light mayonnaise. Will that make you happy?"

"Not really. I want to keep you a long time. You have to make some adjustments."

"Are you going to make adjustments?"

"I don't eat nearly as much as you."

"That's not what I asked."

I didn't have to ask what he meant. We were circling each other. "Hannah's story makes sense," I said. "The two men in Salem killed themselves in a dark ritual in an attempt to live forever."

"It's interesting that they had to die to live forever."

"It's not living. Not really. Their souls carry on, but they have no bodies. They can't eat BLTs ever again. Would you want to live that life?"

"Absolutely not, but I understand reasons for choosing it."

I was dumbfounded. "You can't be serious?"

"Oh, don't look at me that way." He shook his head. "I'm not saying I want to turn into a shade. I'm saying that I can see how it happened."

"Under what scenario would you agree to that life?" I demanded.

"One in which you were in trouble and it was my only way to save your life."

"What are the odds of that happening?" I asked after several moments of contemplation.

"Probably not very good. But I can see other people choosing that life for another reason."

"And that is?"

"Fear. People are afraid to die. Can you imagine being the sort of person who kills and steals? Even if you didn't believe in an afterlife, or punishment from a god or goddess, there would always be this niggling worry."

"I still wouldn't choose the life of a shade," I said.

"I wouldn't either. I want this life with you. That said, the idea of leaving you shreds my heart. I can see someone going that route if they were terminally ill and didn't want to leave a family member."

"That's not what happened in Salem," I pointed out.

"No, but I wasn't talking about Salem specifically. You indicated that you couldn't understand how anybody would go that route. I can think of a few reasons."

I studied his profile, debating. "You know that you wouldn't love me if you decided to turn into a shade."

He frowned. "I'll always love you."

"You can't love me if you don't have a soul."

His expression didn't change. "How can you be sure?"

"That's the way it works."

"Explain it to me as if I'm an idiot."

I laughed, which was probably his intention. "Your soul is who you are." I rested my hand on his chest. "When you die, your body will be put in the ground. That won't be you, though. Your soul is what makes you, you."

He caught my hand and pressed the palm to his lips.

"You lose your soul if you become a shade," I pressed on. "I don't know if you willingly abandon it, but shades don't have souls."

"Do ghosts?"

"Yes. Their soul is what stays behind."

"So ... what fuels a shade?"

That was an interesting question.

"If it's the soul that fuels ghosts, and shades are like angry ghosts, what fuels them?" Landon looked legitimately curious.

"That's a good question."

He smirked. "I stumped my super witch. That's kind of fun."

"I'm not a super witch. Aunt Tillie is."

"Aunt Tillie is powerful, but you're the super witch. She knows it, too." He leaned back and put his arm around my shoulders. "I'll always love you. Forever and always."

"Just don't opt to become a shade and we won't have a problem."

"Fair enough. I ... ." He broke off and narrowed his eyes as he stared across the road. "What is that?"

I followed his gaze, expecting some sort of attack. Instead, I found Aunt Tillie standing on the sidewalk across from Mrs. Little's shop. She appeared to have some sort of animal with her ... and it wasn't small. I started to stand, but Landon kept me anchored to his side. "Let's see what she's doing before we intervene."

"That looks like a bear," I said.

"It's too small to be a bear."

"Maybe it's a cub."

"Then it's probably not dangerous."

I couldn't believe how blasé he was being. "Landon ... ."

"I want to see what she does." He squinted to look inside Mrs. Little's shop. "Willa is in there."

I sat up straighter and peered into the shop window. Aunt Willa was a few feet from the door, conversing at the counter with Mrs. Little. "I don't like that they're chummy," I admitted. "It makes me suspicious."

"I'm suspicious of those two whether they're working together or separately." Landon moved his hand to the back of my neck and rubbed. "Go back to the shades. The guys in Salem did it to themselves because they probably thought they were going to get caught. This was a way for them to evade law enforcement. Where did our shades come from?"

Another question for which I had no answer. "It's possible they've always been here and we simply never realized."

"How could you guys not realize? You're flitting around with magic all the time. It seems to me that you would've stumbled across them at some point, even if only by dumb luck."

"I don't know. They're active now, and there must be a reason."

"You think it's the girls?"

"I don't know. I wish I could be certain they didn't remember anything. There must be a reason Paisley was the first victim."

"Do you think the other girls are in danger?"

"It's a definite possibility. We don't know why Paisley was killed. Maybe Amelia is right and she hooked up with the wrong guy. Maybe none of them remember anything. Maybe this is all a coincidence."

"You don't believe in coincidence."

"Some things are coincidence," I argued. "This feels different."

"What's your next step?"

"Research." That's all we had to focus on. "Until I can figure out how these shades operate, where they came from and what they want, I don't see we have much choice."

"Okay." He nodded. "Do you have the right books?"

"Maybe. I'll get Clove and Thistle on it too. Clove can't do much these days but research. Stormy's great-grandmother was a bust. She can't answer our questions because she's separate from what's going on."

"The answers are there," Landon insisted. "I think you're blocking yourself from finding them because you're so agitated."

"I'm not agitated."

"You're blaming yourself for the girls acting like zombies. We have Brian Kelly running around threatening us. Say what you want — and there's no sense denying it — but I know that you're worried he'll do something to get me in trouble at work."

"I *am* worried about that," I admitted. "He's determined to pay us back. Oddly, he seems more focused on you than me."

"I'm the one who threatened him. I warned him what would happen if he kept messing with you. He has ego issues. He's an insecure man who pretends he's secure. He wants people to believe he's the king of all things, but he's really a peasant selling potatoes."

I cocked an eyebrow. "Potatoes?"

He shrugged. "Or some other root vegetable he has to dig in the ground to harvest. He believes he's bigger than he is, which means he needs people to believe that or his entire sense of self-worth goes down the drain."

"Now who's the shrink?" I teased.

"I've done a lot of thinking about him since he returned. I don't trust him."

"Nobody trusts him. He's a tool."

"Well, he's going to move ... and soon."

"We need to get these shades under control so we can focus on him."

"Definitely." Landon inclined his head toward Aunt Tillie. "She's on the move."

I watched my great-aunt start across the street. I could now see the animal she had with her more clearly. "Is that ... ?"

"A wolverine." Landon straightened and glanced around, seemingly dumbfounded. "Where did she get that thing?"

"Aren't wolverines extinct in Michigan?"

"They were never actually prevalent here. I think the last wolverine sighted here was in 2004."

"How can you possibly know that?"

"I'm a genius. What I want to know even more is what she's doing with that wolverine."

I watched as Aunt Tillie crossed the street. She seemed to be conversing with the animal, which trotted along next to her as through trained. My mouth dropped open when she reached the sidewalk directly in front of the Unicorn Emporium. What had once been a wolverine broke into six smaller animals, and those animals were easily recognizable.

"Skunks." I jumped off the bench and ran to the middle of the street. Landon chased me.

"What are you doing?" he demanded.

Was he kidding? "Do you really think she's not going to do something horrible with those skunks?"

He stood, his eyes moving between me and the skunks. He looked torn.

"If you go over there, she won't stop whatever she has planned," I warned. "I won't be able to share a bed with you if you smell like skunk."

"That's cold. I can't believe you'd banish me from our bed simply because I smell bad."

"There's bad and there's skunk. I can't deal with skunk. If it becomes a choice between sleep and you, I'm going with the sleep." The words were barely out of my mouth before a barrage of wind slammed into me with enough force to lift me two feet off the ground. "What the ... ?"

I careened toward the pavement, an ugly collision in my future, when another burst of magic swooped in from the left and tossed me toward the grass in front of the police station.

I hit hard, the air forced from my lungs, and I rolled to my knees.

"Bay!" Landon, the skunks forgotten, raced in my direction. He looked panicked.

I wanted to soothe him, but I didn't have time. I felt malevolence as

I looked up at the police station window. The shades were all there, grouped together with their gray faces and demonic eyes, and they appeared excited.

Another invisible wave of magic caught me at the shoulder, slamming to the ground again, whispers rolling over me. The shades were excited enough that I could hear them, though their words remained a mystery.

"Bay!" Landon picked up his pace and put his head down. He was going to get to me even if it killed him.

I didn't have time to think, so I forced myself to my feet and extended my hands.

"*Contego.*" I created a shield as the invisible wave circled back for another hit. When it collided with the flimsy shield I'd erected, it sounded like a train running off the rails.

Sparks flew like fireworks on a summer weekend, and the tourists littering the sidewalks broke into applause.

"They don't understand," I said when Landon finally made it to my side. "They don't realize it's real."

"Are you okay?" Landon moved his hands to my face. "What was that?"

"The shades. They're in the police station window."

Landon looked in that direction, his gaze fierce. "Well, that's just great." He looked caught, a little boy who had to make a split-second decision and save the world. "What do I do?"

I couldn't answer him. "I ... don't know." I turned my attention to Aunt Tillie. She stood on the opposite side of the road, her eyes scanning the sidewalk. She didn't speak, but I could practically hear the gears of her mind working.

"They're in the police station window," I called out.

Aunt Tillie shifted her gaze in that direction, her forehead creasing. Then she started across the road. Up until that point, I didn't believe things could get worse.

"Oh, no, no, no." I shook my head and moved to intercept her. Landon caught me around the waist before I could take more than two steps. "What are you doing? They'll kill her."

"She's a super witch, too," Landon insisted. "She can take care of herself."

"I won't leave her."

"Just ... wait." He locked his arms around my waist and focused on Aunt Tillie.

For her part, she didn't look worried in the least. She moved directly to the center of the road and raised her arms above her head. *"Illisus!"* she intoned.

I realized what she was going to do when it was far too late to stop it. "Duck!" I yanked Landon down in time to avoid a spinning manhole cover.

Aunt Tillie's magic exploded in a flood of water as all the fire hydrants on the street began spouting. She spun her hands faster, the magic lifting the water until it was a wall, and then she shoved that wall at the police station.

"Oh, no way." I couldn't allow her to take out the building. All I could picture in my head was Chief Terry losing his second home. I intercepted the spell with one of my own. *"Glacio!"*

The water froze at the exact moment it hit the building, coating it in more than several inches of ice. It looked like something created for a movie. Through it all, I could see the shades. They remained in the window, moving slower than before. It was as if the ice served as a trap of some sort.

"Huh."

"What?" Landon looked bewildered. "Seriously, baby, how are we going to explain that?"

I couldn't worry about explanations when I was struggling to wrap my head around the shades slowing. Then I had an idea. "Give me your gun."

"Excuse me?" Landon's eyebrows practically flew off his forehead. "I will not give you my gun."

"Then shoot the window."

"What?"

"Shoot the window," I insisted. "It's the only way to get rid of them." At least for now, I silently added.

Landon hesitated and then drew his service weapon. "Bay ... ."

He didn't want to fire it. He could get in trouble for discharging his service weapon under these conditions. "Don't worry." I squeezed his hand. "I have another plan."

"What is it?"

Before I could answer, I realized something was hurtling through the air above our heads. When I angled myself to see better, it became apparent that the thing flying through the air was the manhole cover ... and it was hurtling toward the window.

No.

I jerked at the sound of the new voice. It came from the trapped shades. They wanted to escape the window, but the ice was blocking them.

The manhole cover hit with terrific force, bolts of energy cascading from the impact. The glass shattered, and from within the glass I heard the screams overlapping. Then I heard one voice above the rest.

This isn't over.

It was, though. The shades disappeared ... and then everybody on Main Street broke into enthusiastic applause and cheers of delight. They had no idea that what they'd witnessed was real.

My shoulders sank as I looked to Landon. This was not good.

20

TWENTY

Landon stood rooted to his spot, his gun clenched in his hand. Aunt Tillie looked calm, although there was a fierceness in her eyes.

"What happened?" Chief Terry demanded as he raced out of the diner, Hannah at his heels. "What was that?"

"Shades," Landon replied, his eyes moving to me as he holstered his gun. He looked shaken.

"Well, great!" Chief Terry threw up his hands. "Can somebody explain why my building is covered in ice?"

"Shades," Aunt Tillie replied, brushing past him and heading for me.

"And the window?" Chief Terry looked at me, as if registering that I was present for the first time. His expression softened. "Sweetheart, are you okay?"

I had to laugh. Even in his moment of greatest fury he thought of me first. "Shades," was all I could say when he knelt next to me. "They were in your window."

"And attacking," Landon said as he lowered himself next to me. He gingerly began feeling along my back. "They did something that actually lifted her off the ground. I thought they were going to smack her into the pavement."

"They were," I confirmed. "That was the plan. Then something moved me."

"Don't look at me." Aunt Tillie said. "I saw what was happening, but something moved you before I could do anything."

"So, what moved me?" I looked around. "Something shifted me at the last second."

The sound of pounding footsteps drew my eyes to the road, where Thistle was racing toward me. Her hair stood on end and she looked panicked. I tried to stand, but Landon pressed his hand to my shoulder to still me.

"You stay right here until I'm sure you're not hurt," he ordered.

Rather than argue, I nodded and focused on Thistle. "Are you guys okay?" I hadn't even thought about them. They were only two stores down during the attack. "Clove?"

"Clove is fine," Thistle replied, though the wildness in her eyes had me questioning the statement. "I mean ... she's as fine as she can be given the circumstances."

"You mean the freaking ice?" Now that he'd ascertained I wasn't going to keel over and die any second, Chief Terry was back to complaining. "There's ice on my building, people! It's freaking seventy degrees out and my building is covered in ice!"

"Calm down, Esmerelda," Aunt Tillie drawled. "You sound like Margaret. Just chill out." She bent over and stared into my eyes. "You haven't been possessed or anything, have you?"

The question caught me off guard. "Um ... no. Why would you ask that?"

She shrugged. "They're shades. We don't know what they're capable of."

That bothered me more than I was comfortable admitting. "I'm me."

"She's her," Landon agreed. "What I want to know is how much pain you're in."

Surprisingly, I felt okay. "I'm in nowhere near as much pain as I was after the assault in the dining room."

"That doesn't make me feel better." He tilted my chin so I had no choice but to look at him. "They keep going after you."

"I've noticed. I still want to know why I didn't hit the pavement. I mean ... I was going down. I was braced for it. Then something pushed me to safety."

"Yeah, I think I can answer that," Thistle said, drawing my eyes back to her. She glanced over her shoulder, toward Hypnotic. "We saw what was happening from inside the store."

"Great," Landon said. "Why didn't you come out to help?"

Thistle murdered him with a look. "I did. Actually, Clove did, too. I tried to push her back inside, because ... well, you know why."

"We don't need her slammed into the ground," I agreed.

"That's just the thing. I don't know that she would've been slammed into the ground." Thistle looked toward the store again, anxiety lining her face. "We saw you go up in the air. Clove gasped and then — and I swear this is true — her stomach glowed. This ... burst of magic rolled out of her and I think that's what moved you to the grass."

I was dumbfounded. "Are you saying Clove saved me?" I asked.

"She's saying the baby saved you," Aunt Tillie said. "She's saying the baby inherently knew to save you."

That was even weirder than what I thought Thistle had suggested. "But ... how?"

"I don't know." Aunt Tillie stared back at the store. "But it's pretty interesting."

"Oh, you think?" Thistle's snarky side could no longer be contained. She exploded. "We have a magic baby. Yes, I'd say that's pretty interesting."

"You need to calm down too," Aunt Tillie chided.

"We all need to calm down," Landon insisted as he watched the excited tourists across the street talking in hushed tones. "I can't believe this played out in front of the entire town. How are we going to explain this?"

Hannah spoke for the first time. "I don't think you have to worry about that," she reassured. "Everybody in town was thrilled with what they saw. They think it's a witch thing."

"It *is* a witch thing."

"Yes, but they think it's performance art," Hannah explained. "Even if they truly want to believe, they'll chalk it up as a display the town put on."

"She's right," Chief Terry said. "There's nothing to worry about on that front. I don't see anybody complaining."

As if on cue, the door to the Unicorn Emporium flew open and screams emanated from inside.

"Or I could be wrong," Chief Terry muttered.

I watched as three women — including Mrs. Little and Aunt Willa — raced from inside the store, the skunks giving chase. They appeared a little too intent on their quarry. "Aunt Tillie." I could do nothing but shake my head.

"What?" The picture of innocence, Aunt Tillie straightened. "You can't possibly blame me for that. I was busy fighting shades."

"We saw you," Landon said. "We saw the wolverine turn into skunks."

"Yeah, how did you do that?" I asked.

"I have no idea what you're talking about." Aunt Tillie's expression was one of befuddled sadness. "And to think you would blame your poor, old great-aunt of something so dastardly. It's disgraceful. Absolutely disgraceful. I'm horrified you'd say anything of the sort."

"Knock it off." Landon gave her a dirty look. "You're not fooling anybody with that act."

"Definitely not," Chief Terry agreed as he waved his hand in front of his face. "Good grief. That place will have to be fumigated."

Mrs. Little ran in a circle in the middle of the street to avoid the skunk chasing her. "Go away, you foul beast!" She tried to stomp on the skunk and missed.

"Those skunks aren't real, are they?" I asked.

"I have nothing to do with the skunks," Aunt Tillie insisted. "If I did, though, I would say that they will likely disappear in an hour or so. I have no actual knowledge of this, but if I had cast a spell like this, I would've put a time limit on it."

I rubbed my forehead and let out a sigh. "I could hear them this time."

Landon snapped his head back to me. He'd been enjoying the sight of Mrs. Little and Willa trying to hide from the skunks. His smile dissipated in an instant. "They talked to you?"

"They talked to each other. I couldn't make out what they were saying because they all talked at once, but when they realized what Aunt Tillie was going to do with the manhole cover one of them yelled for her to stop. Then, right before they disappeared, I heard someone say it wasn't over."

"Maybe it wasn't the shades," Thistle suggested.

I wrinkled my nose. "Who else would it be?"

"Maybe it was her." Thistle pointed to the building next to Hypnotic. The upstairs level had been a law office at one time but was now empty. I'd heard someone had plans to convert it into a day spa.

At first I thought the window Thistle pointed to was empty, but when I shaded my eyes there was indeed a figure standing in the window watching the scene on the street ... and it was a familiar one.

"Amelia," I said, more in resignation than disbelief.

"Where?" Landon looked toward the window. He was grim when he saw the girl. "Maybe we should go up there and question her."

I grabbed his wrist before he could take off. "That's a terrible idea."

"Why?"

"Because."

He waited for me to expand. When I didn't, he swore under his breath. "I'm going to need more than that, Bay."

"She's clearly here for a reason." I rubbed my palms over my knees, frowning at the pain. I snatched my hand back to stare at the palm and found an ugly scrape from when I'd hit the ground. "Ow."

"Let me see." Landon gently caught my wrist and stared at my palm. "That is ugly." He kissed the mark and then flicked his eyes to Chief Terry. "I need your first aid kit to clean this out."

"Sure." Chief Terry said. "Get rid of the ice on my building and I'll get your first aid kit."

"Oh, will you stop being such a kvetch?" Aunt Tillie demanded, glancing over her shoulder when someone let loose a shrill scream. She grinned at the sight of Aunt Willa at the corner of the building, trapped by two skunks and shielding her face. "That's just terrible," she intoned, the smile never leaving her face. "An absolute travesty."

It would've been funny if we didn't have bigger things to worry about. "My hand is fine. I can clean it at Hypnotic." I grunted as I tried to stand. "Okay, somebody help me up. I feel like an old woman. My joints ache a bit."

"Did you hear that?" Thistle challenged Aunt Tillie. "She feels like you. Help her up."

"Keep it up, mouth," Aunt Tillie shot back. "There's a spot open on my list."

"You have bigger skunks to skin," Thistle shot back.

"Like what?"

"Um ... Clove."

"Oh, right." Aunt Tillie looked at me. "It feels as if that should be your problem," she said. "I handled the shades."

"I think we handled the shades together," I corrected.

"The only thing you did was interrupt my first spell. I was going to drown those bitches, but you turned the water to ice."

Chief Terry's eyes were dark when they locked with mine. "You did this?"

"She was going to flood your building. The ice is better."

"How?"

"A flood would've forced you to tear that building down to the studs to get it operational again. As it stands, all you have to do is wait for the ice to melt."

"I don't like either option." Chief Terry glanced back at the window Amelia had been standing in moments before. "She's gone."

"She probably didn't get what she wanted," Landon noted as he moved behind me and hooked his hands under my arms to help me stand.

"We don't know that she has anything to do with the shades," I argued.

Landon was incredulous. "Are you kidding me? What more proof do you need?"

I shrugged. "I don't know." That was the truth. "She shouldn't be able to control shades, not with magic stolen from Hollow Creek."

"That's your magic," Landon said. "You can control ghosts. She's an evil kid. No, don't bother arguing." He held up his hand to stop me from saying something. "I don't think we can get around the fact that she's evil. This is twice now, Bay. It's not some youthful indiscretion."

"He's right, Bay." Chief Terry said. "This is deliberate. Paisley Gilmore is dead."

"But ... why?" I asked. "Why kill her friend? I can see her wanting revenge on us. If the memory spell didn't last and what we did came rushing back to her, I understand she'd want to make us pay. But Paisley was on her side."

"Maybe Paisley didn't want to go another round with you," Landon suggested. "Maybe Paisley wanted to step back and do the right thing. You've seen those girls. Sophie and Emma are more malleable. They do as they're ordered.

"During the first case, they followed Paisley because Amelia was hidden away," he continued. "Now, with Amelia back, they seem to be following her. Maybe there was room for only one leader."

What he said made sense, but I was loath to admit it. "That doesn't explain her working with the shades. She doesn't have the magic to harness them."

"I think remnants of your magic are floating around Hollow Creek," Landon said. "It's possible she can control the shades with your magic because she has a dark soul, just like the shades do. Even if she can't, she's definitely involved."

There was no other explanation for what had happened.

He massaged my shoulders. "The shades are getting more aggressive and violent. We can't wage war against them on Main Street. Even if the tourists think it's a game."

I rolled my neck and blew out a sigh. "So we have to figure out who's controlling who."

"I'm not following you," Chief Terry said. "Who else would be controlling the situation?"

"There are two possibilities. Either Amelia is controlling the shades or vice-versa. It's possible the shades tapped into something dark in Amelia and are controlling her."

"How would they do that?" Hannah asked. "I'm far from an expert, but it seems that would take a great deal of magic."

I stared at her, gesturing to the street. "Did you miss what went on down here? I mean ... come on. The amount of magic that was thrown around on Main Street five minutes ago is unfathomable. We're lucky we got off unscathed."

"We're lucky we have a magic baby," Landon said. "I told you that kid was going to be born in swirling lights."

I let my eyes drift to Hypnotic. I couldn't see Clove, but I could feel her, even from so far away. Her emotions were a rollercoaster these days, and Thistle and I were often swept along for the ride because we were closest to her.

"We have a magic baby," I admitted, rubbing my forehead. "She's a lot more magic than we thought."

Aunt Tillie folded her arms across her chest. "This is only the beginning. Somebody has to talk with her."

Thistle and I automatically took steps back and spoke at the same time.

"Not it."

Aunt Tillie made a face. "Oh, you're so funny. I can't tell you how funny you are. Oh, wait, you're not."

"We have to talk about the baby as a family," Landon insisted. "May I suggest a family dinner? And we can discuss the shades and how best to deal with them."

It was the pragmatic way to go. Unfortunately, that's not how the Winchesters rolled.

"I'm still not going to be the one to talk to her about giving birth to a glowing baby," I warned. "I don't have the energy to dry those tears."

"Me either." Thistle was emphatic. "This is a job for our mothers."

"Yes. We did the heavy lifting with the shades. They can handle Clove."

"I totally agree," Aunt Tillie said. "It's nice to be on the same page."

I glared at her. I hated when we were on the same side. "Despite that, I'm sticking to what I just said. Mom and the aunts have to deal with this one."

"Then we'll handle everything in one shot over dinner," Landon said.

TWENTY-ONE

Thistle, Aunt Tillie and I went straight to the inn's kitchen. Landon and Chief Terry promised they would watch Clove, keep her away from the conversation, but there was nothing natural about the way they interacted with her. Landon in particular kept staring at her stomach as if a bomb was about to go off.

"So you think Clove's baby somehow stopped your head from being smacked against the pavement?" Mom summed up when we finished relating the story.

"Do you have another explanation?"

"Yes. Aunt Tillie did it and doesn't want to own up to it because she thinks it will make her look soft." Mom pinned Aunt Tillie with a pointed look. "It was you, wasn't it?"

"Since when don't I take credit for being a badass?" Aunt Tillie demanded. "Don't be ridiculous. I would tell you if I'd done it. We don't have time for games."

Mom continued to stare into Aunt Tillie's eyes, her bossiest face on display. After a few seconds, she relented. "Fine. Thistle, tell me exactly what you saw."

"It happened fast," Thistle replied. "Clove mentioned that something was happening on the street. I should point out that she was sitting on the couch when she said it, which means she sensed it rather than saw it.

"We both went to the window and saw Bay lifted from the ground," she continued. "My first instinct was to run outside but it was already too late for that. Clove made this weird sound, like she was gurgling, and then she grabbed her stomach. I saw a spark, kind of a gold energy, rush out of her. The next thing I knew, Bay was on the grass in front of the sidewalk."

"And that's all that happened?" Mom pressed.

"You want more?" Thistle was incredulous. "It's the baby."

"It's not the first time the baby has shown abilities," I added. "Clove's emotions have been all over the place. When she feels something now, we often do as well. She's projecting. And that's on top of her reaction to the runes I drew after Paisley's body was found at the Dragonfly."

Thistle slowly turned to me. "I forgot about that. She said the baby didn't like the runes and then kept talking. I didn't think to question her at the time, but now ... ."

"So, the baby doesn't like the runes." Mom said. "That's a very strange thing to say, but it's not the end of the world."

"We still have to deal with it." There was no way I would let my mother and aunts weasel out of this. "Clove has to be made aware that the baby is ... different."

"She's a Winchester," Twila argued. "Of course she's different. All Winchester babies are different."

"This baby is even more different," I insisted. "I think it's because Sam has witch in his lineage. This baby is getting a double dose."

Mom opened her mouth, as if to argue, and then snapped it shut.

"That does kind of make sense," Marnie hedged. "We talked about it when they started dating, what it could mean for children. We pushed it aside because it seemed unlikely. Sam's witch lines are weak."

"Apparently they're not that weak," I said. "You have to talk to Clove. More importantly, you have to convince her to have the baby somewhere other than a hospital."

Mom balked. "Why us?"

"Because you're the adults."

"Um, last time I checked, you were an adult, Bay," Mom said. "Clove is essentially your sister. You have to deal with it."

No way was I falling for that one. "I have enough to deal with. There are murderous shades out there and a teenaged witch who appears to be using the remnants of our magic against us. I am not going to handle Clove on top of that. You do it."

"You."

"You."

"Oh, I love an adult argument," Aunt Tillie drawled as she made her way to her recliner in the corner of the kitchen. "Nothing better than a mature discussion about the arrival of the next generation."

The fact that Aunt Tillie was calling us immature was sobering. "Mom has to do it," I said. "I have too much on my plate."

"Fine." Mom threw up her hands. "I'll do it."

Now I was suspicious. "You will?"

"Yes," she said, "and you're going to help."

Yup. I should've seen that coming. "I don't want to."

"You're coming anyway." She grabbed my arm and squeezed. "Come on. We're doing it now. We have an inn full of guests this evening. You're going to be inundated with questions because some of them were downtown to see the show you guys put on."

I glared at Thistle, who was edging toward the door. "Don't you think Thistle should come too? If it's a family thing, the whole family should be there."

"Absolutely." Mom froze Thistle in place with a single look. "You're coming, young lady. Don't even try to escape."

Thistle stomped her foot. "I don't want to."

"If you make me chase you, it's going to get ugly."

It was an effective threat, because Thistle fell into step with her mother and moved toward the door. "Fine."

Aunt Tillie cackled from her chair. "Have fun," she called out.

Mom crooked her finger at Aunt Tillie. "You're coming too."

"No, I'm not."

"Yes, you are. You're already on my list because of those leggings. Don't think I didn't notice the backside of them. You tried to be sly this morning and slip them on, but that didn't work. You're coming with us."

Aunt Tillie turned petulant in the blink of an eye. "I would rather not."

"Get up!" Mom's voice was so icy it had me shuddering. "We're doing this right now."

For a moment, I thought Aunt Tillie would continue to argue — it was her way, after all — but she got to her feet. "You're all on my list," she warned. "Every single one of you."

"Yeah, yeah, yeah." Thistle waved the threat off. "What else is new?"

"I've been researching new curses," Aunt Tillie warned. "I've got a few ideas."

"There'd better not be any skunks showing up in my inn," Mom warned. "If they do, a bomb will show up in that greenhouse."

"Oh, you wouldn't blow up my greenhouse."

"Not that sort of bomb." Mom's smile was evil enough that it sent chills down my spine. "We're talking a glitter bomb, one that smells like rancid cupcakes and stains every bottle of wine pink."

Aunt Tillie growled. "Don't even think about it."

"Then get it together. Clove is our priority right now."

WHEN LANDON AND CHIEF TERRY SAW us walking into the library in a crowd, they exchanged amused looks and started toward the door. I wanted to call out to stop them, but I would've made the same choice.

Mom had no problem being the heavy. "Don't even think about it, boys," she announced, causing them to freeze. "Last time I checked, you're part of this family. You stick with the family during group discussions."

Chief Terry issued a whine I'd never heard before. "I don't want to. You're about to talk about lady bits, and I cannot deal with that. I've known her since she was a little girl and didn't have lady bits."

Mom shot him a withering look. "She's always had lady bits. She was born with them."

"You know what I mean." Chief Terry protested. "This is a female discussion. I'm going to the kitchen to eat cookies like a real man."

"And I'm going with him," Landon added.

Mom's eyes narrowed. "Sit. Down."

They didn't even look at each other. Both scrambled for the couch, where they sat with their hands in their laps. Neither wanted to take on my mother. I was impressed with her command of the situation.

"Now, we need to talk to you, Clove." Mom flashed a smile that was straight out of the Grinch cartoon movie.

"Yeah, that will relax her," Thistle muttered.

I couldn't help but agree, but I wisely kept my mouth shut.

"Is something wrong?" Clove's eyes went wide. "Has something bad happened to Sam?"

"He's at the Dandridge, or at least I think he is," Mom replied, taking a seat next to Clove. "I'm sure he's fine. I wish he were here for this conversation, but we have to roll with the punches."

"Is the world ending? If so, I want to be on Aunt Tillie's team for the apocalypse. You're frightening, Aunt Winnie, but she's going to survive and we all know it."

Aunt Tillie pumped her fist. "Ha! I told you all. I'm the Daryl Dixon of the apocalypse."

"What happens if it's aliens instead of zombies?" Thistle demanded.

"Then I'm the Ellen Ripley of the apocalypse."

"And a plague?" I asked.

"Nobody wants to survive that. I've read *The Stand*. That way lies freaky glowing hands and a decimated Vegas. That's absolutely zero fun."

Well, at least she'd given it some thought.

"It's not the apocalypse," Mom reassured Clove. "We need to talk about the baby."

Clove leaned back in her chair and rubbed her stomach, her eyes instantly landing on Thistle. "You told them." Her tone was accusatory.

"I felt like I had no choice," Thistle said. "What happened today was a big deal."

"The baby doesn't like the shades," Clove explained. "She didn't mean to hurt Bay."

"Of course she didn't." Mom patted Clove's hand. "She loves Bay because you love Bay. We're not worried the baby wants to hurt us. On the contrary, we think the baby is going to be something special."

Clove smiled. "Of course she is. She's a Winchester ... though she's going to be a Cornell."

"She's going to be a Winchester," Aunt Tillie fired back. "All babies in this family carry the Winchester name."

"Not this baby." For the first time in I couldn't remember how long, Clove stood up to Aunt Tillie. "Sam has a right to pass on his name to our baby."

"Then make it Mitzi Cornell-Winchester," Aunt Tillie said. "The Winchester name must be in there."

"I kind of like the name Mitzi." Clove adopted a far-off expression. "It's pretty."

"No," Thistle and I answered at the same time.

Clove scowled. "You guys are no fun when it comes to naming babies. Sam and I have already talked about it. Whatever the baby's first name ends up being, the last name will be Cornell. Winchester will be the middle name."

"No." Aunt Tillie stamped. "That's a mistake."

"Then it will be our mistake."

Aunt Tillie opened her mouth again, but Mom silenced her with a look. "Clove and Sam have the right to name their baby. You don't get a say."

"If this isn't about naming the baby, what is it about?" Clove demanded. "If you're not worried that the baby is trying to kill Bay, what's the problem?"

"The problem is that the baby is much stronger than we anticipated," Marnie replied, perching on the arm of Clove's chair and stroking her head. They looked like clones of one another. I knew exactly how Clove would look in twenty-five years. It was eerie.

"Why is that bad?" Clove whined. "Bay is much stronger than anybody thought she would be when she was little."

"We're not saying it's bad," Mom insisted. "Stop jumping to the worst possible conclusions, Clove. We're saying we have to deal with it."

Clove's face was blank. "What do you mean?"

"We love you," Marnie started. "We love you very much."

Clove's lower lip started to tremble. "Am I dying?"

"Oh, you guys are worse at this than Bay and I would've been," Thistle snapped. She leaned over, resting her hands on her knees, and stared directly into Clove's eyes. "You have to have the baby here."

Clove immediately balked. "No way. I'm not doing a home birth. I want to go to the hospital, where there are drugs and epidurals."

"That's not an option." Thistle said. "I'm sorry to be the bearer of bad news, but here it is: You have to have the baby here in case it's born in glowing light or somehow zings someone with magic during the birth. We can't explain a glowing baby to random nurses and doctors."

"No!" Clove vehemently shook her head. "I'm having the baby in the hospital. I need drugs."

"Drugs aren't good for the baby," Marnie pointed out.

"Who cares?" Clove was adamant. "Drugs are good for mommy. If I have a stoned baby for three days, it will be fine. She'll survive."

"You'll survive a home birth," Mom said. "Some of the covens have wonderful midwives. We'll get you the very best."

"Absolutely not." Enraged, Clove hopped to her feet. I hadn't seen her move that fast in weeks. "I am not having this baby at home. It's not going to happen."

"You are." Mom folded her arms over her chest. "We can't risk the baby doing something that draws attention at the hospital. What if somebody wants to swoop in and study it? Do you want your baby turned into a lab rat?"

Clove worked her jaw. "No. But I need drugs."

"Don't worry about that," Aunt Tillie said with a hand wave. "I have plenty of pot. We'll just get you stoned." She risked a glance at a disapproving Chief Terry. "It's legal now. You can't stop us."

"I don't want to get stoned," Clove whined. "I want an epidural. I don't want to feel it."

"I had an epidural," Twila noted. "I still felt it. Have you seen the size of Thistle's head?" She pointed for emphasis. "Even with an epidural, you're going to feel that."

"Thanks, Mom," Thistle said dryly. She was calm when she held out her hands to Clove. "I know you're upset about this, but it really is the best thing. You won't remember the pain."

"Oh, I hate this." Clove threw herself on the couch and started to cry, big sobs wracking her body. "My life is over. You guys have taken my only hope."

"Well, that's not dramatic or anything," Aunt Tillie drawled.

"You haven't even given birth, you crazy old bat," Clove hissed. "What do you know?"

I pressed my lips together and turned, surprised to find that Landon had moved to my side. "Things are getting heavy," I noted.

"So I see." He brushed his fingers against my cheek and held them up so I could see the pads were wet. "You're crying."

I wasn't as bothered about the fact as I should've been. "It's because Clove is crying."

"I hope you don't feel the other things Clove feels when she's in labor and can't control her magic or emotions."

Oh, well, crap. I hadn't even considered that. "We need to find a midwife who can give her an epidural," I said, my voice carrying across the room.

"I'm right there with you." Thistle looked horrified at the thought. "I am not going through labor with her and getting nothing out of it."

"Oh, shut up over there," Mom warned. She focused on Clove. "You guys are being ridiculous babies."

She was right, but still ... . I met Landon's gaze. "If I have to go through labor I'm going to be really angry."

"You're not the only one. I feel your pain too, remember?"

"Right." I rolled my neck, my eyes falling on the window of the door. There were no shades present, something I was relieved about, but I was reminded that we had more than one thing to worry about. "We need to have a seance on the bluff tonight."

"W‍HAT?" Mom's eyebrows drew together. "Are you kidding me? Why would we want to have a seance now?"

"We need to talk to those shades, and I think we're going to need a lot of magic to force them to come to us."

"But ... ," Mom began to protest.

"We have to do it," Landon insisted. "The sooner we get rid of these shades, the sooner you guys can come up with a plan for Clove ... and I would prefer the plan not involve torturing my future wife in the process."

Mom looked tired as she stroked Clove's hair. "We'll conduct a seance. You're the expert."

I didn't feel like an expert, but we were running out of time. Something had to be done before somebody else was hurt. I didn't want it to be a member of my family.

"Dusk," I said. "Everybody needs to be there."

TWENTY-TWO

I was nervous when it was time to head out to the bluff. I hadn't eaten much, which bothered Landon, but my stomach was too jittery to inhale the meatloaf my mother and aunts had cooked.

"We'll have cake in bed when this is done," Landon said as we walked to the bluff. Everybody else had already left the inn. "We'll be naked when we eat it."

A laugh bubbled up, and I was relieved it cut through some of the tension. "That sounds like a plan."

He caught my hand before we crested the final hill. "Don't do anything crazy."

"Like what?"

"Like ... put yourself in danger."

"I'll be fine."

"Make sure you are." He squeezed my hand. Hard. "Remember that proposal I gave you out here."

"The one that no man will ever be able to match," I teased.

"I meant every word. I want you to be you. I accept the witchy stuff. I need you to not die on me. It will break me."

"I won't die on you." I meant it. "This is a conversation, nothing more."

AMANDA M. LEE

He brushed my hair away and pressed his forehead against mine. "We need answers and you're the one who is going to get them for us. I just don't want things to get crazy."

"Aunt Tillie will be with us. It's going to get crazy."

"That's exactly what I'm afraid of." He gave me a kiss and then resumed walking. "Let's do this."

CANDLES LIGHTED THE BLUFF. Clove, with Sam standing as her protector, stood away from the circle.

Mom, Thistle and Marnie painted lines on the ground with a can of spray paint. I wasn't familiar with the design, something Aunt Tillie had come up with.

"Are we ready?"

Mom lifted her eyes and nodded. "As ready as we're going to get."

"The older witches will hold a circle behind us," Aunt Tillie explained. "You and I will be at the center. Clove will be left out of it completely."

"That makes sense," I said.

"What did she say that makes sense?" Thistle demanded. "She just lumped me in with the old witches."

"Hey!" Mom's eyes flashed with annoyance. "I'm not old. I'm in my prime."

"*I'm* in my prime," Aunt Tillie said. "You need to get over yourself. We all have a job to do. Bay is at the center. It's her show."

"Yes, Bay is the center of all our worlds these days," Thistle drawled. "I can't tell you how much I love it when my life revolves around her."

"Shut up," Landon muttered, drawing Thistle's glare.

"Don't tell me to shut up!"

Marcus, who had been standing with Sam and Clove, moved to Thistle's side. He was the calmest member of our family, the only one who preferred avoiding fights, and was eager to stop us from falling apart now. "Let's not do this," he suggested. "There's no need to fight."

"There's always a need to fight," Aunt Tillie shot back. "This particular fight is stupid, though," she added. "We're here for a reason."

I blew out a sigh and released Landon's hand. "You should go stand with Chief Terry and Hannah."

"I would rather stick with you," he said.

"I know, but ... it's safer for you to be with them, away from the circle."

"If it's safe enough for you to be in the circle, then it's safe enough for me." The tilt of his chin told me he wasn't going to back down. "I think I should be with the center-of-the-world group."

Aunt Tillie snorted. "Only you would call it that."

"I'm in this, so I'm going to stand with you."

"How thrilling for all of us," Aunt Tillie drawled, her eye roll pronounced. "Do what you want. Let's get moving. I want to stream *The Mandalorian* before bed tonight. Baby Yoda is my spirit animal."

Somehow that seemed fitting. "Okay. Let's get to it."

Hannah cleared her throat from her spot near Clove and Sam. "Um ... I don't want to be the newb here, but what exactly is going to happen?"

I had to tug on my limited patience to stop myself from yelling at her to shut up and watch. My nerves were frayed enough that I might've lost it. Instead, I offered her a wan smile. She was trying to help, which meant that it was unnecessary to fly off the handle.

"It's a ritual," I explained, searching for the right words. "This is a ghost trap." I pointed to the lines that had been painted on the ground. "We're not dealing with normal ghosts, but this should still work as a trap."

"We'll pool our magic," Aunt Tillie said. "Bay is a necromancer. She should be able to call the shades to the circle. They'll be trapped here as long as we want."

"Or as long as the magic holds out," I added.

"And then what?" Hannah's face was blank. "What do you expect to happen?"

"We need answers." I thought of Amelia's face in the upstairs window. "There's a human component to what's happening in Hemlock Cove. We need to know who is involved so we can break whatever spell has been cast and send these shades on their way."

"I still don't understand."

"We don't really understand either," Mom said. "Bay is trying to get answers. We can't come up with a plan of attack until we know what we're dealing with."

"I get that part." Hannah's expression was strained. "I don't understand how Bay can call the shades here whether they want to come or not. Why not just destroy them now and put an end to them?"

"I don't know how to do that," I said. "I can call ghosts. I can order them around. Shades are different. I'm not sure they'll follow my commands."

"Then how do you know you'll be able to call them here?"

"We don't," Thistle replied. "But if we do manage it, we'll be able to trap them here for at least a little bit. They'll fight the effort. We'll ask questions and hopefully they'll answer. Then they'll either escape or whoever created them will call them away. At least that's what we think."

"I see." Hannah was thoughtful. "It all sounds very convoluted. I can't believe you're capable of any of this."

"Sit back and enjoy the show," Aunt Tillie said. "We're masters at getting things done for a reason."

She sounded more certain about what was about to happen than I felt. It didn't matter. It was time. "Everybody get in position."

Landon moved to stand behind Aunt Tillie and me as we stood just outside the circle. Thistle took one of the four corners with my mother and aunts. She looked angry — probably about being paired with an older generation — but she didn't complain. She nodded when we made eye contact.

"Here we go." Mom lifted her arms. "I call upon the power of the north. Bring strength, determination and resilience."

Marnie was next. "I call upon the power of the east. Bring love, devotion and loyalty."

Twila was third. "I call upon the power of the south. Bring grace, acceptance and peace."

Thistle was last. "I call upon the power of the west. Bring anger, retribution and hate."

Landon jerked, the last incantation confusing him. Shades were unhappy souls. They were angry, and we needed the anger.

"Now," Aunt Tillie instructed.

I pressed my eyes shut and extended my hands. "Come," I intoned, allowing the magic to roll off me.

I felt resistance straight away.

No.

We won't come.

You can't make us.

I was in no mood for games. "Come," I repeated, expelling more magic. "You don't have a choice."

"What's happening?" Landon demanded. "Why isn't it working?"

"Chill out, drama queen," Aunt Tillie instructed, closing her eyes. "They're resisting."

Hannah spoke from somewhere behind me. "I thought she was in control."

"It's different," Clove said. "They're not normal ghosts."

I pushed the voices out of my head and focused on my task. The shades resisted, but they sounded fearful enough that I knew I would be able to maintain control of them if I exerted a little more effort. "Now!" I yelled when I felt another tug on my magic.

A bright swirl of light appeared in the trap, four forms struggling against taking shape. Aunt Tillie lent her magic to mine and we trapped two of the shades. The other two escaped.

"Oh, holy ... ." Hannah was breathless. "There are ghosts here."

Not ghosts, I wanted to tell her. What we had in front of us were different.

"Hello," I said as the shades struggled against the invisible cage we'd conjured. "It's nice to see you."

"Oh, good grief." Aunt Tillie made an exaggerated face. "Don't play nice with them. Smack them around some."

I ignored her and glanced between the faces of the dead. One of them — the female — looked familiar. "Do I know you?"

"Let me go!" She struggled mightily against her constraints but lacked the strength to break free.

"That's Sandy Strawser," Landon said. "You remember. I worked her case about six months ago. You saw the photos of the crime scene."

I searched my memory. "You're the woman who killed your children." I vaguely remembered the story. "You said you thought they were possessed by demons."

"That was a lie," Landon insisted. "She drowned her children in the tub and claimed mental illness. We uncovered the fact that she was having an affair with a married man and he didn't want to deal with children. She thought he would leave his wife if she killed her kids."

Now it was all coming back to me. "She went in for an evaluation," I said. "She tried to fool the professionals by acting out multiple personalities."

"Yeah." Landon's lips twisted into a sneer. "When we questioned the guy she was seeing, he admitted to the affair. He said he was never going to leave his wife. He only said the thing about the kids in the first place because he thought it would get her to back off. He feared she would say something to his wife, so he tried to appease her ... and it backfired."

"She died in prison?" I was trying to remember.

"The county jail," Landon corrected. "She was found stabbed to death in her cell." He grew quieter. "There was some mystery as to what happened to her. Some assumed one of the guards allowed another inmate into her cell to kill her. More than half her blood was missing."

"She was killed by someone who used her blood to feed," I said. "Another shade."

"Pretty much," Landon confirmed. "Knowing her, she probably volunteered for it because she didn't want to spend the rest of her life in prison."

That made sense. "What happened to the guy she was having an affair with? He died under mysterious circumstances a few weeks later."

Landon rolled his neck until it cracked. "He had a farm accident, fell on a thresher."

"Which means someone could've killed him the same way and tried to cover it up," I said.

"Yes."

"Is this him?"

Landon shook his head. "I don't know who that is."

Honestly, it didn't matter. I understood the sort of people we were dealing with. Only dark souls agreed to become shades. And they attracted other shades.

"I guess it doesn't matter." I folded my arms across my chest and regarded the male shade with a thin-lipped grimace. "We would like to chat with you."

"I don't answer to you," he growled, throwing himself against the walls of the trap in an attempt to break free.

"It won't last long," Aunt Tillie noted, stooping to study the lines on the ground. "They're either too strong or the trap is too weak."

"Maybe both," I acknowledged, wetting my lips. "Who is your master?" I asked.

"We don't answer to you," the male shade repeated. He threw himself against the wall, barely taking a moment to regroup before doing it again, eliciting sparks.

Landon moved closer to me. "Is that normal?"

Nothing about this situation was normal. "Not really."

"Then let them go."

He had to be joking. "Why would I do that?"

"So nobody gets hurt."

"It will be fine," I reassured him, returning my focus to the shade. "You have a master. I want to know who it is."

"Did you hear that?" Sandy cackled. "She wants to know who our master is. Like we're just going to tell her."

"You *will* tell me." I generated a gust of magic and sent it toward her. She went rigid when it hit. "You're living under different rules than I am," I said. "I can do whatever I want. You're trapped."

"Not for long." The male shade threw himself against the cage walls again. This time I saw the trap flicker. It held, but another blow or two and the shades would escape. I stepped into the cage with the shades and caught the man by the throat, using my left hand to exert control on the female and pin her against the cage walls.

"What's happening?" Sandy whimpered as she fought against the magic. "What is this?"

"Witches," the man barked. "They're unholy witches."

"You say that like it's a bad thing," Aunt Tillie drawled.

I ignored the banter. "Who is your master? Show me!" I burrowed into the shade's mind, forcing my way through layers of memory and hatred. My head felt light with the flashes I saw, my shoulders heavy with the weight of the horror. I kept digging.

"Bay!" Landon tried to jump over the barriers of the trap but Aunt Tillie stopped him with a wave of her hand, the magic knocking him sideways.

"She's the only one who can go in there." Aunt Tillie said. "The shades will kill you."

"Get her out!" he demanded.

"Chill out," Aunt Tillie ordered.

"Get her out!"

I heard the panic in his voice but was beyond helping him at the moment. I only had a short amount of time before the shades would escape.

"Tell me who your master is," I ordered, staring hard into the shade's eyes. There was nothing familiar about him and yet I couldn't help feeling as if I should know him. "Someone started this chain of events. I want to know who."

Defiance lit his eyes and he fought my magic.

"Give me something!" I poured more magic into him, probably more than was wise, and he began to fray.

"It's too late," he cackled maniacally as he dissipated. "You can't hold us. You don't have the strength."

As frustrating as it was to admit, I had no choice but to release him. He was gone within a split-second, Sandy following close behind. Once they were gone, all I heard were whispers and gasps behind me ... and the beating of my own heart.

"Son of a Goddess!" I viciously swore and kicked the nearest candle, ignoring the look of reproval from my mother. I found Landon studying me with a mixture of fury and sympathy. "Are you going to yell?"

He shook his head. "I kind of want to but I don't think that will help."

"Likely not," I agreed. "Still, if you want to yell, I have it coming."

He nodded in agreement and then crossed to me, wrapping his arms around me and resting his cheek on my forehead. "We're going to fight about this eventually."

"But not today."

"Not today," he agreed. "You don't need any additional strain."

He kissed my forehead, swaying as the area behind us exploded in uninhibited chatter. I tuned them out and focused on the sound of his heartbeat. Finally, one voice rose about the din.

"So ... wine party?" Aunt Tillie asked.

Mom smiled at her. "You read my mind."

And just like that the mood on the bluff shifted from bitter disappointment to relaxed amusement.

I cast one more look to where the shades had been trapped and then nodded at Landon's unasked question.

"We might as well get drunk," I conceded. "We don't have anything else going for us right now."

Landon slipped his arm around my shoulders and kissed my temple. "We have each other."

I smiled. "Forever and always, right?"

"Yup. Forever and always."

TWENTY-THREE

"I'm dying."

I kept the covers wrapped over my head the next morning, refusing to even peek out when I felt Landon rustling next to me.

"Me, too." His voice sounded raspy.

I lay still and allowed my body to register the myriad complaints it would lodge over the upcoming hours. "My arm hurts," I realized, finally pulling the covers down to take a look. I frowned at the bruise near my elbow. "Did I get in a fight last night?"

Landon chuckled. "I don't believe so." He rolled to look, his eyes going dark when he saw the mark. "Did the shades do that?"

"The shades didn't lay a hand on me," I reminded him.

"You laid a hand on them."

"I did."

"I don't believe that was part of the plan." His tone was accusatory.

"Landon, we had limited time." I was in no mood for an argument. "I had to do what I had to do. As you can see, I'm fine."

"You're bruised," he groused, gently taking my arm. "These look like fingerprints, as if somebody grabbed you."

I let the memories of our drunken bluff post-seance party wash over me. "I think it was Thistle. Aunt Tillie was chasing her with promises of a bloating curse and she was trying to get away. I vaguely remember Thistle trying to hide behind me."

Landon snorted and rolled to his back. "Now that you mention it, I remember that as well. I can't believe she grabbed you that hard."

"I'm a delicate flower. I bruise easily."

"I know." He slipped his arm under my waist and tugged until my head was on his shoulder. "I don't like it."

"I think you would be happiest if I was never hurt."

"Yes."

"This is just a minor thing."

"The shades aren't." Now that we weren't trapped in a haze of drunkenness thanks to Aunt Tillie's wine, he was ready to voice his opinion on what happened the previous evening.

"I don't like that you barreled into that circle, Bay."

I had no patience, so my response was edgier than I would've liked. "What should I have done? They were going to escape. I had to make use of the time we had."

"Let them escape."

"We need to know why they're here, who is controlling them, what their ultimate goal is. We need answers. I tried to get them."

"Is it possible they're not being controlled?"

"What do you mean?"

"Maybe they're here of their own volition. Maybe they're just in the mood to haunt us and we should be focused on eradicating them rather than hunting them."

"That doesn't feel right."

"What does feel right? It seems the rules regarding shades vary. They're not like Floyd."

I shook my head. "Floyd was a poltergeist."

"Which is fancy speak for a really angry ghost."

"Pretty much. He was more powerful than a normal ghost, fueled by rage. Shades are fueled by darkness." I ran my fingers over Landon's bare chest. I didn't even remember getting undressed for bed the previous evening. Looking around the bed, it was obvious we'd shed our clothes walking through the bedroom and just fell where we landed. That was also the power of Aunt Tillie's wine. "Sandy Strawser was there last night," I reminded him. "She was an evil woman. Her essence was coveted by someone to use as a weapon."

"How can you be certain of that?"

I shrugged. "It's just a feeling, Landon. That's all we have to go on right now. I'm doing the best that I can."

"I'm not giving you crap for it."

"You're not happy with what happened last night."

"Because I love you. I need to keep you in my life forever. I don't question your instincts. I just ... can't stomach the idea of losing you."

"You won't lose me."

"How can you be sure?"

"Because some things are meant to be. I firmly believe we were always meant to find one another. That's why we crossed paths as kids. That's why we found one another at the right time as adults. I think if we didn't find one another at the corn maze that day we would've found each other at a different time.

"Things worked out exactly as they should," I continued. "Even though I thought you were a criminal hanging out with other criminals, I was drawn to you. I felt this incredible sense of ... yearning ... whenever I looked at you."

I felt his lips curve against my forehead. "I felt it, too. I looked at you and wanted something I'd never wanted before. Hannah told you that I was dedicated to the job above all else. That changed when I met you."

"That's because I'm awesome."

He laughed, as I'd hoped he would. I hated it when he was too serious. "You're definitely awesome. You still have to be careful. These new powers of yours are helpful and I'm glad you have them, but I want you to tread lightly, Bay. You're not omnipotent."

"Nobody is. Well, Aunt Tillie thinks she is."

"Eventually we'll have a kid or two and I'll be angry forever if you're not around to raise little witches with me. We both know I'm going to be an indulgent father. Our kids will be so spoiled nobody will be able to tolerate them if you're not around to play bad cop."

I glared at him. "That's not funny."

"It's not meant to be funny. Somebody has to be the disciplinarian."

"Why me?"

"Because you've got a lot of your mother in you."

"That doesn't seem fair ... and it might be the meanest thing you've ever said to me."

This time his laugh was raucous. "Fine. We'll take turns being bad cop. I need you with me to do it."

"Landon, I have no intention of leaving you." I meant it. "I knew I would be okay last night. You don't have to worry about me being reckless. I'm the good one in this family."

He tightened his arms around me. "That's not saying much."

"No, but it's true. I'm always going to come home to you."

"Good." He brushed his lips against my forehead. "I have big plans for us. I see a fat baby or two in our future. I see trips ... and retirement ... and adventures. I can't do all of that alone."

And that, I realized, was his true worry. "You won't be alone. Even if something happens to me — and it won't — you'll never be alone. You'll always have my family ... and yours."

"That's not enough. I need you."

I blamed the hangover for the tears pricking the back of my eyes. "I need you, too."

"Of course you do. I'm a catch."

I snorted. "And humble."

"Yeah, well ... humbleness is overrated." He pressed his lips to mine and sighed. "I'll defer to you on this because you're the expert. Just ... be careful. Something feels off about this entire situation."

"I agree. We need to start breaking this down."

"We need breakfast first." He dragged a hand through his unruly hair. "That's the only thing that's going to kill this hangover. We also need to check on Hannah. She's not used to the potency of Aunt Tillie's wine. She was sucking it down last night."

"We warned her." I smiled at the memory. "I believe you told her a story about tiny soldiers trying to explode your brain from the inside the first time you got drunk on the wine."

"That was right before Aunt Tillie convinced her to strip naked and dance on the bluff."

I'd forgotten about that. "She's going to be embarrassed. Thankfully you and Chief Terry were gentlemen and didn't look."

"I'm always a gentleman."

"You're ... something." I poked his side. "Come on. We should shower and head up. Now that you've reminded me of the naked dancing, I think it's best we're there to greet Hannah. She's going to be having a rough morning, and Aunt Tillie is likely to make it worse."

Landon's smile grew wider. "We can always count on Aunt Tillie for that."

"She's a professional," I agreed.

THE DINING ROOM WAS FULL WHEN WE finally made it to the inn. Landon wisely filled travel mugs with coffee for the walk, so we'd managed to take the edge off before we joined the others. But the din from the laughing guests agitated my already brewing headache.

"We were starting to wonder if you were going to join us," Mom chastised as we sat in our usual spots. "You're late."

I checked the clock on the wall. "We're, like, three minutes late."

"Late is late." Mom looked to Landon. "Only those who are on time get bacon."

"Don't torture me," Landon moaned as he poured glasses of juice for both of us. "I'm a man on the edge. I found my pants on the front porch. I don't exactly remember how they got there."

Chief Terry tossed him a dark look. "Don't be gross."

"I'm not being gross. We were way too drunk to do anything fun last night. I'm just confused about why I started stripping during the walk. I found my shoes on the driveway."

"It's the wine," I said, glaring at Aunt Tillie. "The wine is evil."

For her part, my great-aunt looked none the worse for wear. She was bright-eyed and eager as she mixed scrambled eggs with hashbrowns and then forked it over toast. "Don't blame the wine. It's the drinker who is the problem, not the alcohol."

"Yeah, yeah, yeah." I focused on Hannah's empty chair, my stomach doing an uneasy roll. "Has anybody seen her?"

Mom shook her head. "No, but I'm pretty sure she got sick last night."

"She took over the bathroom on the second floor and we heard her puking through the door," Chief Terry added. His eyes were glassy and unfocused. "I think she was there for half the night."

"We should let her sleep it off," Mom said. "I put aspirin and bottles of water outside her door."

Landon rubbed his chin, debating. "Should we wake her? She does have a job to do."

"Leave her be," I replied. "We're not even sure what's going on. Until we're absolutely certain that we need her, we should let her rest."

"I agree with Bay," Mom said as she sat. "The girl is new to Aunt Tillie's wine. She's going to wish she'd listened to us when we told her to stop. She'll be worse than all of us."

"I'm fine," Aunt Tillie offered. "I feel great."

"That's because you're evil and the wine doesn't affect evil people like it does the rest of us," Landon drawled. "By the way, there's no reason to brag. It makes us like you less."

Rather than be offended, Aunt Tillie grinned. "Aw, is 'The Man' feeling queasy this morning?"

"Shaky is more like it," Landon replied. "I'll be fine after breakfast."

That was a bolder prediction than I was willing to make. "Give Hannah a few hours. We're not even sure where to focus this morning. If we come across something that will help us, we'll deal with it then."

AT THE OTHER end of the table, the guests who had checked in the previous day were sharing an intense conversation. They weren't interested in what we were saying in the least.

"I like the kissing booth," a younger man said. "How great is it that they have a booth set up for that?"

I flicked my eyes to my mother and found her shaking her head. "What's wrong?"

"Nothing." She cleared her throat to get the attention of the two couples. "I should probably make introductions. They fell by the wayside last evening." She introduced everybody at our end of the table and then singled out the two couples. "This is Tony Sexton and his wife Samantha. They're here on their fifth wedding anniversary from Grand Rapids."

She turned to the other couple, who looked to be in their forties. "And this is Phyllis and Randy Hamilton. They came from Wisconsin. Apparently they're all big fans of the festival downtown."

"It's amazing," Samantha enthused, her eyes sparkling. "It's so quaint. It's a witch festival in a witch town. Who doesn't love that?"

Aunt Tillie's hand shot in the air.

Mom pretended Aunt Tillie was invisible and gave the couples an indulgent smile. "The festivals have taken on a life of their own. I wasn't sure that it was a good idea to have nonstop festivals throughout the year, but they've turned into big crowd pleasers."

"That's because everybody loves carnival food," Landon offered. He was mixing hash browns and eggs with bits of bacon. "Elephant ears are a special kind of magic."

Tony chuckled. "I ate one of those. I paired it with ice cream – amazing."

Landon nodded in agreement. "See, Bay, I'm not the only one who thinks elephant ears and ice cream belong together."

I fought the urge to roll my eyes. "You think elephant ears can be paired with anything. I believe I watched you eat them with chili last year."

"And I stand by that decision."

"The whole town is great," Samantha said. "I can imagine living here. I'm an accountant, so I wouldn't be able to make a living in a town this small, but if I could I would move here."

"My wife loves witch stuff." Tony said. "She's absolutely over the moon about it. When we read a story about Hemlock Cove in The Detroit Free Press, we had to check it out for ourselves. I'm pretty sure we'll be back."

"Oh, definitely." Samantha bobbed her blond head. "I want to come back for Halloween but understand you're already booked."

"We are. I'm sorry." Mom said. "That's our busiest time of the year. We book a full year in advance for Halloween."

"Don't be sorry." Samantha waved her hand. "I just wish we would've thought ahead. This Halloween is out, but we definitely want to come back next Halloween."

Tony agreed as he squeezed his wife's hand. "We plan to have kids in two years, so if we come back next Halloween that might be our last hurrah as a couple. We want to live it up right ... which is why I love that kissing booth."

Samantha made a face. "I didn't like the guy running it. He was creepy."

I lifted my chin and stared at her. "What do you mean?" Todd Lipscomb was officially on my radar. If he didn't clean up his act, I had every intention of making his life a living hell.

"He was fine," Tony said hurriedly. "I think it was part of the act. He just might not be as good an actor as everybody else in the town. It would make sense to have some people pretending to be evil."

Landon flicked his eyes to me, something unsaid passing between us. "How was he acting?" He tried to be nonchalant with the question but couldn't carry it off.

"Is something wrong?" Tony asked, straightening in his chair. "Is there something wrong with that guy?"

"Not that we know of," I lied. "I wasn't aware that anybody in town was acting evil. They usually save that for Halloween to ratchet up the atmosphere."

"That makes sense." Tony visibly relaxed. "Maybe he was practicing."

"Maybe." I forced a smile. "Can you tell me what he was doing?"

"He was talking to himself – and was really crabby," Samantha volunteered. "He kept talking as if there was someone else there, saying things about needing more power and evil women trying to steal his life. It was weird."

"I think we were lacking context," Tony explained. "I believe he came up with an entire backstory that he was playing out and we missed the first part. I kind of wish we hadn't, because it sounded like he put a lot of effort into the story, something about evil witches messing with his mind."

I pressed my lips together and pushed my eggs around my plate with my fork. Tony and Samantha were buying into the mystique of the town. I knew better when it came to Todd.

"We'll talk to him about doing a better job with his stories," Mom offered, taking control of the conversation. "We don't want the tourists to be confused."

"Todd is a ... unique ... soul," Marnie said. "He doesn't always stick to the script."

"We don't want to get anybody in trouble," Samantha said hurriedly. "We just found him talking to himself to be weird. He seemed really angry. Everybody else has been very friendly and welcoming."

"He won't be in trouble," Landon reassured her. "We'll just explain that he should spread the story out over a longer period so people can follow the narrative."

"That's smart." Tony happily slathered a slice of toast with jam. "Everybody should be on the same page with their stories."

Landon looked at me. "Absolutely. You read my mind."

TWENTY-FOUR

"I think we know where we're going to spend our morning," Landon said when we'd retreated to the library after breakfast.

I nodded, my mind already working furiously.

"He could be involved," Landon continued. "He tried to put everything on the girls the last go-around, but he could've been more involved when we wrote him off as a perverted idiot."

I leaned against the door jamb. I was thinking something entirely different.

"Bay?" Landon finally noticed I wasn't engaging in the conversation. "What's wrong?"

"Do you think I did this to them?" I blurted out.

Landon's eyebrows furrowed. "Do I think you did what to them?"

"I opened them up. I modified their memories. Maybe they've all been overtaken by shades ... and it's because of what I did."

"Baby, you didn't do this."

"You don't know that." The more I thought about it, the more sense it made. "They were in control of themselves before. They all had ulterior motives for what they were doing. Every single one of them, including Todd. We modified his memory with the others because we couldn't figure out a way to take him in and let the girls go. I think I did this."

"No." Landon grabbed my shoulders and then released them, opting to rub his hands up and down my arms in a soothing motion. "You didn't do this."

He couldn't know the truth of it. I couldn't either. "I think it's possible."

"I don't."

"How can you know?" I asked. "You're not familiar with shades."

"I know you. You wouldn't have done this."

"Not on purpose," I agreed. "But I'm not infallible. What if I hollowed them out with the memory spell? I could've created room for other creatures to take up refuge."

"But ... ." He trailed off, reading the serious expression on my face. "If you did, it was an accident," he insisted.

"That doesn't mean I'm not responsible."

"Bay ... ." He looked as if he didn't know whether he should dote on me or chastise me.

"We have to visit Todd." There was no way around that. "If he's been taken over, then it's my job to fix this."

"How are you going to do that?"

It was a good question. "I have no idea."

"Then we'll play it by ear." He rested his forehead against mine. "It's going to be okay."

He couldn't say that with any degree of certainty. He would believe it because he likely figured it was necessary for me. He looked as worried as I felt.

"We should head out now." I opted for stoicism. If I fell apart, he would, too. "We need to check him out. We should've been monitoring him more closely the whole time."

"We didn't want to be close to him," Landon pointed out. "We figured if we spent too much time watching him that people would get suspicious. There was a method to our madness."

"We still have to make sure."

He nodded. "Okay." His lips were warm against mine when he

offered me a brief kiss. "Please don't blame yourself for this. It's not your fault."

It felt like my fault. Still, there was no reason to assign blame ... at least not yet. "Let's head to town. We should probably take separate vehicles in case we have to split up."

He didn't look keen on the idea. "Bay ... ."

"It's fine," I said. "I'm not going to melt down." I mostly meant it. I could, however, promise nothing.

"I'll follow you." He grabbed my hand before I could walk away from him. "No matter what, this isn't your fault."

I really hoped that was true.

I PARKED AT THE NEWSPAPER OFFICE AND met Landon at the festival. He'd parked his vehicle in front of the police station, exchanged several words with Chief Terry, and then headed directly for me. I was already leaning against the fence watching Todd when he caught up.

"Do you see anything?" he asked after a few seconds of silence.

"No, but that doesn't necessarily mean anything. I'm hardly an expert at identifying shades that have taken root in people."

"Okay." He stared hard at Todd. "I guess we need to talk to him."

I could think of at least a hundred things I would've preferred to do. "That's the only thing we can do."

He linked his fingers with mine and fell into step with me. "If he's gross, I'm going to pop him one. You've been warned."

I wasn't opposed to Todd getting a fist to the face. As we closed the distance, I watched him. He seemed normal, smiling and waving at guests, but now that I knew he had a thing for teenagers I found everything he did disgusting.

"There's my favorite couple." Todd beamed when he saw us. "You haven't been by in weeks. Usually I can count on you two sneaking into the booth at least every other festival, but I think it's been three since you've stopped by."

"We've been making out at home," Landon said with a smile. I knew it wasn't a real one but Todd either didn't notice or didn't care.

"Yes, but the booth is specially designed for lovers." He moved his hands up and down, as if trying to sell us something great. "This is the booth to end all booths. How long do you guys want in there?"

I hesitated and then shook my head. "Actually, we're not here for the booth today."

"Oh, no?" Todd waved at a pair of tourists walking behind us. "That's too bad. I particularly like when Landon loads up on elephant ears and chases you into the booth."

There was an edge to his words, but his smile remained friendly.

"We're here to talk to you," Landon said. "We talked to a few guests last night, individuals staying at the Overlook. They mentioned that you weren't in the best of spirits when they were here yesterday."

Todd frowned. "Did they say I was unpleasant? I'm never unpleasant."

"They mentioned that you were talking to yourself."

Todd snorted. "I wasn't talking to myself. I was trying to get my new earpiece to work. It's Bluetooth and it's very particular."

"Why would you need an earpiece?" I asked. "Since when is that part of the deal here?"

"Since Margaret Little, that witch, decided we all needed to be available to her twenty-four hours a day."

I was caught off guard. "What?"

"Haven't you heard? She doesn't think the festivals are organized well enough so she created this phone channel that we all have to check in on once an hour. If she feels that we're not working fast enough, or if there's a gap in the festival offerings, she barks at us through the earpiece." As if to prove it, he pulled out a blue earbud. "She made us buy these. They weren't cheap."

I took the earbud and frowned at it. "I hadn't heard."

"And you were talking on this yesterday?" Landon challenged. "The guests we talked to said you were acting evil."

"Have you ever talked to Margaret Little? The woman is nothing but evil. I told her the earbuds were a bad idea. It's like being haunted but by people who are alive. I don't want to talk to her on a normal day. When I'm busy with work, I especially don't want to talk to her. I was probably snapping at her."

Landon flicked his eyes to me. "Well, that is ... understandable."

"It is," I agreed.

"She's a pain. I might've called her a witch, which isn't professional, but the tourists can hardly complain about that given where we are." Todd retrieved the earbud. "I'm sorry the guests were upset. I didn't realize anybody heard me. I was trying to be discreet."

"Mrs. Little doesn't do discreet," I mused.

"She doesn't. She's looking at a mutiny. We didn't agree to make her the boss."

I looked to the left where a hint of movement had caught my eye. There, Amelia stood watching us, her expression dark. She didn't even try to hide her disgust. There was anger reflected in her eyes, outright hatred positively rolling off her. Todd seemed oblivious to her.

Landon's hand moved to my back as he followed my gaze, his fingers stiff as they trailed up and down my spine. "Well, it sounds like it was just a mistake then." His smile was wan. "We were just checking that there wasn't something wrong."

"Nothing is wrong," he reassured us. "I am sorry that I put off some of the guests. I'll make sure not to do that again."

"That would be great." I tugged on Landon's belt loop. He needed no prodding. Amelia was our next stop.

"Have a good day." Landon offered up half a wave as he fell into step with me. "Do you think it's her?" he asked in a low voice when we were clear of Todd.

"She's been acting weird. If she's not working with the shades, or taken over by them, she's involved some other way. We have to talk to her."

"Do you think she'll run? I'm too hungover to chase a teenager."

"I thought you were a prime piece of beef."

"I am, but Aunt Tillie's wine makes me feel young when I'm drinking it and old when I'm recovering ... like 'hand me my cane' old. I need a day to get back to my normal self."

The picture he painted made me laugh. "You'll be sexy even when you need a cane."

"Without a doubt," he agreed. "I'm the sexiest of the sexy."

Amelia had drifted to the corner of the street, positioning herself in front of the Unicorn Emporium. Her gaze was defiant as she regarded us.

"Amelia." Landon had his FBI face in place as he stood in front of her. "Where are your cohorts today?"

"Who would that be?" Amelia asked blankly.

"Sophia and Emma," I provided. "I never see you without them."

"We're hardly joined at the hip," she said dryly.

"You are ... or you were," I corrected. "Maybe something has changed in the last few weeks to upset the dynamics of your group."

Amelia's eyes narrowed. A chill ran down my spine. She was no longer hiding behind feigned innocence. She wanted me to know that there was more to her. I reached forward and clapped my hands on either side of her head.

"What are you doing?" She immediately began struggling. "Stop that!"

Landon lobbed a panicked look over his shoulder. After a few seconds, I released Amelia and took a shaky step back.

"Well?" Landon prodded.

I felt sick to my stomach, and only part of it was remnants of the hangover. "She remembers," I said hollowly.

"Did you think I didn't?" Amelia's eyes flashed with fire. "Seriously? Did you think I didn't remember what you did to me?"

"Is she one of them?" Landon demanded. "Does she have a shade inside of her?"

Amelia's expression changed in an instant. "What are you talking about?"

"There's no shade in her," I said, letting loose a shaky breath. "She's all teenager ... and altogether angry."

"Can you blame me?" Amelia's tone ratcheted up to shrill. "You messed with my mind. You ... changed who I was."

"Look, you didn't just do a bad thing. You're a bad person. I saw that in your head at Hollow Creek that night. You're lucky we let you off as easily as we did."

"What could you have done to me that was worse?" she demanded.

"We could've killed you." Even I was surprised at how chilling my voice sounded.

Amelia swallowed hard. "We didn't do anything."

"You hurt Marcus," Landon shot back. "You tried to hurt Bay and her family. You were going to hurt your own families. You're not some innocent teenager playing harmless games with her friends, so stop acting like you are."

Amelia's lower lip jutted out. "I just want to live my life."

"Actions have consequences," Landon argued. "You hurt people. You tried to paint yourself as a victim when you were behind everything. You wanted to position Todd Lipscomb as your sacrificial lamb, which would've ruined his life."

"He's a pervert. I don't care about protecting perverts."

"And I don't care about protecting sociopaths," Landon seethed. "I would've been fine if they ended you at that creek. Bay wasn't okay with it, though. You owe your life to her."

"I don't owe her anything." Amelia crossed her arms over her chest, defiant. "She ruined my life. She messed with my mind. As soon as I figure out a way to make her pay, I will."

"Does that mean you have nothing to do with the shade problem now?" I demanded.

"I don't even know what you're talking about," Amelia growled. "Why would I care about curtains?"

My stomach clenched as I studied her closer. "She's not possessed, and I don't know that she's part of this."

"We saw her," Landon insisted. "She was watching when you were attacked yesterday. She had to be part of it. There's no other explanation."

There was one other explanation. "She was drawn by the magic." I understood at least part of it now. "You sensed the darkness in the shades. You've also been spying on us, maybe going so far as to visit the inn."

"You took my magic," Amelia hissed.

I chuckled. "You took magic that didn't belong to you and used it to harm people. That magic was never yours. It always belonged to us."

"It was mine," Amelia insisted. "I was going to use it to get out of this stupid town. You made sure that wouldn't happen. You ruined my life."

"I'm pretty sure you did that to yourself," Landon shot back. "You're the villain in this story. Bay is the hero. I don't feel sorry for you."

"Even though she raped my mind?"

I hated that she used that word. "I did what I thought was right. You were a danger, to yourself and this community. I'm not sorry for stripping your powers or modifying your memory. I am curious, however, about how you managed to overcome the spell."

"I'm not sure. It started with nightmares — that very first night — and then I started having them during the day," Amelia explained. "It was like a wall coming down. If I fought hard enough, I could see more ... and more and more. Eventually the entire wall came crumbling down."

Landon focused on me. "Is that possible?"

"I think anything is possible. She was stronger than the rest. We knew that from the start. I should've dosed her harder."

"I won't let you do it again," Amelia warned, extending a finger. "I won't let you change who I am again."

I wasn't certain it would be necessary. Amelia alone wasn't strong enough to topple us. "Do the others remember?"

"No, and I've tried to jog their memories. They're completely useless. Zombies."

"That's why you pretend to be disengaged, too," I said. "You're following their lead." I really had changed them, I realized. Amelia had been faking, but the others were really that disassociated from their lives. "You wanted to hide among them. You slipped up a few times when we were visiting."

"Yeah, and I'm not happy about it." Amelia shook her head, as if collecting herself. "It doesn't matter. I'm going to get revenge on you and your entire family, especially that crazy old lady."

That nudged a smile out of me. "If you want to take on Aunt Tillie, that's up to you. You won't win. I would think you would've figured that out by now."

"I'm not afraid of her."

That was bold talk, the sort of which I didn't believe. It didn't matter, though. All I cared about for today's purposes was the fact that Amelia wasn't involved with the shades. She was a problem, but one for a different day.

"I look forward to your attempt. For now, you should know that it's not wise to run your mouth. You should keep what you know to yourself."

"And if I don't?"

"No one will believe you ... but Aunt Tillie will go after you."

"I'm not afraid of her."

"Then you're dumber than you look."

25

TWENTY-FIVE

"She's dangerous." Landon stopped at a festival kiosk for iced teas and then directed me to a table at the outskirts of the action.

"She *is* dangerous," I agreed. There was no reason to pretend otherwise. "She's also scared."

"Of what?"

"Me."

Landon held my gaze for a moment and then broke into a wide grin. "My badass future wife is terrorizing the town's teenagers. I love it."

I shot him a dubious look. "I'm not Aunt Tillie."

"No, but you're powerful, Bay. Amelia knows that."

"But she might not care." I glanced to where she still stood across the street, her back to Mrs. Little's shop and glaring at us.

"I think she cares." Landon said, looking at Amelia. "Do you think she remembers all of it?"

"I do, and that's the problem. The girls splintered over their memories. Amelia doesn't care about Sophia and Emma. She can control them. Paisley was more apt to resist."

"Do you think she killed Paisley?"

My initial reaction was to dismiss the possibility outright. Then I reconsidered. "I just ... don't know."

He patted my hand and sipped his iced tea. He glanced over when Chief Terry approached us. "Is something wrong?"

One look at Chief Terry's face told me that he was indeed concerned about something. "I got a call from Steve Newton about fifteen minutes ago. He's on his way."

My heart rolled. "Why?"

"I'm not exactly sure. He asked that I be available for a meeting. He wants Landon present ... and Hannah."

That didn't sound good. "Did you call the inn?"

"Hannah is awake and feeling ragged. They're slapping her back together. The meeting is in two hours."

"Well, great." Landon exhaled heavily and dragged a hand through his hair. "Whatever he wants, it can't be good."

I was one step ahead of him. "You know it's Brian."

"I don't know that." Landon kept his tone even, likely in an attempt to keep me from freaking out. "We have more than one enemy. It could've been Amelia."

"What could've been Amelia?" Chief Terry asked as he slid onto the picnic table bench next to me. "Did I miss something?"

Landon filled Chief Terry in on our conversations with Todd and Amelia. Chief Terry started swearing before Landon wrapped it up.

"Well, that's just freaking great," he grumbled, lifting his eyes to the sky, a gesture he did when I was a kid and he was trying to keep from yelling at us after catching us doing something stupid. "This is not good, Bay. You have to do something."

"What am I supposed to do?" I was surprised at how pragmatic I sounded. "Do you want me to kill a teenager?"

Chief Terry looked around to make sure nobody had heard. "Of course not. Don't be ridiculous."

"Look, Amelia is angry. Actually, she's downright furious. But she knows she's not strong enough to take us on."

"She's a teenager," Chief Terry said. "Just because she's aware of it doesn't mean she believes it."

"Oh, she believes." I flicked my eyes to where the girl continued to glare. "Because of what happened, she understands about power. She knows that she wants it back."

"Why not just go to Hollow Creek and do what she did the first time?" Landon asked. "Is there anything stopping her from turning those shards into another round of magical mayhem?"

I nodded.

His eyebrows hopped in surprise. "There is? What?"

"Me. I didn't just modify her memory. I bound her powers, just like I did with Dani Harris before I allowed her to leave town."

Landon stroked his chin. "Wait ... did I know you did that?"

"I don't remember telling you I did it, but it seemed the thing to do."

"I thought her powers weren't real," Chief Terry argued. "You said she collected magic from Hollow Creek and shaped it into something it wasn't. If that's the case, how can you bind a magical being?"

"That was the easy part. The hard part was digging in those girls' brains and deciding what to keep and what to get rid of. There's a reason I fashioned things so they would have intense headaches if they tried too hard to remember."

Landon stirred. "Amelia mentioned a wall."

"I couldn't really remove the memories. I had to bury them. Apparently she was strong enough to dig for them." I thought about what I'd said. "Or I did a poor job of constructing the spell and it wasn't difficult at all."

"I'll believe the former," Landon said, resting his hand on top of mine.

"I could've screwed up," I said. "Until that night, I'd never modified anybody's memory in that manner. I mean ... there were a few memory spells I messed around with as a kid, but Aunt Tillie has always done the heavy lifting on that front."

"I still don't believe it was you," Landon argued. "You did fine with the other girls."

"Or maybe Sophia and Emma are weaker than Paisley and Amelia."

"Do you think Paisley remembered, too?" Chief Terry asked.

"I don't know. I've been trying to figure out why she had to die and I come up with nothing. Did Amelia kill her friend because she didn't remember? Paisley was stabbed several times."

Chief Terry nodded. "Five."

"Doesn't that speak to overkill?"

"And we're back to *Criminal Minds*," Landon noted with a wink.

"I'm just saying that five wounds indicate a frenzied attack. If it was a calculated murder, one stab should've been enough. Two at the most."

"Unless we're dealing with teenagers. Bay, no matter how worldly Amelia seems, she wouldn't have been comfortable killing Paisley. Maybe she panicked and wanted to make sure she was dead so Paisley couldn't tell anyone."

"And then what?" I challenged. "Did Amelia drive to Paisley's house, kill her parents without leaving any blood behind and dump the bodies on her own with no magic at her disposal?"

Landon bit his lower lip. "Maybe Sophia and Emma helped her."

I tried to picture the three girls moving bodies. "That only works if they managed to drag the Gilmores' bodies into the woods. Can you see the three of them doing that? They might like having the occasional cocktail in the woods, but they're not going to spend hours out there digging graves. It's not as easy as it looks on television."

Landon arched an amused eyebrow. "How do you know that? Did Aunt Tillie force you to bury bodies when you were a kid or something?"

"Not bodies. Wine." I answered before thinking better of it and then gave Chief Terry a guilty look. "Sorry."

Confused, Landon switched his attention to Chief Terry. "What is she sorry about?"

"I caught Tillie in the woods when the girls were little," Chief Terry replied. "She was out by my deer blind. It was dumb luck that I found her."

"Not so much," I countered. "Aunt Tillie purposely picked that spot because she believed someone would have to be stupid — or have a death wish — to go anywhere near your blind."

"Of course she did." Chief Terry rolled his eyes. "Anyway, they had shovels and guilty expressions on their faces. Bay was about nine. She burst into tears when she saw me."

"Then Clove followed suit," he continued. "Clove, of course, was manipulating me. Bay was upset because Tillie instructed her to lie."

Landon smiled. "Let me guess. Rather than make Bay cry harder, you swallowed whatever story they told you."

"I didn't swallow it. I knew Tillie was burying something illegal. It could've been wine or pot. I let them off."

"You're a big softie." Landon's grin was wide. "Picturing you rolling over and showing your soft underbelly to three little witches and their crazy great-aunt makes me warm and cuddly all over."

Chief Terry murdered him with a look. "Keep it up. I'll throw you in jail if you're not careful."

"On what charges?"

"I'll make something up." Chief Terry's eyes sobered when they connected with mine. "I knew you girls were up to no good even then. It was my choice to let you go. Don't feel guilty."

He made me laugh. "I don't feel guilty ... and it was definitely wine she buried. She made a killing on the stuff she sold near your blind."

"I've always loved her entrepreneurial spirit," he said dryly.

"We've gone off on a tangent," I noted. "I'm just saying there's no way those girls dug graves."

"I have to agree with Bay," Chief Terry said. "Everything would have to line up perfectly for them to carry that out. Someone would've seen them removing bodies from the Gilmore house."

Landon didn't appear bothered to have his pet theory shot down. "Then what happened? If the girls didn't do it, are they free and clear of this?"

"They can't be," I answered. "Not entirely. Their relationship with Paisley puts them in the thick of this."

"Do we assume that Amelia is the only one who remembers?" Chief Terry asked. "Is it possible the others do?"

"Amelia pretty much came out and said that Sophia and Emma don't remember. I'm guessing that makes her frustrated."

"Emma and Sophia are acting out of sorts," I said. "They're flat and uninterested in life. I did that to them. Amelia is pretending to act the same way, but she's slipped. Twenty minutes ago, she didn't even pretend to be removed from it all."

"Not even a little," Landon agreed. "She was angry. We asked her about watching when the shades attacked and she admitted to following us. She denied being in cahoots with the shades."

"Cahoots?" I smirked at Landon's shrug. "Yeah, the 1920s called. They want their word back."

He pinned my feet between his under the table. "You know what I mean."

"Do you believe her about the shades?" Chief Terry asked.

"I do," I said. "She saw we were under magical attack yesterday. I don't think she saw the shades. Knowing we have a magical enemy trying to take us out has emboldened her."

"To what end?"

"She wants revenge." I looked at Landon for confirmation. "She believes we took something from her."

"Technically we did," Landon pointed out. "Three weeks ago, she was magical and had a plan that she thought would deliver everything she wanted. She can't see past her needs and wants."

"You think she's hoping to join forces with whoever controls the shades," Chief Terry mused. "I guess that makes sense."

"I'm betting she will go home and research shades," I said. "She wasn't raised to be magical. Everything those girls managed to pull off came from instinct, books and the internet. She likely realizes she can't wield magic as long as I'm alive. I am responsible for binding her powers."

Landon frowned. "Wait ... ."

"I'm not afraid of a teenager," I reassured him.

"You should be," he snapped. "Teenagers are irrational creatures. In fact, when we have kids of our own, I'm going to request we never have a teenager."

I blinked several times in rapid succession. "So when we have a daughter she's going to jump from twelve to twenty overnight?"

AMANDA M. LEE

"No. She's going to stick at a cute age forever. I'll pick the age when I find one I like."

I had to press my lips together to keep from laughing.

"I'm serious," he insisted. "You're a witch. You can figure out how to freeze our kid at a cute age."

"You realize if we have a seven-year-old forever we'll never be alone again."

His eyes went wide. "Oh."

Chief Terry chuckled. "Let's worry about your magical offspring later. We need to focus on the demon teenager glaring holes into us. Landon is right. She's wily enough to have called Steve. We need to be prepared."

"That's fine," I said. "I still think it's more likely that Brian called. He believes Landon messed with his business prospects. He wants nothing more than to hurt Landon. Brian thinks Landon is his adversary. He thinks I'm Landon's pawn."

Landon held my gaze for a long beat. "You're right."

"I'm always right."

"Kelly thinks I stole that newspaper to set you up to make money for me." Landon rubbed the spot between his eyebrows. "He's convinced I set this all up."

"You have to be ready in case Steve asks you about marrying a witch." Something awful occurred to me. "You might have to distance yourself from me to protect your job."

Landon jabbed a warning finger in my direction. "Don't say things like that. I won't do that."

"But if Steve thinks there's something hinky going on ... ." I trailed off, dark possibilities pushing to the forefront of my brain.

"There's nothing Kelly can do to force me away from you."

"He could tell your boss tall tales and force an investigation."

"Do you really think Steve is going to drive here to demand I break up with you because Kelly told him some wild tale about Aunt Tillie cursing his penis to turn green and break out in sores?"

"Stranger things have happened."

"No, they haven't." He looked momentarily frustrated and then softened his expression. "Bay, why would he call Hannah into a meeting about my future marriage?"

Reality smacked me in the face. Hard. "Oh."

He shot me a knowing look. "Odds are this has something to do with the case."

"I'm with Landon," Chief Terry said. "It has to do with the case. But if Steve wants answers on those runes, we have nothing to give him."

"Then we'll tell him that," Landon said. "We'll tell him where we are and go from there."

Chief Terry looked at me. "You can't come to the meeting."

"Yeah. I'm pretty sure I figured out that Landon can't take his fiancée to a meeting with his boss. I'm not an idiot."

"I never said you were. I just don't want you doing anything stupid ... like rushing into the office and throwing yourself on an invisible sword in an attempt to save Landon. Stay out of this until we know more."

I'd been raised by busybodies, so that was easier said than done. "I'll be good," I promised. "I won't do anything stupid."

"What are you going to do?" Landon asked. "We know that Amelia isn't behind the shades, but she could be working with them. If she isn't already, she could soon join them."

I glanced between a still glowering Amelia and the newspaper office. "I think I'm going to tap some ghostly help."

Landon followed my gaze to the office. "You think Viola can help with this?"

"Probably not, but I have to at least ask. I'm stuck while you're in your meeting anyway."

Landon leaned forward and stared directly into my eyes. "You're going to stick close to town until we can regroup."

I feigned shock and hurt. "You act as if you don't trust me."

"I know you. If you get an idea in your head, you'll run off and test it. I prefer you wait for me."

I took pity on him. "I won't run off. Besides, I won't be able to focus on much of anything until I know Steve doesn't want to bust you for marrying a witch. I promise to stay close to downtown."

"Good enough." Landon stuck out his lips in exaggerated fashion for a kiss.

I gave him what he wanted. "We're closer," I whispered before pulling back. "I feel as if we have all the pieces but they're not arranged properly."

"*All* the pieces?"

"Okay, maybe we're missing one."

"It's a big piece."

"Yeah, but once we have it the rest will slide into place."

"Just as soon as my boss is out of town we'll start looking again."

"I'll dig in with Viola and wait it out."

"I'll call as soon as I can and tell you what Steve really wants. We're still good here, Bay. There's no reason to freak out."

"I'm a Winchester. Sometimes the only thing I can do is freak out."

"I don't think this meeting will be anywhere near as terrifying as you believe."

I desperately hoped he was right.

TWENTY-SIX

Landon sent me back to the newspaper office with a box of food, including some maple-bacon flavored hard candy he found at a kiosk and demanded I hide it from Aunt Tillie.

"She'll hex it to make me act like a fool."

I wanted to point out he already acted like a fool when bacon was involved, but it seemed unnecessarily combative at this point. "I'll guard it with my life," I promised.

He caught my chin before I could walk away. "The thing I want guarded most is you."

"Are you telling me to leave the candy behind if something bad happens?" I asked with a laugh.

"Of course not. You have two hands. You can throw magic around with one and protect my candy with the other." He grinned as he leaned in to give me a kiss and then sobered. "Don't run off without me."

"I won't." I meant it – mostly. "As long as you stop hovering and focus on your job."

"Fine." He gave me another kiss. "Do me a favor and don't obsess about this," he ordered as he headed for the police station. "It'll be fine."

"I'll do my best." I remained rooted to my spot and watched as he crossed the lawn, not missing the fact that he looked at least three times to where Amelia had been standing before he reached the door. Hannah joined him there. She looked dressed for success, but even from this distance she was pale. I hoped Steve's visit wouldn't add to what I was certain was a monster of a headache.

With nothing left to do but fret, I carried Landon's box of goodies to The Whistler. The security system he'd insisted on installing seemed like a goddess-send now, what with a killer lurking and Brian's determination to make my life miserable.

I dropped the box of candy on my desk, smirking when I realized there was rope licorice at the very bottom. That was my favorite. Landon could take it or leave it. Even in the middle of a crisis, he went out of his way to make sure I had comfort food.

I left the licorice on my desk — it would be a treat for later — and went looking for Viola. I found her in the kitchenette watching television, as was her way. She didn't bother looking up when she heard me.

"You tell him, Judy," she snapped at the television. "He stole that woman's scooter and her hat. People saw him wearing the hat and nothing else in the neighborhood, which means he's a pervert. Nail him."

I drew my eyebrows together and tried to figure out what was happening on the screen. "What are you watching?"

Viola finally dragged her eyes to me. "*Judge Judy*. Do you know who that is?"

I nodded. "Aunt Tillie rails weekly about her having a show in which she gets to punish people."

Viola snorted. "Sounds like Tillie. Although ... ." She trailed off. Viola was never what could be considered sharp. Sometimes watching the gears in her mind work was painful.

"What is it?" I asked.

"I was just thinking how a television show where a witch gets to dole out hexes to jerky people would get a million viewers. I might find Tillie impossible to get along with — don't ever tell her I said that — but other people would eat her up."

"Yes ... and then likely spit her out," I agreed. "She has a certain presence that can't be denied. I think giving her a television show would be a mistake, though. She would get off on the power and punish the innocent as well as the guilty."

"That might be even funnier."

"Yeah, I'm not keen on giving her too much power." I went to the Keurig and flipped it on to make some coffee. "I need your help." I felt awkward broaching the subject when she was watching *Judge Judy*, but getting the formalities out of the way was best.

Viola's eyes filled with suspicion. "What sort of help?"

"It's difficult to explain."

That obviously wasn't good enough for Viola. "Is it the sort of help where I can't say no and you force me to do your bidding?"

Guilt rolled into a ball in my stomach and started churning. "I would really rather not go that route."

"You've done it before." Her tone wasn't accusatory as much as matter-of-fact. That didn't make me feel any better.

"I have, and I regret it ... kind of."

Viola hiked a ghostly eyebrow. "Kind of?"

"I needed help to save my family," I reminded her. "I called you guys because I felt I had no other choice."

"You could've asked. I would've helped even though I despise Tillie."

"I didn't feel I had time to ask. On top of that, I didn't think you would say yes. You hate Aunt Tillie."

"I like you."

The simple statement caught me off guard. "Thank you. I really am sorry. I just ... panicked."

Viola's expression softened. "I guess that's allowed. Even I've panicked a time or two."

"I remember the time at that one festival when the bee flew into your bra and stung you. You were so surprised you started flapping your arms and knocked Mrs. Little into the punch bowl."

Viola grinned. "That was a fun day. Margaret melted down and blamed the bee incident on Tillie."

"She blames everything on Aunt Tillie."

"In Margaret's defense, Tillie has gone out of her way to torture her for years," Viola said. "Margaret is a real pill — one of those horse tranquilizers that makes you gag — but Tillie has made Margaret's life miserable. I don't know anybody who would come out the other side of that mess sane."

As much as I didn't want to admit it, she had a point. That didn't mean I would take up for Mrs. Little. The woman was horrible. She'd earned everything Aunt Tillie had thrown at her.

"You said you had something you wanted me to do," Viola prodded, drawing me back into the conversation.

"Are you familiar with shades?" I asked.

"You have blinds on the windows," she said.

I kept my smile in place. "I'm talking about ghost shades."

Viola's expression remained blank. "I don't know what that is."

I broke it down in simple terms. "Evil ghosts. That's essentially what we're talking about."

"I've seen a lot of ghosts who could've been considered evil during their lives."

"You're a good person," I said. "In life, you might've been a little scattered — and your association with Mrs. Little always annoyed me — but you were a good person. There are certain ghosts who can't make that claim. They're rotten to their core. They're also sometimes controlled by people.

"They can take over human beings," I continued. "They can wedge their dark souls into another person and take over, live that individual's life."

Viola looked fascinated. "That's like living another life, a second one."

"True, but it's not a real life. It's more of a half-life. You have to drink the blood of others to survive in this form."

"Why is that?"

"Because the human body wasn't designed to house two souls ... and blood is essentially power. It's always comes back to the blood."

Viola cocked her head in a manner that told me she was thinking hard. "I'm not one of those souls?"

"Definitely not."

"But they're in town?"

"At least a few. I'm guessing we're dealing with about ten of them."

"What do they want?"

That was the question of the day. "That's what we're trying to figure out. They attacked me yesterday in the middle of town. They've moved on me at the inn, too."

"It sounds like they're fixated on you."

"I think they are. That's likely by design."

"Because of what you can do? The ghost thing, I mean."

"It's possible. It's also possible this is payback for something else."

"Okay. What do you want me to do?"

"See if you can find them."

"And then what?"

"Then come back and tell me what you find."

"That's it? No fights or anything?"

I shook my head. "No fights." *At least not right now*, I silently added. If a fight was necessary, I would broach that subject later. "I only need to know where they are ... and maybe how many of them are running around."

"I think I can do that." Viola flashed me a smile. "It's like we're partners in a television show. I'm the smart one and you're the ... um ... sidekick."

She was the smart one? That stung on about three different levels. "You're the smart one," I agreed.

"Then I shall find these shades and report back to you with due haste." She saluted, which felt unnecessary, but I saluted back.

"Good luck."

"I don't need luck. I've watched every episode of *Alias*. Twice. I've got this." With those words she was gone, leaving me alone in the office with only *Judge Judy* for company.

"Aunt Tillie really would be better at this job than you," I mused as I turned off the television. Hexes as punishment? It sounded mildly amusing. Aunt Tillie would jump at the chance. She also would abuse her power ... and drive my mother batty.

I hummed to myself as I cut through the building on the way back to my office. Viola might've been a ditz of the highest order, but she was diligent when it came to assignments. She might find the shades. What would happen after that was anybody's guess. It was also possible that the shades could stay hidden from Viola. I had no idea the extent of their powers. Still, it was worth a shot.

I was so lost in thought that I almost didn't notice the figure standing in front of the desk in the lobby as I passed. I'd locked the door behind me — another thing Landon insisted on before separating — so nobody should've been capable of getting inside the building. Unfortunately, once I recognized the figure glaring holes into me, I wasn't all that surprised.

"What are you doing here?" I stood on the other side of the desk and fixed Brian with a furious look. "You're not supposed to be here."

Brian snorted. "I can't believe you just said that with a straight face."

He wanted me to be afraid. Well, he was messing with the wrong witch. "This is my building."

"Only because your boyfriend stole it from me."

"Landon didn't steal anything from you." I was beyond furious. "You moved on me. Either you didn't realize the town would stand with me or you didn't care."

Brian's eyes narrowed. "You set me up. You had me fire you because you knew it would work out in your favor."

That was the most ludicrous thing I'd ever heard. "I didn't set you up. You did it to yourself. William stipulated in his will that you had to keep me on. You tried to oust me the first chance you got."

"You wouldn't get with the program," Brian seethed, clenching and unclenching his hands. "I told you what we needed to do to save the newspaper. You refused to get on board with my plan ... and now I've lost my family's legacy."

"You didn't want to save the newspaper," I argued. "It brings in good business, especially considering how other newspapers run so close to the margins these days. The Whistler has a built-in advertising pool that brings in steady income. You wanted more."

"Is that so terrible?"

I shrugged. "It's unrealistic. This newspaper can't deliver what you want it to. Your grandfather realized that. I think that's why he demanded you keep me on. He knew you wouldn't be able to wrap your head around the businesses in this town."

"Is that what you think?" Brian's tone was cold, to the point I reassessed my situation. He'd effectively cut me off from the exit. That felt deliberate. This felt more dangerous than I initially grasped.

"Obviously you feel differently," I said. "I don't know what to tell you, Brian. I don't know what it is you want to hear."

"I want my business back."

"No."

"No?" His eyes went wide, and for a moment I thought his pupils were much larger. I wrote it off as a trick of the shadows, but a small flame of doubt niggled at the back of my brain.

"It's my newspaper." On this one point I would never back down. "I put the stories together. I deal with the advertisers. I schedule profiles ... and business stories ... and I lay out the front page. You never did any of that."

"I was the brains. You were the labor."

"And yet now I'm both."

The growl that gurgled up in his throat had my blood running cold.

"You stole my business," he seethed. "You stole my birthright. You and that second-rate FBI agent. You cast a spell on him. That's how you got him to steal my newspaper. At first, I thought it was him. Now I realize it's you. You made him do what he did."

I worked my jaw, uncertain. "I don't know what you mean," I said.

"Don't lie to me!" Brian exploded and took a menacing step toward the desk. My heart rate picked up. "You're a witch," he insisted. "I knew the truth before I left. Your aunt cursed me a few times."

"I ... think you should probably lay off the drinking before five o'clock," I offered softly. "You're talking nonsense."

"And you're lying. I get it." He shifted his head so I could get a better view of his eyes in the limited lobby light and my heart shuddered when I saw they were black. "I didn't understand when I was here before. I couldn't figure it out."

My throat was dry. "You couldn't figure what out?"

"All of it. I didn't understand why my grandfather included you in my inheritance. I didn't understand why everybody in this town seemed so enamored with you. Even I was enamored with you for a few minutes ... and then you brought in the fed.

"What do you see in him?" he continued. "I've been over this in my head a million times. I figured if I couldn't beat you, I could join with you and take control of the newspaper that way. But he was always in the way."

"You've been taken over by a shade," I said. "Did you make a deal with him? Did you call him to you?" A horrible thought occurred to me. "Did you do this just to get back at me?"

Brian exhaled heavily and looked to the ceiling. "Everything always comes back to you, doesn't it, Bay? This entire town is your playground and the rest of us are supposed to bow as you lord it over us."

"That's not true."

"No?" Brian brought his eyes back to mine. "Things are about to change, Bay."

My stomach rumbled. "How do you figure?"

"Because I no longer have to wonder how you stole my life. I've given up trying to figure it out."

"Then why are you here?"

"To take it back."

I stretched out my fingers, aching to use my magic. "You're not taking anything from me," I said. "You should just leave now."

"No."

"No?"

"No," he confirmed with a snake-like hiss. "I'm here to take back what's mine. You'll no longer be part of the equation when I'm finished."

"Then I guess this was inevitable." I flung a cloud of blue magic at his face. "*Obscuro*," I muttered before bolting to the right.

He viciously swore as he tried to peer through the murk I'd created. I was already in the hallway, lying in wait and prepared to strike.

If he thought he was going to attack me on my turf, he had another thing coming. He was done taking things from me.

27

TWENTY-SEVEN

Landon would've wanted me to run.

Instead, I slipped into the hallway and erected a magical barrier to pen Brian in the lobby while I remained safe on the other side.

I had questions, and only he could answer them.

"What was that?" Brian called out when he'd recovered from the confusion spell I threw at him. A normal human wouldn't have been able to throw it off so easily. The shade inside him had an easier time ... and yet it had confounded him for at least fifteen seconds. I could likely use it again if necessary.

"What was what?" I asked, knowing full well he was only talking to me in an effort to ascertain where I'd gone. I couldn't make out his features under the limited light in the lobby, but I saw his head snap in my direction.

"That ... spell," Brian seethed as he stomped in my direction. "What was it?"

"Oh, a little of this." I remained still in the darkness and watched in satisfaction when he slammed into the invisible wall I'd erected.

"Son of a ... !" He swore when colliding with the magic, his body doing a little dance as the energy zapped him. "What is that?" He almost sounded shrill.

"You're in my world now," I said. I knew he wouldn't be able to see me in the dark hallway. Landon had once hidden in the same alcove that I now stood in, jumping out to terrify me. He'd been trying to teach me a lesson about safety. Of course, because he was Landon, it had turned into a sexy game of hide-and-seek that ended on my office couch.

The outcome would be different this time.

"No, this is my world," he snapped, raising his fingers and glossing them over the barrier. "It's my world and you stole it."

"Nobody stole anything from you. You lost it."

"Your boyfriend stole it," Brian hissed, his voice reminding me of the snake in *The Jungle Book* cartoon Disney released long before I was born. "It was mine and he bullied me into selling it to him ... and for almost nothing."

"You tried to oust me, and Chief Terry rallied the townsfolk," I countered. "You underestimated their loyalty to me."

"Yes, loyalty to a witch. Do you think they would've stood by you if they knew that little tidbit?"

I cocked my head, considering. "Yes," I replied. "They would've stood by me."

"They love you that much, do they?" He sounded furious when he tested the barrier again and singed his fingers, waving them quickly to fan the heat and then sticking them in his mouth to alleviate the pain. He was a like a small child with a too-hot slice of pizza.

"The people of Hemlock Cove made a business decision," I said. "They did what they had to do when they turned this town into a tourist destination. They saved it. They're well aware that they need the newspaper if they want it to keep thriving. You couldn't give them what they needed."

"I'm a good businessman."

"You're a little boy playing at chief operating officer. You don't understand the reality of this business."

"And you do?"

"I understand more than you think." I angled my head to keep an eye on him. "I want to play a game with you, Brian," I said. "Are you up for it?"

"Is this like that movie *Scream*? Don't they play games in that movie? Are you going to kill me?"

"There's a very good chance, but right this second, no. If I was going to play horror movie games with you, I would channel my inner Aunt Tillie and go *Saw*, not *Scream*. I like the quips in *Scream*, but the kills in *Saw* are more my style."

His grimaced. "What's the game?"

"I'm going to ask you a question. You're going to answer it honestly. Then I'll do the same for you."

"Why would I play?"

"You have questions. You might know I'm a witch, but you don't understand all of it."

He was quiet a moment, the only sound coming from the barrier as he tested it again. "Fine."

He agreed far too easily. "Just like that?"

"Just like that," he agreed. "You don't think I know what you're doing, but I do."

"Oh?"

"You believe you'll be able to use your phone to call your boyfriend here. That's why you're dragging this out. I believe he's otherwise engaged ... what with his boss coming to town and all."

I narrowed my eyes in the darkness. "I knew it. You're the reason Steve is in town."

"I might've placed a call." Brian chuckled. "Does that bother you?"

"You're messing with his livelihood."

"He stole mine."

"You did this to yourself. If you'd followed William's wishes you'd still own the newspaper. Of course, you would've run it into the ground by now and gone bankrupt."

"So smug," Brian sneered, grunting when he slammed his fist into the magical barrier.

"You're not powerful enough to take down that wall," I told him. "You can't get to me."

"How can you be so certain?"

"I've been at this longer than you. Do you want to play the game or not?"

He hesitated and then nodded. "Sure. Let's play."

"WHEN WERE you taken over by the shade?"

He laughed. "Of course you'd want to know about that. You've always been a busybody."

"You have to follow the rules," I insisted. "I have questions. So do you. I won't answer yours unless you answer mine."

"Fine." He sounded bitter. "When I left this place, I had no idea what I was going to do with my life. I had a clear plan before your boyfriend ripped what was mine away from me. I was aimless when I left ... and I had a persistent case of chlamydia that refused to clear up. I would get it treated, think I was fine, and then three weeks later — like clockwork — it returned."

I had to press my lips together to keep from laughing. "That's Aunt Tillie. If you haven't gotten over that yet, you probably won't. You have to learn from your mistakes to overcome the curse."

"That mean old terror just likes torturing me. I have plans for her."

My heart rolled. "She's better than you. You can't take her."

"You'd be surprised what I'm capable of. I'm going to kill you first, so you won't have to watch her die."

I figured that was the ultimate goal. Hearing it out loud like that made me uncomfortable. "Go back to your story," I prodded. "I want to hear how this happened."

"There's not much to tell." Brian was blasé. "I was bitter, angry, and forced to take an office job at an insurance agency."

"The horror," I intoned, rolling my eyes.

"It *was* horrific. I was desperate to get out of there, but I had bills to pay. I had rent. So, even though I hated every horrible person in that building — I could hear them snickering behind my back about losing my grandfather's business — I had to tough it out."

Did he really hear people snickering behind his back, or was that the paranoia talking? "And then what happened?"

"My boss pulled me aside. He said he'd been watching me and it was obvious I was unhappy. He asked what was going on, and before I knew it I was spilling my guts to him. Instead of telling me to get over myself, which I expected, he told me to get my revenge. He even offered help."

My shoulders jerked at the last part. "He was a shade."

"I've answered your question." His voice was cold. "It's my turn."

Even though I wanted to press him further, I nodded. A deal was a deal, after all. "Shoot."

"How many people have you killed?"

That wasn't the question I was expecting. "What?"

"You heard me. How many innocent people have you taken out of this world so you can continue to rule it?"

"That would be zero."

"Don't lie."

"I haven't killed any innocent people."

"Is that what you do? Convince yourself that you're on the side of good and they're on the side of evil? It's not murder if they're evil, right?"

"I mind my own business until evil tries to take over."

"Who decides who is evil?"

"I believe actions decide."

"What if I told you that you're the villain in my story? You're the evil one. How do you feel about that?"

"Sorry for you."

"Why?"

"You're delusional. I had nothing against you until you moved on me."

"Are you honestly saying that you liked me even though you believed I was incompetent and didn't deserve my grandfather's business?"

I hesitated, his words striking a chord. I shook my head. "You're being ridiculous," I said. "I didn't hate you from the start. You might've convinced yourself of that, but it's not true. I only wanted to do my job without you breathing down my neck."

"And I wanted to do my job without you taking it from me. Which of us is the villain, Bay? I don't believe it's me. You were accused of killing someone. You were working against me from the start."

He was stuck in a bitter spiral. There was truth in his words, but not the sort of truth that others could see. There was no convincing him that he was wrong.

"Let's talk about the shade," I insisted.

"We're not done talking about you."

"I answered your question. It's my turn."

"Fine." I heard the zing of the barrier again. He continually tested it. As long as he kept trying, I didn't have to worry about what he was doing.

"Your boss at this insurance company, he was a shade," I pressed. "How did he sell you on this?"

"He didn't have to sell me. As for being a shade, I don't know what that means. I'm not an expert on your witchy ways."

"You have a dark soul inside of you."

"I have a lost soul inside of me. It's a powerful ally. I give the soul a place to rest, take refuge, and recover after a hard day. In return, the soul helps me."

"Helps you do what?"

"Does it matter?"

"I'd like to know."

"The soul helps me better myself," he replied. "It keeps me on task. How else do you explain me making enough money to buy the lake house in less than a year? The old Brian couldn't do that."

Something about the way he said it tipped me off to the truth of things. "You're not Brian."

"On the contrary, I am Brian Kelly."

"You're not the real Brian." My mind was a minefield of possibilities. "You're the thing that took him over."

His bloodcurdling cackle made me glance over my shoulder to make sure I wasn't about to be attacked from behind.

"The fact that you're just figuring that out is ... so cute," Brian said. "He made it sound as though you're a super witch I would have trouble taking down. You've been nothing but easy from the start."

"Is Brian still in there?"

"Brian is a sleepy boy. He pokes his head out from time to time, we chat, and then he goes back to sleep. Don't worry about him, he's where he belongs ... and I'm where I belong."

"How long have you been with him? Were you here in Hemlock Cove the first time?"

"I was not. The story is true. I just told it from his point of view."

"He let you in."

"He did. It works out better that way. If he fights the process I can never truly be in control. I had to convince him that I had his best interests at heart."

"He's paranoid," I noted. "How did you convince him that you would win the battle for him?"

"It wasn't difficult. When someone wants something so bad they're willing to give up a part of themselves to get it, all you have to do is show them what they want and tell them how you're going to get it for them."

"Yes, but even if you were to somehow get the newspaper, Brian wouldn't be the one enjoying the spoils of the victory."

"That is very true. Deep down, he doesn't care. He just wants you to lose."

"What sort of shade are you?"

"I don't believe in being pigeonholed."

"You're not a normal shade, but you're constrained by the same rules." Something occurred to me. "Paisley. You killed her and drank her blood."

"Paisley was a victim of circumstance. She was in the wrong place at the wrong time. I didn't want to kill her, but she refused to stop shadowing me ... especially when she figured out what I was. She wanted a powerful friend, too. She had a bit of revenge she wanted exact. That's how we got hooked up in the first place."

And that's when the final piece slipped into place. "Paisley remembered, too."

"Too? Who else remembers? Am I missing something?" He sounded far too intrigued for my comfort.

"That doesn't matter. What did Paisley say to you?"

"You stripped her powers, stole what was hers. We had that in common."

"That magic was never hers. She couldn't wield it properly."

"I saw that from the start. She, however, didn't want to hear it. It was much easier to fuel her paranoid delusions and tell her what she wanted to hear than get her to see the truth."

"You started hanging out with them from the moment you arrived." I thought back to the night Aunt Tillie and I had glamoured ourselves to visit the party spot behind the Dragonfly and stumbled across Brian. "You were grooming them from the start."

"An interesting choice of words – *grooming*."

My stomach heaved. "You're the person Paisley was seeing. Her friends said it was a secret, but she couldn't stop herself from bragging. It was you."

"And that's why she had to go. Truly. She refused to keep her mouth shut. She prattled on and on about how she wanted to get revenge against you. I preferred when I thought I could use all four girls. In the end, only Paisley turned out to be truly helpful. Even when I snuffed out the light in her eyes and told her she would be sustaining me for weeks, she was still helpful."

I thought I might throw up. "You're disgusting."

"I'm a survivor."

"Tell me about the other shades."

"They're not my doing. I'm here on a specific mission. I promised Brian when he surrendered his body to me. I plan to carry out that promise." He pressed as close to the barrier as he could and leered directly at me, proving he knew where I was the entire time. "I hear witch blood is delicious."

I debated trying to take him out now. I didn't want to put the populace at risk if I ran away and he followed. I'd never dealt with anything like him. Rather than risk him fueling on Winchester blood, I decided to retreat and gather my witchy forces.

"I think you'll have to go without tonight." I stepped out into the hallway. "Your time here is done."

"You're not as powerful as you think."

That made me laugh. The shade was limited. He only knew what Brian knew, and that was precious little. "You keep telling yourself that. Our next meeting will be all the sweeter because of it." I started down the hallway. There was another door at the far end of the building and I planned to escape through it and rendezvous with Landon at the police station. After that, we would call in the reinforcements.

"Where do you think you're going?" Brian called to my back. "We're not done."

"Oh, we're done." I didn't bother looking over my shoulder when I reached the door. "The next time we meet, you'll be dying. You might want to start running now."

"I'm not afraid of you."

"Then you're dumber than you look." I pushed open the door, thinking I had a clear escape, and then my heart lodged in my throat when another face appeared directly in front of me.

"Hello, Bay." Rosemary stepped through the opening, her eyes lit with green fire as her fingers extended. "I've been waiting for this for a long time."

Before I could respond, she jolted me with a burst of magic I recognized from when the shades attacked at the inn. I flew back, slamming into the wall, and then began to slip to the floor as my vision wobbled.

"We have some things to discuss," she said brightly.

28

TWENTY-EIGHT

The blow hurt, but not enough to incapacitate me. I scrambled so my back was against the wall so as not to worry about being attacked from behind, and murdered Rosemary with a death glare.

"Why am I not surprised?"

Rosemary's lips curved into a smirk. "I don't know, Bay. Why aren't you surprised?"

"I've known you were evil since we were kids."

Rosemary hunkered down on an even level with me. "Rosemary was never evil. She just wanted to be included in all your wacky Winchester games. Willa poisoned her mind. Are you really saying you didn't know that?"

I was jittery as I regarded her. "You're not Rosemary." It was a statement, not a question. Now, looking into the depths of her glowing eyes, it was obvious Rosemary had fled. What had taken over her body was something else entirely.

"No, I'm not Rosemary." She let out an evil laugh and then stood, her gaze going to the other end of the hallway, where Brian paced and cursed my existence. "I don't suppose you can drop whatever that ... thing ... is, can you?"

"I don't suppose so." She had to be crazy if she thought I would put myself at that sort of disadvantage.

"I guess it doesn't matter." She dusted off her hands and shot me a pitying look. "I wanted to take you out anyway."

I wasn't afraid to die. Sure, it wasn't on my list of things to do in the next fifty years, but I didn't fear the other side. I wasn't going to allow her to kill me without a fight. "Who are you?"

"Does it matter?"

"It does to me."

"I'm ... more than one thing," she replied. "I'm beyond anything you can imagine."

I snorted. "That sounds like something Aunt Tillie would say."

"Yes, well, she's an impressive specimen. Always has been. But age has worn her down. The most fearsome witch in the Midwest is now a clown who spends all her time dishing out petty revenge to people beneath her."

"I think she likes it."

"Which speaks to her mental state." Rosemary scuffed her shoe against the floor and then shook her head. "It doesn't matter. She kept the balance of power here off center for decades. It's her age that allowed for this."

I was taken aback. "What does that mean?"

"I was here long ago but didn't stay despite what this town has to offer. Now I'm back and the living conditions are much better."

"Have you fought Aunt Tillie before?" The mere possibility had my mind buzzing. "Will she recognize you when she sees you?"

"I've never fought her. I knew better than to take her on. But like I said, she's not what she once was."

"You should say that to her face."

Rosemary's chuckle was low, drawn out, and tinged with evil. "You're so amusing. Even now, when I've told you that she's diminishing, you believe she'll walk through the door and save you."

I didn't believe that. I didn't even hope for it. I wanted Aunt Tillie to be safe. Whatever entity had taken up residence in Rosemary was dangerous. "How long have you been inside of Rosemary?"

"Long enough."

"That's not an answer."

"What answer will make you feel better?" She cocked her head and regarded me with overt amusement. "Do you want to hear that I took her over yesterday? That she had a vulnerable moment and couldn't hold me off? That she's somewhere close, just beneath the surface, fighting to escape?"

I ground my molars together. "I don't really know if that would make me feel better," I said. "I just want the truth."

"Rosemary has been ... struggling ... for some time," she replied. "The weight of her grandmother's expectations and her mother's indifference had her feeling sorry for herself. She met Brian here, as you recall, and when he enacted a plan to get back at you for stealing his newspaper, he enlisted her.

"He romanced her, pretended to care about her, and gave Rosemary the things she'd always yearned for," she continued. "Rosemary thought he really cared for her. Even when he showed up one day and was markedly different, almost as if another person was living in his skin, she believed he was her salvation."

The amusement flitting across the thing that had taken over Rosemary's face turned my stomach. "Somehow the thing inside Brian convinced her to open herself up to possession," I surmised.

"That's an ugly word. She's not possessed. She's simply sharing herself with another individual."

"Except you're the one in control here," I argued. "You have all the say in what's happening. Does Rosemary even grasp what's happening?"

"Rosemary had no idea what she was agreeing to. She only knew that Brian wanted it, so she gave in. Now she spends all her time walled off in a prison of her own making. She doesn't want to know what he's doing. She doesn't want to know what I'm doing. All the better for me."

"Because?"

"Because there's nothing I hate more than a vessel that rebels against the process."

Something about the way she stated it piqued my interest. "You've been in other people before."

"I prefer thinking of them as vessels."

"If you strip them of dignity, make them things instead of people, it's easier for you to ignore what you're really doing."

"And what's that?"

"Raping them. You're erasing what they were, forcing them to be what they're not, and taking away their choice. You're pretty much the evilest of the evil. What I want to know is how you got this way. You weren't always a disembodied soul looking to invade people."

"I certainly wasn't," she readily agreed, smirking. "I was human once. A long time ago. Before your Tillie even graced this earth. I knew your grandmother, Caroline. She made a name for herself selling potions and spells when it was unheard of for women to run their own businesses.

"Your grandfather was a philanderer of the highest order," she continued. "He embarrassed your grandmother, even going so far as to bring another child home. I was one of the women he spent his time with, so I got to know him extremely well."

A germ of suspicion invaded my mind. "Are you Willa's mother?"

She laughed, the sound light and playful. The spark of evil in her eyes told me that I'd guessed correctly. "Why would you assume that?"

"You have to be obsessed with us for a reason. You've followed Aunt Tillie multiple times, which indicates that you've come to Hemlock Cove more than once."

"I visited Hemlock Cove only once. But Walkerville was my home for a time."

I searched my memory. What did I know about Willa's birth mother? Even when Aunt Tillie dropped the bomb regarding Willa's true parentage, she never filled us in on the salacious details.

"You abandoned Willa to be raised by my great-grandfather and great-grandmother," I said.

"I didn't abandon her." Her expression shifted from delight to fury. "I was a single mother in a time when you couldn't be a single mother.

I demanded that your great-grandfather leave your great-grandmother and marry me. Decorum dictated he do so."

"I'm guessing he said no."

"He said it would cost too much to divorce your great-grandmother. I didn't realize it at the time, but she was the primary breadwinner in that home. She owned the house. She made the money. She raised the children."

"He had nothing to offer you," I mused. "That must've been a hard reality to swallow."

"It was impossible."

"You had no choice but to leave Willa with my great-grandmother. You would've been branded and forever disparaged if you tried to keep her."

"Your great-grandmother promised to take care of her. Then I left town."

"You never saw Willa again?"

"I was ... otherwise engaged." Her smile was back. "I moved to Detroit and got a different job, the sort that paid well but had an age limit. I put my dancing moves to good use."

I nodded in understanding. "You lived a hard life."

"And when I returned to Walkerville to check on my daughter I was not greeted with open arms. I was told to leave and never return."

"I take it you didn't follow those orders."

"Oh, but I did. I moved to Bay City and got a job as a waitress. By then I was past my prime for dancing. I spent my nights slinging drinks and putting up with wandering hands ... and sometimes tongues. It was demeaning, but it allowed me to embrace my rage."

I could pretty much figure the rest of it out. "You died, but your soul didn't pass over. You were too angry to allow that to happen."

"I drank myself to death," she confirmed. "My liver gave out and I died in a puddle of my own vomit. I never did have that all-important moment of clarity when I was alive. I managed it when I emerged for my second life, though."

"And then what? Did you try to reclaim Willa?"

"Reclaim her? No. But I did go to see her. Your great-grandmother saw me ... and Tillie. They banished me from the land. The spell was strong enough that I couldn't overcome it."

"But you kept coming back to test it."

"Yes." She nodded. "Even after Willa left, I returned. I owed your great-grandmother a debt that I never managed to repay."

"Wait ... ." I was confused.

"I didn't want to reward her with anything good. Don't think that. The debt I owed her was death. She died on her own before I could make it a reality."

"Well ... I guess that's a bummer for you."

"I still wanted to pay back her offspring."

The realization of her true motivations was a kick in the ego. "This was never about me. It was always about Aunt Tillie."

"Oh, look, you finally figured it out." She rolled her eyes. "You're the new power in this town. I have to take you out if I want a clear path to Tillie."

"And Rosemary? Why take over your own great-granddaughter's body? Don't you have any shame at all?"

She snorted. "I don't know this girl. I don't care about her. A blood tie makes it easier for a soul to take up permanent residence. Rosemary isn't strong enough to fight me off. She's already given up and retreated to a corner of her brain where I can't communicate with her. It's best for everybody concerned."

"Except Rosemary."

"Give me a break. You've never cared about Rosemary."

"She's not my favorite person, but I don't want her to suffer."

"She's not suffering. She's been removed from this world."

"And will you return her body when you've seen your revenge scheme through to the end? Will Rosemary have another shot at life?"

"This is my body now. I'm not giving it up."

I was fairly certain I understood everything. "Your dark soul connected with his dark soul." I pointed to the lobby, to where Brian paced. "He gave in to your friend first and brought Rosemary along for the ride. Then, along the way, you collected other souls.

"You've been killing people for the blood," I continued. "You need to feed. Even though you're not truly alive, the blood sustains you."

"So smart," she sneered.

"I just want to understand."

"To what end?" She looked legitimately curious. "What do you think this will do for you?"

"Probably nothing, but I can't rest without answers."

"Fine. Finish it. What else do you need to know?"

"Brian was messing around with Paisley. He wanted to use her because she managed to tap into our magic once before. She turned out to be a disappointment, though."

"She did."

"What about her parents? Where are they?"

She shrugged. "Who can say?"

"You can. You're responsible for whatever happened to them."

"They're in the woods, not far from where their daughter died. They followed her to the clearing and saw what happened. As Brian handled her, I took care of the parents. We buried them and returned their vehicle to the driveway so it would look as if they were taken from the house. They're in the woods, if anybody ever bothers to look."

"Why leave Paisley in the open and hide the bodies of her parents?" I asked.

"I can't believe you're this slow." She heaved out a sigh. "We wanted to draw you in. We wanted you focused on Paisley rather than us. I needed to keep you off your game."

"And then what?"

"This." She gestured to the hallway. "We're here to end you."

"What makes you think you have the power? It's just you and me. If I'm the new power as you say, you don't have the strength to take me out."

She leaned over and rested her hands on her knees, her round face splitting with a wide grin. "What makes you think I'm alone?"

Alarm bells went off in my head and I snapped my eyes to the hallway, where Brian had been pacing. He was gone, which meant he was

AMANDA M. LEE

on his way to the door Rosemary had used to enter the building. He was on his way to me.

"Crap." I scrambled to my feet, prepared to fight, but nobody walked through the door. "Where is he?" I asked.

"He's coming." Rosemary didn't look particularly bothered. "He should be here any second."

After another sixty seconds, I glanced at her again. "Are you sure?"

"Of course I'm sure." Despite the words, irritation radiated off Rosemary, and in a moment of fury she started toward the door. "What is he doing out there? How long does it take to walk between two doors?" She disappeared through the opening, leaving me with a choice.

I could drop the barrier and try to escape through the front door of the newspaper or follow her and try to best her. There really was no choice. I had to end this now. I raised my hand as I stepped through the opening.

I was focused, determined, and when I looked along the paver stones that made up the back walkway, I almost missed what I should've seen days before. There, in the corners of the stones, were the runes from the trees left near Paisley's body.

There were four of them littering the stones. I only had a moment to wonder why. The stones had been there since long before I took over the business. William had built that walkway. Was he somehow involved in this? Did he know what was to come?

I would have to ponder that later, I reminded myself.

Rosemary, her back to me, scanned the area surrounding the door. "Where did he go?" Bewilderment was wild on her face as she turned.

I caught her before she could register how close I was, slamming both hands to either side of her head and freezing her in place. "*Congelo!*"

Her body went rigid as I searched through the dark corners of her mind. I was looking for one thing.

I found Rosemary — the real Rosemary — sitting in a library when I started kicking down doors. She seemed surprised to see me.

"What are you doing here?"

"Helping you." I felt sorry for her, but I didn't like her. "You've got to fight your way free. I can't do it on my own."

Rosemary hesitated. "I ... don't know what you mean."

"I'm going to expel her," I replied, grimacing when I felt the shade fighting back. "I'm going to force her out. When I do, you need to take control. Whatever happens, you can't let her back in."

Rosemary's lower lip quivered. "I didn't realize what was happening. Brian said ... ." She trailed off.

"Brian knew what was going to happen. He took advantage of you. But now you have to take control when I say it's time. Do you understand?"

For a moment, Rosemary looked so conflicted that I thought she might turn me down and continue hiding. But she nodded. "Yes."

"Good. Get ready." I sucked in a breath and increased my magic. "Now!"

I slammed back into the real world and tightened my grip on the flailing shade. *"Apage!"*

It took everything I had to shove the shade out of Rosemary's body, and when the dark apparition took shape on the other side of Rosemary's limp body, there was rage in her eyes.

"I'm not done with you!" she roared as she tore in my direction. She never made it. A magical net landed on her before she rushed more than a few feet.

Instinctively, I threw up my hands to protect myself, but when she didn't touch me I turned to see who had stopped her.

Days from now I would wonder if Aunt Tillie's appearance at that moment was destined. Her magical grip on the shade, her fingers squeezing the life out of the ghost even as the dark soul tried to escape, seemed meant to be.

"Where did you come from?" I demanded, watching with grim detachment as the shade started fraying at the edges. "What are you doing to her?"

"What has to be done." Aunt Tillie narrowed her eyes and glared at the shade. "I need to put an end to this, and you're going to help."

I was resigned. "What do you want me to do?"

"What your instincts tell you to do. You're a necromancer, Bay. You can end this once and for all. You just need to call on the right form of magic. And you need a poppet."

I'd forgotten about that. A quick glance at the bushes told me I had more than a few to work with. Thistle had been making garden gnomes on and off the last few years and I'd taken to placing them outside the building as decorations.

I set my jaw and nodded. Aunt Tillie was right. I did know what to do. "Okay, but then we have to find Brian. He's infected, too."

"No need to worry about that." Aunt Tillie's lips curved in evil delight. "Your boy toy has him on the lawn in front of the newspaper. Landon keeps losing control of his fist. It's kind of funny."

"How did you know?"

"Viola. You told her to find shades. She found them ... and then warned us what was happening."

"I guess I owe her."

"No, you owe me. Now, let's finish this. I have some games I still want to play with Willa."

Only Aunt Tillie would think this was the appropriate time for torture.

"I'm coming." I stepped toward them, raising my hands. Aunt Tillie was right. I did know what to do. Thistle's art would live on forever now, just in a different way than any of us had foreseen.

TWENTY-NINE

We left Rosemary unconscious on the ground — really, what else could we do? — and headed toward the front of the building. Sure enough, Landon had Brian on the ground, and the fury in my fiancé's eyes made me cringe.

"Landon?"

He jerked up his head. "Bay." He let out a relieved breath. "You're all right."

"Yeah." I smiled as I moved closer to him, dropping to my knees and cupping his chin with my hands. "Are you okay?"

"I've been better. I was afraid for you, but when I saw Kelly coming out of the newspaper ... ." He trailed off.

"You had to stop him."

"I was going to kill him."

"Why didn't you?"

"Because that's not my job." His eyes were brimming. Despite that, he didn't let go of Brian's wrists even as the other man bucked beneath him. "Give me a kiss."

"Do you think this is the right time?"

"I need it."

I leaned in and smacked a loud kiss against his lips and then pulled back to stare at a furious Brian. "It's good you didn't kill him. He's possessed."

"Are you sure?"

"Yeah. We just knocked a shade out of Rosemary and destroyed it. She was possessed as well."

"Are you planning on doing the same to him?"

"Do you have a better idea?"

"We could lock him up and charge him with Paisley Gilmore's murder."

It was an intriguing option, but I shook my head. "I don't think we can do that."

"Why not?"

"He may be a tool, but he's no murderer."

"He might not have been in control of his faculties, but his hands wielded the weapon that killed Paisley Gilmore."

"And Rosemary's, which killed her parents. They're out in the woods behind the Dragonfly, by the way. She admitted that before I entombed the shade in one of Thistle's garden gnomes. It's the one that looks like Gene Simmons from KISS. They were following Paisley because they thought something was up with her. Turns out they were right. They tried to intervene when Brian was killing her, but Rosemary ended them ... and then fed on their blood."

Landon made a face of disgust. "Lovely." He shook his head. "Okay, I'm not sure what to do about this. I need to talk to Terry. Before that, you need to get rid of this shade."

I nodded. "I've got it. I know better what to do this time." I pressed my hand to Brian's chest and prepared myself, my eyes flitting between the garden gnome that looked like a frolicking fairy and the one that looked like a deranged clown. The choice was clear. "Aunt Tillie says Viola warned her that something was going on. Did she do the same for you?"

Landon was silent a moment, focused on struggling Brian, and then nodded. "I heard her."

"That's another bout with ghosts." I was more amused than worried. "You're becoming a regular ghost whisperer yourself."

"I would rather discuss that later. Let's handle Kelly and figure out how to deal with the Gilmore situation."

He couldn't accept the reality that this kept happening to him. He was fine when I was magical. Now that it was happening to him ... well ... it was too much for him to bear. "Sure." I paused. "It's going to be okay."

He managed a rueful smile. "Isn't that my line?"

"Yes, but this time you need to hear it."

"I think you're right. You can repeat it to me when you're naked and feeding me bacon in bed later. I'll likely be more open to hearing it then."

TWO HOURS LATER, ROSEMARY SAT IN the Overlook's dining room, staring into space, an untouched cup of tea in front of her. Despite my protestations to the contrary, Landon and Chief Terry had taken Brian into custody. They had enough evidence against him regarding Paisley's murder to hand the case over to the prosecutor. There was nothing else they could do.

For her part, Rosemary was a morose mess.

"I don't understand how this happened," she said, her eyes bouncing between Aunt Tillie and me. She was unnaturally pale, dirt smudging her cheeks. She looked like a completely different person from the one who attacked me at the Whistler office.

"You opened yourself to it," I explained, looking to the door. Aunt Willa was reportedly on her way, Mom and my aunts waiting for her in the lobby. Apparently they wanted to have a discussion with her before she saw Rosemary.

"But ... I didn't."

"You must have," I insisted. "The shade couldn't have gotten a foothold inside of you if you didn't open yourself to her." I hesitated and then blew out a sigh. "She said that Brian made the request of you."

"He did, but ... I was trying to make him happy. That's all I wanted."

Aunt Tillie stirred. "I think there's a lesson in there for you."

"What lesson is that?"

"You need to worry more about yourself and less about others. If someone suggests something that's likely bad — oh, say like allowing an evil spirit to take you over — perhaps you should put your foot down and say no."

"I didn't know it would turn out like this." Rosemary sounded pathetic. "I just ... wanted to make him happy."

"I think you wanted to make yourself happy and you thought Brian was the only way you could do it," I countered, thinking back to what the shade had told me. "You were lonely, abandoned by your mother. She never took proper care of you from what I can tell, and often left you to fend for yourself. You were also oppressed by your grandmother. Brian was your escape."

"I love him."

"I'm not sure you ever knew him."

"We're engaged."

I looked to Aunt Tillie, who held out her hands and made a face. "Brian is in jail right now. I'm not sure he won't be staying there." I opted for the truth. "He's ... in big trouble. The smartest thing for you would be to distance yourself from him."

Rosemary's mouth dropped open. "But ... we're in love."

"Again, I don't know that you ever met the real Brian. Even if you did, he was never going to be the person you wanted him to be. He only hooked up with you because he thought he could use you against us."

"I want to believe there was more to him than just a revenge plot and lies."

"Well, that's something you'll have to deal with yourself." I refused to coddle her. "It's time you picked a path and struck out on your own. You can be your own person, Rosemary. You don't have to do what Aunt Willa tells you to do."

Rather than gain strength from the statement, Rosemary dissolved into tears. "She's going to be so mad at me."

Disgust rolled through me, and before I could decide what I wanted to say in response, I heard footsteps on the hardwood floors.

I found Aunt Willa standing in the open doorway. She looked stricken.

"What's happened?" she demanded. "What did you do to my granddaughter?"

I opened my mouth to tell her exactly where she could shove her accusations – we still had days of shade cleanup from the mess Rosemary and Brian had created – but Aunt Tillie placed a hand on my wrist to still me.

"I've got this," she said, flicking her eyes to her half-sister. "Let me do this."

It was probably a mistake — Aunt Tillie could never be considered gentle — but I was too tired to argue. I nodded and leaned back in my chair.

"I'm going to give it to you straight," Aunt Tillie said. "Rosemary was possessed by an evil shade. Apparently it was your birth mother, although I never got a chance to talk to her to confirm that. Why she would lie about that is beyond me, but never say never when you're dealing with evil.

"Rosemary allowed the shade to take her over at Brian's behest," she continued. "He willingly embraced his dark side to go after us because he's a bitter little troll with a pencil eraser for a penis. He's in jail, likely headed for prison.

"Bay freed both Brian and Rosemary from the shades possessing them. She did this after they both tried to kill her. I should point out that Bay would've been well within her rights to kill them. I believe you owe her a thank you."

Aunt Willa was incredulous. "Excuse me?"

"You heard me." Aunt Tillie refused to back down. "Rosemary is only alive because of Bay. Her life is a freaking train wreck. You should recognize that, because your life has always been a train wreck."

"I don't think I like your tone," Aunt Willa hissed.

"I don't think I care." For once, Aunt Tillie wasn't in a joking mood. She was deadly serious. "Brian Kelly is at the very least going to be named a suspect in Paisley Gilmore's murder. That will make him a pariah in this town. If Rosemary chooses to stay with him — which is a mistake — it will reflect badly on her and you. Do you want that?"

"He's not a murderer," Aunt Willa insisted. "I would know."

"You can't even see the truth of yourself," Aunt Tillie fired back. "How can you see him when you're oblivious about yourself?"

"I'm ... not." Aunt Willa studied Rosemary's profile. Her granddaughter was a disheveled, shaking mess. "I don't understand how this happened."

They were the same words Rosemary had spoken. "She allowed it to happen," I snapped. "You helped it happen. There's a lot for you two to break down. Just for the record, no matter what she says, she knows what occurred. She remembers. She was there. You can talk to each other about that, argue to your heart's content, but we're done with you."

Aunt Willa rolled her eyes. "You've always been an ungrateful girl. It's because you were raised by an ungrateful ass." She gestured to Aunt Tillie. "I don't believe a word you've said here today."

"That's your prerogative." I turned my attention to the kitchen door as it swung open, smiling as my mother handed me a baggie full of bacon. "Thank you."

"Terry called," Mom said. "He's on his way home. He said Landon is going straight to the guest house."

That was my cue. I pushed myself to a standing position. "I need to get home."

"We're not done here," Aunt Willa argued. "We're nowhere near done."

"Oh, we're done." I was fed up with her and everything she represented. "I have nothing left to say to you. As it is, it's going to take days to clean up the mess your granddaughter left in our town. You need to go."

"You can't just kick me out of town."

"I can, and that's what I'm doing." I started for the hallway. "You have three days. Pack up and get out."

"Or what?"

"Or I'll have every ghost in town haunt you."

"Is that a threat?"

"It's a promise."

"She'll make them sing show tunes," Aunt Tillie warned. "Bad ones. You'll never know peace again."

Aunt Willa worked her jaw, searching for words. "This isn't my fault," she moaned. "I didn't know."

"You might not have known, but it is your fault," I countered. "Now it's time for you to do the right thing and fix what you broke. You can't do it here, though. This is my town."

Aunt Tillie smirked, but didn't speak.

"Where are you going?" Aunt Willa demanded. "We're nowhere near done."

"I'm going home to feed my fiancé bacon and make wedding plans," I replied. "He's earned a mental break. It's time you took responsibility. You're just as much to blame for this as Brian and Rosemary are."

"This is not my fault!"

I was too tired to keep pressing the issue. Instead, I met Aunt Tillie's gaze. "Can you take it from here?"

She grinned and bobbed her head. "This is why two super witches are better than one. It would be my pleasure to finish this up."

For once, I wholeheartedly agreed with her.